# ANGEL DOWN

## LOIS GREIMAN

Angel Down
Copyright © 2017 by Lois Greiman
Print ISBN: 9781548475819

NYLA Publishing
121 W. 27th St., Suite 1201, New York, NY 10001
http://www.nyliterary.com

# Praise for Lois Greiman

"Dangerously funny stuff."
*Janet Evanovich*

"Simple sexy sport may be just what the doctor ordered."
*Publishers Weekly*

"Lois Greiman is a modern day Dorothy Sayers. Witty as hell, yet
talented enough to write like an angel with a broken wing."
Kinky Friedman, author of *Ten Little New Yorkers*

"What a marvelous book! A delightful romp, a laugh on
every page."
*MaryJanice Davidson, NYT bestselling author of the Undead series.*

"Amazingly good." (Top Pick!)
Romantic Times

"L.A. psychologist, Chrissy McMullen is back to prove that
boobs, brass, and brains make for one heck of a good time…
laugh out loud funny…sassy…clever."

tongue-in-cheek, comical suspense guaranteed to entice and entertain."

*Book Loons*

## Chapter One

Wild Turkey rippled like amber waves inside Gabriel Durrand's whiskey glass. Ambient noises dimmed as the palpable scents of civilization drifted seamlessly into earthier odors. The desert crept into his consciousness on a carpet of darkness, swallowing him by slow degrees.

Sweat dripped into his eyes and trickled down his back, hot and slick, slipping into the waistband of his cammies. But he remained as he was, unmoving, barely breathing because this was it. He could feel it in the cramped muscles of his shoulders, on the itchy nape of his neck. They'd been living in this damned sandbox for five weeks now. Followed a hundred leads. Planned a dozen missions, but this would be the last.

They'd finally run the bastard to ground. Abdul Wakil Ghafoor. Rapist, murderer. Soon-to-be corpse.

It was oh-dark thirty. Sometime between too early and just about fucking time. The desert was as quiet as death. His comrades were nearby, but almost invisible. A squad of men with exceptional training and unsurpassed skills. He knew each of them as well as he knew himself.

Jairo…the little Latino, strong as a bull, quick as a fox. Snipes…

sharpshooter and new daddy, so proud it'd make you laugh if it weren't for that dumb-ass niggle of jealousy every time he pulled out the photos.

Intel…the genius.

Shep…

Close behind him, Shepherd's stomach rumbled. The rangy Okie shifted his rifle, trying to ease the jacked-up tension that had been building in them all for a month. "If this fucker makes me miss breakfast, I'm gonna kill 'im twice," he murmured.

Shepherd…the ass…and Gabe's wingman since boot camp.

"Quit your fucking swearing," Gabe mouthed, and Shepherd grinned, teeth so white they nearly glowed. But they were well hidden, hunkered down behind a wall the color of puke. Forty feet away at one o'clock was a squat farmhouse constructed of the same material. Light spilled at a sharp angle from the building's only window. Sporadic laughter could be heard coming from behind the closed door. Ghafoor had a hell of a sense of humor. As did his guards. There was nothing funnier to them than spilling American blood. But the hilarity would end tonight.

Intel had traced them here.

Reynolds had given the orders; no planes, no Humvees, no noise. Just a half-dozen seasoned Rangers armed with guts and patriotism.

This would be a coup to negate the growing list of Middle Eastern snafus because this was an OFP. Their own fucking program. No one knew they were there. Not their mothers. Not their lovers, and sure as hell not the shit-bricks in Washington.

Off to their left, Reynolds raised his arm. Camouflaged warriors eased out of nowhere, tightening the perimeter like a noose around Ghafoor's scrawny neck.

A new Land Cruiser stood nearby, shining in the moonlight. Reynolds motioned toward it, one quick jerk of his head. Snipes crept forward, M-4 at the ready as he reached through the open window, retrieved the keys, then nodded once and knelt, taking cover behind a chromed wheel.

The rest of the detail found new positions, just as invisible, but closer now, every rifle trained, every muscle tensed.

Reynolds pointed to Intel, crouched as he was behind an ancient, wind-gnarled olive tree.

Just about ready, just about there.

Intel hunkered back, entirely unseen, his voice loud and clear in the dark silence, an echoing Pashto warning to lay down their guns, to give themselves up.

Then the Land Cruiser exploded. It leapt toward the sky on a rocket of flame. Fire engulfed Snipes like a glove. He shrieked, high-pitched with agony. The sound was chopped short as the vehicle landed.

Scraps of metal rained from the sky. A flaming shard struck Gabe, ripping the rifle from his hands. He threw himself onto the sand, clawing for his frags, but his fingers were slippery. Unwieldy.

Gunfire burst over them, torpedoing from behind. Reynolds grunted and spun, hitting the ground like a loosed boulder.

Gabe scrambled around in a circle, spinning on his belly. White-hot gunfire ripped at them from a dozen inky locations, and through his skewed night vision goggles, he could see the blackened faces of the men who had outwitted them.

To his right, Intel stepped out of cover and opened fire. Two Sunni rebels stumbled backward, bodies jerking to the staccato beat of his weapon. For a moment, the lone tree seemed to crackle with silver energy, then it split, ripping down the middle. Splinters burst into the air like fireworks. Intel leapt away, miraculously unscathed, rifle raised in astonishment.

"Get down! Get the fuck down!" someone screamed, but before the words ended, Intel toppled backward, twitching erratically in the exploding light.

And in that same eerie glow, Shepherd leapt forward. Gabe watched him race across the desert in slow motion, a hunkered, camouflaged sprinter on a heavy treadmill of sand. Powder-puffs billowed up from his boots as he labored toward Intel's twitching body. Firelight echoed off his rifle as a dozen Taliban aimed to kill.

Gabe found himself on his feet. He didn't know when he'd located his rifle. Didn't interpret his own actions. Didn't hear his own incoherent roar as he raced toward the duo by the fractured tree, M-4 chattering as he ran.

Someone shrieked a truncated curse. Shepherd dragged Intel to his feet. A splinter the size of a pistol muzzle was protruding from the wounded man's throat, but he was still convulsing, limbs jerking out of rhythm, like Pinocchio gone mad.

"Let's go!" Gabe shouted and crouched down, spattering gunfire into the anonymous blackness.

"Help me!" Shepherd rasped.

But Intel had gone limp. "Too late!"

"The hell it is!" Shepherd barked. "Grab his—"

Gabe leapt to his feet and swung. The butt of his weapon struck Shepherd's temple like a thunderclap. He stumbled back, shock stamped across his face as Intel's body slumped to the ground. And then Shepherd fell, too, stunned and motionless. For one horrified moment, Gabe delayed, barely hearing the harsh beat of the guns behind him. Then he threw himself atop Shep's prostrate form and opened fire.

It was a nightmare of chaos, of pain, of terror and blood and anger and guilt.

But finally the noise ceased, though the pain continued, throbbing like a bitching ulcer.

"You okay?"

Reynolds was bent at the waist, holding his stomach. In the periphery, someone was weeping, guttural gasping sobs that slowed gradually, becoming softer, intermittent.

Gabe nodded, though he couldn't remember the question. Blood was dripping onto his leg with mind-numbing regularity.

"Are you sure?" someone asked, and with those words reality seeped like acid into his aching brain.

He raised his eyes, letting the surroundings take hold of his faulty consciousness; the Blue Oyster, a semi-seedy club on the outskirts of MacLean, Virginia. A club where he'd been told to meet an agent named Eddy. An agent who could help save Shepherd's ass. But Eddy hadn't shown.

Instead, a woman stood beside his table. She was blond and slim. *Cute* would be the term his sister would use, and that with some derision. The Durrand women didn't do cute.

"Sure," he said and drew himself fully into the present, locking the past behind him in maximum security.

The woman frowned, seemed to consider leaving then decided against it. "You spilled your drink."

It took him a moment to glance down, longer to realize she was right. Blood was *not* dripping onto his thigh as he had assumed. It was whiskey. A neat means of losing consciousness by the quickest possible route.

"I'm fine," he said and righted his glass, but she didn't move away, forcing him to say more, to attempt civility. "Don't I *look* fine?"

She scowled. Ginger-colored freckles were scattered across her pert little nose like wind-blown confetti, and her face was shaped like a heart, making her look as if she'd just whistled off the streets of Mayberry U. S. A.

His hands were trembling. He shoved them under the table for safekeeping. "Devastatingly handsome?" he asked. It was a line Linus Shepherd might have delivered. If Linus Shepherd were still around. If he hadn't been such a damn fuckup.

Suddenly Gabe's eyes stung and his throat felt tight, but Rangers didn't cry. Sometimes they got shit-faced and brawled in the street like rabid dogs. Sometimes they shot the tires out of their own damn vehicles, but they did *not* cry, and he'd left his Beretta at the hotel. So he would do none of the above.

"Yet boyishly charming?" he asked.

"Sure," she said, then, "I'm sorry. I didn't mean to bother you. I just thought you might... I'm sorry," she said again and retreated to a table behind him and to his right.

He let her go, refilled his glass from the handy bottle nearby and wondered why the hell he was such a damned wienie. She was built like an all-American Barbie, for God's sake, and he wasn't *dead*. Not yet.

At least that's what Shepherd had said before shipping off to Bogotá with Miller the Moron. Before half of Miller's men had come back in body bags. Before Shepherd had gone MIA.

Goddammit! Gabe gritted his teeth against the hard rush of memories. Against the pain and guilt and hopelessness.

But he *wasn't* dead. Not yet, he remembered, and closing his eyes for an abbreviated eternity, grabbed the Wild Turkey by the throat and rose to his feet.

# Chapter Two

Linus Jeremy Shepherd didn't bother opening his eyes. He'd
just awakened from a dozen vicious dreams, but he knew
where he was—in hell. Caught, abandoned, chained like a
slavering hound.

He didn't test his bonds but shivered instead, chilled by the
tropical heat. Or maybe it was a fever. He'd been shot. Again.
Which was just damned unlucky. Or it could be that Durrand was
right for once, and Shep was an idiot.

He smiled grimly at the idea of admitting the truth and wished
like hell Durrand were there to give him shit about it. And maybe,
while ol' Gabe was hanging around, the damned know-it-all could
get him the hell out of there.

Yeah, that'd be sweet. They'd take down these rebel bastards,
bullets buzzing like mosquitoes. Then they'd fly home, first class,
Wild Turkey at their elbows and long-legged stewardesses cuddled
in their laps. Shep might even join the mile-high club….again.

Curling more tightly beneath the reaching branches of some
big-ass deciduous, he shivered spasmodically and scowled into the
mud, confused. Maybe they weren't called stewardesses anymore.
Dammit, everything was fucked up. But things were really FUBAR

if he couldn't remember the important stuff. What was their pc title? Air commanders? Flight assistants? Flight attendants! That was it. He smiled, teeth chattering, dreams drifting mistily past as leggy fly-girls strolled through his boggled mind. He didn't want to piss anyone off. Especially not the big-haired blonde with the sassy come-and-get-me smile.

He didn't want to do anything but make her happy.

And maybe, if he were really lucky, survive the night.

## Chapter Three

Strawberry blond. That's what she was, Gabe thought. She glanced up at his approach. Her eyes were green, her brow furrowed. The expression made her look like a perturbed school-girl, bent forward as she was, pen poised over a square cocktail napkin. It was in pristine condition but for her blocky handwriting.

"I wanted to apologize," he said and motioned jerkily with the Wild Turkey back at his just-abandoned table. "About before. I'm not usually so antisocial." That was probably not true, he thought, but she didn't seem to notice.

"No problem." Sliding the napkin out of sight, she crumpled it in her fist. "I didn't mean to interrupt," she said, and despite the fact that his life was going to hell with the speed of a damned torpedo, he almost smiled, because she hadn't been quite quick enough removing the napkin; he'd read the first line.

"Drafting a resignation letter?" he guessed.

"No. Not at all," she said and cleared her throat. "You want to have a seat?"

"A Dear John letter?" he asked.

She shook her head and glanced away as he sat down. "Why would you think that?"

"Oh, I don't know. Acceptance speeches rarely begin with 'Dear Dickhead,'" he said.

For a moment, he thought she'd sputter a denial, but finally she smiled. A little flushed and as fresh-faced as a Girl Scout. "All right," she said. "I *am* resigning. Sent the email three hours and…" She checked her wrist. It was absolutely devoid of a watch. She shrugged, unconcerned. "…seventeen minutes ago."

He stretched out his aching right leg. "Resigning from what?" he asked.

"My desk job," she said and took a sip. "Do you want to know why?"

"I'm going to assume it's because your boss is a dickhead."

"That's right." She leaned forward suddenly, and in that moment of abrupt animation she reminded him of every woman who made life worth living. Or a living hell. "And do you want to know why he's such a dickhead?" she asked but continued before he could respond. "It's because I'm a woman."

"Are you sure?"

She leaned back in her chair, brows raised. "Am I sure that's the reason, or am I sure that I'm a woman?"

He was pretty confident of her gender but didn't mention the fact. "Seems to me people are dickheads for all sorts of reasons," he said.

She watched him as he drank. Her eyes had softened a little. Maybe he'd rushed to judgment. Maybe they weren't *just* green. Maybe they were forest green. Or fresh asparagus green.

"What'd they do to *you*?" she asked.

He flexed his right hand, almost tempted to tell her, to let her pity cushion the pain but he tested a lie instead. "They passed me over for a promotion."

"Me, too!" she said and smacked the table with enough force to make him wonder how much she'd had to drink.

"Yeah?"

"Yeah. That's why they're dickheads."

He watched her mouth form the words. He couldn't help himself. Perhaps it was because he was wasted. But perhaps it was because there was something about hearing obscenities fall from her sweet-cherry lips that was weirdly erotic. Not that he could do anything about eroticism at that precise moment.

"Because I'm qualified," she said and slammed down the remainder of her drink with a scowl. "I'm more than qualified."

Probably true, he thought. She seemed to have all the qualities an employer could want: intelligence, integrity, compassion… looks. Or maybe those were the attributes *he* wanted.

God, how drunk *was* he?

"I'm sorry. I shouldn't be whining when you…" She paused. "What's your name anyway?"

He was almost tempted to try another lie. As if taking a new identity could clear out the past, could pave a new future. "Gabriel," he said. "How 'bout you?"

"Jenny."

"With an *ie*?"

She shook her head, jiggled the ice in her glass. "A *y*."

"You look more like an *ie* to me."

"Maybe I'll have to reconsider," she said and motioned for another drink. Her blouse gaped a little at the neck; the waiter seemed to appear instantaneously, like a character in a kid's pop-up book.

"Thanks, Walt," she said. Burly and florid, Walt nodded once before returning to the bar. "I don't usually imbibe," she admitted once they were alone again. "Mom was an alcoholic. At least, that was Dad's opinion."

"I'm sorry."

"Oh. No," she said and waved off his sympathies. "She wasn't…I mean…*Dad* was the psycho. But he was hardly ever around anyway."

"Divorced?"

"Thankfully."

He lifted his drink in some kind of idiotic salute. "Mine, too."

"Your mom ever get over it?"

He shrugged, thinking of the woman most referred to as Sarge. "Ma kind of defies description."

"Give me a for instance," she said.

He considered remaining mute. There was lots to be said for mute. Such as, it generally didn't get you shot or make you look like a dumbass. But he spoke anyway. "For instance, she'd kick me from here to Christmas if she knew I wasn't making a pass at you."

"I don't think…" she began then paused. "What?"

He'd been wrong. She wasn't cute. She was gorgeous. Almost too good to be true. If the bastards in Basic wanted to send the perfect woman to test his willpower, she'd be the one.

"She doesn't hold with self-pity," he said.

"So why haven't…" She paused but spoke again in a moment. "Are you gay?"

He choked on his whiskey, coughed twice then wiped his mouth with the back of his left hand.

"Don't get me wrong," she added, angel eyes wide as forever. "I'm not homophobic or anything. One of my best friends…"

"No," he said.

"You're not gay?"

"Someone would probably have informed me by now if I was."

For a second, she looked ready to continue that line of questioning, but finally she shook her head. "I don't know what's wrong with me. I don't usually act so weird."

"Sometimes the dickheads get to you."

"I guess so." She shrugged. The movement shifted her blouse a little more, showing the slightest bit of cleavage. And wasn't that interesting—turns out half a barrel of whiskey wouldn't limit his ability to do something about her eroticism, after all. But there were other things to consider. For instance, she appeared to be slightly younger than his combat boots. "I kind of thought he was my friend." She glanced at her drink, causing a shiny lock of hair to fall across her cheek. He could imagine it slipping soft as a sigh through his fingers. And with that image in his mind, he realized his combat boots were pretty damned mature for their age.

"The dickhead?" he guessed.

"Yeah."

"Sometimes even friends screw up."

"*Especially* friends," she corrected, and he nodded.

Their gazes met and held. Something sizzled through his inebriated system. Sexual tension maybe. Then again, it might be alcohol poisoning.

"Well…"

They spoke in unison, then drew identical breaths and laughed at the chemistry that bubbled between them, as harmless as nitroglycerin.

"I should get home," she said and motioned for the nearby waiter, but Gabe shoved a fifty into the man's hand and shook off her protests.

"My pleasure."

She looked pretty steady as she rose beside him. "Well…I wouldn't want to ruin your pleasure."

He caught her gaze. She embodied an odd meld of shyness and bravado that he found dangerously appealing. Matched with her sugarplum smile and slim, rocking body, she was all but irresistible.

But he *would* resist. He'd been trained to resist. To overcome. To *lead the damned way,* as the Ranger credo said.

Pushing back the flagrant flow of memories, he lifted his left hand to the small of her back and ushered her toward the door. "Can I call you a cab?"

"No. Thank you. I only live a few blocks from here."

"You don't plan to walk," he said and glanced out the window. By the glare of the overhead lights, he could see it was beginning to spit some kind of viscous precipitation.

"I'll be fine." She turned, but somehow he had moved closer than he'd intended. Her hip brushed his crotch. Her shoulder grazed his chest, and when she inhaled, they shared the same breath. "I'm...ummm..." Her voice was quiet, and there suddenly seemed to be a distinct lack of oxygen. "I'm tougher than I look," she said, but her words were little more than a kitten-soft murmur.

"Yeah?" *Sparkling repartee, Durrand.* But what did he expect? He could barely breathe. Thinking was out of the question. "Listen." His voice sounded oddly raspy, as if it intended to cold-cock his good sense and blindside his best intentions. "I don't think you should get involved with someone like—" he began.

But that's when she kissed him.

# Chapter Four

Her lips met his like a pile-driver. Her fingers were in his hair, and damned if he had any choice at all in the matter. Hormones were slewing up like loosed geysers and suddenly he was driving her backward. Her spine smacked the wall, but she was too busy squeezing his ass to notice.

Need, too long ignored, torpedoed through him. They stumbled into the women's restroom. No one there. Just a mop. A bucket. Three empty stalls. The nearest banged open as they crammed inside. He struggled to lock the door, but her fingers were on his chest, distracting him. How many hands did she have? She was already peeling his buttons open, making such mundane matters as privacy seem asinine. He groaned as she kissed his nipple, rasped something inarticulate as she struggled with his belt buckle. But there was no time for nonsensical noises. Her breasts were calling to him. Teasing, begging.

He reached for her buttons, but they were traitorously small. He was sweating like a turret gunner by the time he got the second one open, and then her breasts were there, mounded above the frothy lace of her bra. He groaned as he cupped them in his hands, growled as he reached around to yank her close, but in that moment, he felt something hard and smooth brush his fingertips.

A pistol was tucked into her waistband.

Sanity sluiced in on a cold tide of memories and betrayals.

Yanking out the gun, he shoved it against her jaw before she could draw another breath.

"Who the hell are you?" he snarled, because suddenly he knew the truth. He'd been a moron. Again. She *was*, in fact, too good to be true. The perfect woman sent to tempt him. But it hardly mattered, because he was sane once more.

She tilted her head back another notch. Her sugar-won't-melt expression was gone, replaced by narrowed eyes and pursed lips as she held her breath and eased her hands cautiously away from his half-bared chest.

"What's going on?" she whispered.

He gritted his teeth against his own idiocy. "Where'd you get the weapon?"

"Colonel Edwards."

"He your commander?"

"My father."

"Who sent you?"

"Sent me?" She shifted her gaze toward the stall door, but he moved the pistol a quarter of an inch and shook his head.

"What were you supposed to do?" he asked. "Drug me? Shoot me? Why? Is this about Tehran?"

"Listen. I'm sorry. I don't know…" She shook her head. "I can get you some help. Just put down the gun."

He scowled. "Help?"

"The agency has a good therapist."

He snorted, not failing to see the humor of the situation. "Tempting offer, but I'm in kind of a hurry. Shep…" He stopped, thoughts jamming tight in his brain. "That's why you're here," he said and croaked a laugh. "You plan to stop me. Well, fuck that! I'm going after Shepherd. I don't give a shit what—"

"I think you should."

He cocked his head. "What's that?"

"Shepherd." She nodded agreeably. "I think you *should…*" she began then slammed the stall door against his injured hand. His fingers went instantly numb. The gun sailed through the air, arced upward then splashed into the toilet. The solid sound of lexon meeting porcelain jerked them into simultaneous action.

He reached for her a fraction of a second before she struck, ramming the heel of her hand into his eye. He staggered backward, cursing as agony exploded in his head. Her knee came up like a piston. He blocked it with his thigh. New pain screamed up his wounded leg, but even through the red haze, he realized she was already dipping into the bowl.

Yanking himself beyond the misery, he grabbed her about the waist, but she slammed against him, driving him backward. They flew through the door together, him dragging her with him as he crashed onto the linoleum. Air whistled from his lungs, but she was already on her feet, already scrambling back toward the nearest stall.

He rose with a growl, lurching toward her, and in that instant, she jerked about, positioned on one knee and gripping the pistol with both hands.

"Stay right there!" she snapped and rose, feet spread, arms extended.

Water dripped from the muzzle of the pistol. It was an ASP. Miller the Moron's weapon of choice. Gabe did as he was told. Right thigh grousing like a bitch, he raised his hands and nodded at her unexpected success. "Who sent you?" he asked again.

"One inch closer and I'll shoot you dead. I swear to God I will." Her voice trembled. The ASP did not.

He forced himself to think. It was about damned time. "Not quite as affectionate as you were a minute ago," he said, and when her cheeks flushed with color, he laughed.

Her brows dipped, drawing together. "Is this some kind of training drill?"

"Sure," he said, mind circling hazily through the mire of

whiskey and pain. "In fact…" he began, but a thought struck him like a frag grenade. "Shit!" He felt dizzy with the realization. "Miller set this up, didn't he?"

She eased over to the wall, motioned him toward the sink.

"He doesn't want anyone to know he fucked up," he said and stepped toward her.

"Don't come any closer!" Her voice was shaking in earnest now. He took another step, driven by rage, by guilt, by a wild wash of emotions he had no time to assess or regret. "I'll shoot! I will," she rasped.

He stopped, inadvertently remembering a dozen times Shepherd had saved his ass. "Well, if you're going to do it, lady, now's the time," he said, but she hesitated, and in that moment, he lunged.

Maybe she would have pulled the trigger if given another moment, but despite everything, he was still damn quick. He smacked the grip of the ASP. It soared into the air. He caught it in his left hand, then took a step back and watched her.

She was pale now. Pale and shaken. But her chin was up, her full lips pursed.

"Didn't your mother ever tell you to shoot first and make nice later?" he asked.

"You won't get anything out of me," she said.

"You sure?" He took a step forward, and in that instant, she bolted.

Grabbing the mop that leaned against the nearby wall, she swung it like a baton. It whistled through the air, catching the ASP's muzzle, but he jerked back and steadied his aim before she could swing again.

They were faced off like badgers.

"I've never shot a woman before. But I'm open to new experiences," he said.

"Tell me what this is about," she ordered and raised the mop like a bamboo shinai.

How damned drunk was she? "You know I've got the gun, right?"

"*My* gun," she snarled, and goddamned if murder didn't gleam in her eyes.

"Why are you—" he began, but suddenly the restroom door swung open. A woman stumbled in, already unbuttoning her jeans. She staggered to a halt when she saw him, jerked her gaze to the gun then scuttled back into the hall, high-heels clicking like castanets.

"You're not getting any more than my name," rasped the mop wielder.

"Jenny, I believe you said. With a *y*. The obviously deranged daughter of Colonel Edwards. The question is, how you know Miller," he said, but a disturbing worm of a thought was niggling his saturated mind. It was slippery, just out of reach, but it was there.

"That woman's going to call 911," she said, jerking her head toward the restroom door. "This place will be crawling with cops. If you know what's good for you, you'll put down the weapon and give yourself up."

The irritating thought was beginning to hum insistently. He tried to drown it with a question. "What do they call you?" He was buying time, but a snide little voice suggested he was out of cash, and maybe, just maybe, out of his mind. "What do you go by, at your desk job?"

"I told you, I'm not giving you any more—" she began, but someone called from the far side of the door, loud and abrasive.

"Hey, Eddy! Eddy, are you in there?" And suddenly, the puzzle pieces clicked shakily into place.

Reality seemed to set the world in slow motion, making everything as clear as vodka: her face, the dingy restroom, Gabe's own glaring stupidity.

He'd made a big-ass mistake. Had propositioned and subsequently threatened Eddy, the one agent Reynolds had recommended. The agent now pissed enough to split his head open with a mop handle. Which meant that Shepherd was shit out of luck, even if he *were* still alive.

# Chapter Five

G abe straightened slightly and nodded once at the mop-wielding woman across the restroom from him. Sure. Of course. Murphy's Law was bound to make its presence felt today. "You're Eddy?" he asked.

She blinked. Eyes more fresh mint than asparagus now, they were as wide as a doe's and doll-bright. "Put down the pistol."

He *should* probably do that, he thought, but couldn't quite manage to make his muscles unclench. 'Cause the kicker was, he might be entirely wrong about the mop-wielder's identity. Again. "Eddy," he repeated, still holding the ASP's cool grip in both hands. "You know Captain Reynolds?"

"Eddy!" Someone pounded on the restroom door again. "Hey! Everything okay in there?"

She scowled, the affronted expression that of a toddler. "Captain Reynolds?" She straightened a little, too. "You mean Uncle Lou?"

Uncle Lou? *Uncle* Lou? He felt his breath catch in his throat. Captain Reynolds stood six feet, eight inches in his stocking feet. If he ever *had* stocking feet, which he did not because he'd been gestated in combat boots. Probably was born with six mags of ammo packed into his pistol belt, too. Gabe had known Reynolds for fifteen years and had never once called him anything more personal than "sir."

Edwards' scowl darkened, going from petulant toddler to angry teenager.

"Eddy! I'm coming in," someone yelled from the hall.

She drew a deep breath, never breaking eye contact. "Just a minute."

"Your uncle Reynolds said I might find you here," Gabe said. The idea of Captain Reynolds being avuncular would have made him laugh if he weren't pretty sure a show of humor would get his nuts kicked into his larynx.

"Did he tell you to attack me in the ladies' room, too?" she asked.

He shrugged, going for casual, but the motion pulled the aching muscles tight across his shoulders and back. "Actually, he suggested the men's room, but I thought…what the hell…a change of venue might be nice."

"Eddy?" The voice from the hall sounded more quizzical than frantic now.

"Everything's fine, Walt," she said and dropped her voice. "I think."

They had reached what used to be called a Mexican stand-off in less pc times. Gabe drew in a lungful of air and forced the muzzle of the ASP toward his knees.

Relief or something like it shone on the girl's farm-fresh features. "I'll be out in a second," she called, then *sotto voce*, "if you give me my sidearm." She narrowed her aspen green eyes at him. "Otherwise, I'll see that you're court-martialed before sunrise."

"I'm afraid my schedule's kind of tight right now."

She tilted her head at him.

"I don't have any time to spend in the brig."

Her cheeks were flushed, her expression determined.

"I don't want this to get messy," he said.

"Well…" She shuffled her feet a little. "You should have

thought about that before you stole my ASP and threatened my life."

He watched her carefully, assessing her weaknesses. She longed to be tough. No doubt about that. But would she risk the lives of others? He didn't think so. "Walt seems like an okay guy. I wouldn't want him to get hurt," he said and did his best to sound ominous.

Apparently, it worked because she inhaled sharply. "If you give me my sidearm we can walk away unscathed. No one the wiser. We'll never have to see each other again."

He gave it a moment's thought then lifted the ASP, dropped its ammo into his pocket, and handed her the pistol.

She took it in a hand as slim as a lightning rod then tucked the weapon back into the waistband of her trousers.

"After you," he said and nodded toward the door.

She raised her chin a notch as if considering his challenge and turned, back straight, movements stiff.

"I'm sorry, Walt." She was apologizing before she reached the hallway. "I didn't mean to worry you. I was just…feeling a little dizzy."

"Hey." Walt's voice was as deep as a well. "Guess I better cut Mindy off. She thought you was with some guy but—" He stopped, brows ricocheting off his receding hairline as Gabe stepped up behind Edwards.

"Oh…" She cleared her throat. "This is…ah, Gabriel." Even the tips of her ears were red now, and her voice had lost a little of its velvety rasp. *Maybe thinking you're about to die in a ladies' room on the seedy side of town will do that to a girl.* "He uhh…" She paused, dropping the verbal ball.

Gabe fumbled for a second, then picked it up and dashed for the end zone as best he could. "I followed her in to make sure she didn't faint."

Walt narrowed his eyes. He was approximately as wide as he was tall, and would have made a kick-ass drill sergeant if he decided against being an attack dog. "So everything's all right?" he asked.

"I'm sorry if I worried you," she said. Her tone suggested that she felt guilty about troubling him, despite the fact that she'd been fighting for her life just moments before.

It could be that Jenny Edwards had an overdeveloped conscience.

Walt narrowed his eyes, gave Gabe a warning glare and shifted his attention back to Edwards. "Well, I guess I'll see you next week then, Eddy."

"Next week," she said and turned woodenly toward the door.

Gabe wasn't sure if he should follow her or stay behind and let Walt beat the crap out of him. He delayed momentarily, debating that, but following her seemed marginally better. He turned and did just that. She'd left her coat, a cute little red number, on a hook near the door and stopped to swing it over her shoulders. He reached up to assist as Walt lumbered back behind the bar.

"Don't touch me," she snarled then smiled at Walt as she tugged her hair from beneath the plaid collar. "Good night," she called and pushed through the door.

Gabe followed her outside, careful not to crowd. He might be wrong, but he thought he sensed a little bitterness. "Don't you want to know what this is about?"

She kept walking. "Seek help," she suggested.

He almost laughed. "Wish I could, but if Shep's not dead already, he doesn't have much time left."

She took another few steps then stopped and pivoted toward him. "Did you lie about your name?"

That wasn't the gambit he'd expected. "It's Gabe. Gabriel Durrand."

"What branch?"

He paused a second, doing his best to keep up. "Army."

She swiveled away with a snort. He stiffened at her derisive tone and wondered why? It wasn't as if the Army had made all his dreams come true. Nightmares more like. Lots of nightmares. And that was only when he was lucky enough to be able to sleep at all.

"I need a language specialist," he said, striding up beside her.

She kept walking.

"And somebody with computer skills."

"Because this Shep's in trouble," she said.

"That's right."

"Where is he? In the brig for attacking an innocent woman in a restroom?"

He didn't bother to tell her that his leg still throbbed where an *innocent* woman had kneed him. It seemed a little petty, considering the circumstances.

"Colombia," he said.

Her brows lowered a little. Two snowflakes and some other snotty form of precipitation settled onto her honey-toned hair.

She stopped finally. The abruptness of the motion suggested she might still be a little tipsy. "You a Ranger?" she asked.

He felt an instantaneous swell of pride. A flush of embarrassment followed close on its heels. Some day, maybe after he was dead, he would grow up and realize that Ranger might be synonymous with chump. "Yeah."

"Shepherd, too?"

He nodded and felt his throat seize up at the mention of the man's name. "He was working a private op."

"Is he your brother or something?"

For a fraction of a second, he considered trying to clarify their relationship, but since Shep's latest idiot move, Gabe couldn't have been madder even if the dumbass was blood kin so why bother with lengthy explanations.

He simply nodded.

She turned away. "Not interested then."

He stepped up after her. "Why the hell–"

"Psychoses tend to be hereditary."

He didn't know whether to laugh or cry, and ended up

deciding that he'd do best to avoid both. "I was told you were a decent terp."

She raised her brows.

"An interpreter. I heard you were pretty good."

"Pretty good?" She stopped short, Nyquil eyes blazing.

He drew back a little. "I believe adequate was the word used."

"*Vete al diablo,*" she said and pivoted away.

The words sounded kind of sexy coming from her tart strawberry lips but he had to assume they weren't complimentary. "Listen, I know we didn't get off to the best start but–"

She spun back toward him. "What part of *vete al diablo* don't you understand?"

"All of it." Frustration burned him like acid. "That's why I need a damned translator."

She stared at him a second then ground her teeth and pivoted away.

He grabbed her arm, but she jerked out of his grasp and faced him with a snarl. "Don't even–"

"Sorry." He raised his hands again. "Listen…" He drew a deep breath, trying to calm himself, to slow down. "He's not my brother. He's just a… He's just a guy who keeps making stupid decisions."

She glared at him. "You lied?"

"He's the 'or something' you mentioned."

"You lied."

He ground his teeth. "It'll be an easy job. Safe. I just need help for a couple weeks. Just long enough to get him out of trouble."

"My father used to say that you'll never learn to stand on your feet if you don't spend a little time on your knees…with an AK-47 pressed to the base of your skull."

Was that sexual? Or spiritual? God, he wished he were just a little less drunk. "Well, I'm sure that's very…prophetic, and as soon as I find Shep I'm going to give that due consideration, but right now—"

"Why do you even care about him if he's such a loser?"

He glanced to the side and blinked, but not because he was

going to cry. God no. "We go back a ways." She was staring at him. He felt his hands shake and tried to refrain from saying more. "And it might...there might be some danger."

She pursed her Blow Pop lips at him. A trio of young women were laughing as they crossed against the light. Laughing as if they didn't have a care in the world.

She nodded crisply. "I'll think about it," she said and turned away.

It took every ounce of willpower he possessed to let her go. But nothing could have prevented him from speaking again. "We're out of time," he said.

She didn't glance back. "*You're* out of time," she reminded him and kept walking.

## Chapter Six

E ddy gave Damian three rapid-fire jabs to the midsection then danced back. He swung to the left, but she ducked, dodged, then kicked up, slamming her heel into his lower regions.

He groaned weakly.

"That's right," she snarled. "Touch me again and you'll be singing soprano for the rest of your pathetic life." Turning jauntily, she walked away with a swagger that would have made Eastwood proud.

The tattered punching bag she'd dubbed "Damian" made no clever retort.

Sweat dripped from Eddy's neck and slipped into her sports bra, but she didn't mind. She liked to sweat. It counteracted the vague fringes of the hangover that threatened and made her muscles loosen and flex. It geared her up, pushed her past the polite boundaries that were as much a part of her as her freckled nose and knobby knees. She may have inherited her father's Kelly green eyes, but her apologetic demeanor came strictly from her maternal side. Perhaps her mother's easy pliability had been one of the characteristics that had most attracted Colonel Edwards in the early days of her parents' relationship, but in the end, when her mother began to feel the need to spread her fledgling wings, it had torn their family asunder like a house of straw. In retrospect, maybe it wasn't surprising that Eddy had silently vowed to be tough. It was rather shocking, however, that she had failed so miserably.

She closed her eyes as memories of the recent evening screamed through her mind. What the hell had she been thinking? Or rather, had she been thinking at *all*? It wasn't as if she made a habit of attacking men in restroom stalls. Neither did she generally agree to consider absurd propositions offered by the aforementioned men.

True, the alcohol she'd imbibed had probably adversely affected her decision-making abilities, but those effects had long ago faded, leaving her reluctantly sober and dismally uncertain.

Indecision gnawed at her. Should she accept Durrand's challenge? Maybe his entrance into her life was providence. She'd wanted field experience since the day she'd first considered becoming a spook. Hadn't she? Or had that just been another lie she'd told herself while safely hidden behind her computer monitor?

Obviously, this wasn't a decision to be made lightly. But with whom could she discuss it? Her mother, though intelligent and caring, would see little but the risk factor. Her father, on the other hand, might well see the value in her following through. It might, as he was apt to phrase it, put some hair on her chest. But unless mandated by a court order, she preferred to avoid speaking to Colonel Edwards. On the other hand, each of her friends would look at the situation through their own lens, when what she needed was objectivity. Someone to give it to her straight.

She practiced her Eastwood glare a moment longer and was blessed with an idea.

In another moment, she was dialing the phone.

The familiar voice on the other end of the line was atypically breathy.

"Ms. France?" Eddy scowled, wondering if she had gotten the

wrong number. The woman's tone lacked its usual workmanlike quality. But maybe that was to be expected at 0200 hours. Then again, she had no idea what time zone—or even what country— the operative lived in. "I'm sorry if I woke you. Shall I call back at another—"

"Who is this?" The words were husky, a little brusque. Ms. France, apparently, had *not* been raised by a soft-spoken pacifist.

"Edwards, Jennifer," Eddy said, converting to a military stiffness she sometimes hid behind in uncertain circumstances.

There was a moment's delay then, "Calling from Langley?"

"Not this time." Eddy refrained from clearing her throat. She wasn't doing anything wrong. Sylvia France was a private citizen, an intelligence gathering individual who worked for the highest bidder. "This is for my personal edification."

"Very well, I'll bill it separately. Is that acceptable?"

"Yes." The conversation felt strange, making Eddy feel twitchy. She half wished she had done more research on her own; she was something of an IT expert in her own right, but Silvia had been known to obtain more information in ten minutes than others could in a week. So she punted, reaching for some kind of socially acceptable small talk. "How are you doing this morning, Ms. France?"

"I've been better," the other woman said and muffling the phone, rasped something low and quiet before speaking to Eddy again. "I hope to be so again soon."

"Oh. Oh!" Eddy said, suddenly understanding the situation; Sylvia France was not alone. But it didn't matter. Eddy wasn't an adolescent. She was twenty-seven years of age and not as innocent as she looked. She'd been told by a number of people that such a thing wouldn't even be possible. "I'm..." She was floundering badly. "I'm so sorry I bothered you."

"No need to be.

"Omar,"—Sylvia's voice was very low. A little hoarse —"don't stop.

"What do you need, Edwards?"

A man moaned. Apparently, Silvia wasn't the only one hoping to improve her circumstances in the very near future. The idea made Eddy fidget like a toddler, but she could hardly hang up now.

"I need some information," she said.

"I assumed you weren't calling for a kidney transplant," Sylvia said then sucked in a long, shuddering breath.

Eddy forced a chuckle and closed her eyes. What was wrong with her? She was a grown woman, wise to the ways of the world. Educated. Liberated. Accomplished.

"Now, Lance!" Sylvia growled.

Eddy blinked as a blush rose to her unseen cheeks. Okay, maybe she *wasn't* wise to the ways of the world, at all. Good gosh, she could barely remember the last time she'd had a *date,* and Silvia France, a woman whose voice and name suggested she was well into her sixties, was, apparently, having a threesome.

"There, Robbie." The words were barely a whisper. "Right there!"

Okay, *not* a threesome. Eddy covered her face with her hand. "Maybe I should call back later." Her voice sounded very small.

"Yes."

"Okay. In the morning then, right after–"

"Yes, yes, yes."

Eddy's cheeks burned hotter. She cleared her throat. "All right. Well…thanks."

"Thank *you,*" Sylvia breathed. Then, "Now, what can I help you with, Edwards?"

Eddy remained mute. There were rustling noises in the background.

"Edwards?"

"Um…yes." She glanced down at the walnut secretary she'd found while antiquing with her mother in upstate New York. The room was cozily decorated, her workspace as neat as a double shot of whiskey, but she felt strangely out of place. "I need intel on a man named Gabriel Durrand."

"Middle name?" The woman was all business suddenly. It was disorienting. Like driving through a blizzard into a dazzling blue sky day.

"I don't know."

"Civilian? Military? Political?"

"Military. Army. Ranger, I think, but maybe—"

"Gabriel Bertram Durrand." There was almost no breathing room between the question being asked and the answer being given. "Born in Greenville, Tennessee on June 3, 1982. Nine pounds eight ounces.

"Yes. Goodbye." The farewell blended almost seamlessly with the rest of the narrative.

"That weight puts him in the ninety-fourth percentile of national births." She sounded almost bored, as if it were noon on a workday and she had nothing to do but sort out Eddy's problems. "He had a slight speech impediment in second grade. Sustained a scar on his left hand from a glue gun incident while in kindergarten."

Eddy swallowed the urge to ask if she was being serious, but in her experience, Silvia France was always serious. Until tonight, Eddy hadn't been entirely sure she was human.

"One sister. Kelsey Ann Durrand, age twenty-nine, second lieutenant in the Army. Has a niece named Zoey. No father listed. Mother is Sergeant Ostroot Durrand. Gabriel graduated middle of his class from Engsbrook High School. Played rugby at the University of Michigan where he majored in engineering and dislocated a shoulder. Enlisted in 2002. Received a silver star for gallantry while serving in Iraq. Was promoted to second lieutenant three years ago. He was wounded in a skirmish in Kabul." She paused, probably skimming the dozen computer screens she was reported to have spread out in front of her like a geisha's painted fan. "Shipped out for a special-ops mission in March of this year during which every member of the team was either wounded or killed."

"Including Durrand?"

"Looks like he took shrapnel to his right hand and leg."

Eddy winced involuntarily. "Anything else?"

"That mission garnered both a recommendation for an award *and* a formal complaint."

"Who filed the complaint?"

"Looks like it was…" She hesitated a moment. "A Lieutenant Linus Shepherd."

Shep?

"And the recommendation for the award?"

"Lieutenant Shepherd again."

A dozen questions struck Eddy at once. "Do you know why?"

"It appears that Lieutenant Durrand saved Lieutenant Shepherd's life."

"And the complaint?"

"Looks like the same reason was listed."

Eddy scowled at the black square of her window. "Does that make any sense to you?"

"I could venture a guess but it would be strictly conjecture and no more valid than yours."

"Okay." Eddy sat in silence, mind spinning. She needed time to sort things through on her own, but she wasn't entirely sure how to extract herself from the bowels of their rather absurd conversation. "Goodbye" seemed a little abrupt. "Carry on" somewhat suggestive. "Well…" Eddy said and managed not to clear her throat. "Have a good night, Ms. France."

"I already did," Sylvia said and hung up.

## Chapter Seven

"Frank!" Gabe rubbed his forehead with this free hand and wished to hell the room would stop spinning.

"Yeah."

"I asked what you know about Jennifer Edwards."

"Dude, it's three o'clock in the morning."

"I'm aware of the time, Frank. I'm also aware of the fact that I didn't inform Colonel Estevez that you have a picture of—"

"Shhh, Jesus, man, what's wrong with you? This line isn't secure."

"Then give me some intel."

"Okay, okay. Geez. Who's this girl you want to know about?"

"Jennifer. Or Jenny. With a $y$. Edwards."

"I take it you struck out, again?"

"I didn't..." Gabe began but stopped himself before things spun completely out of control. "Just tell me what you know." It occurred to him that he should have checked her out before racing half-cocked into the Blue Oyster eight hours earlier, but a recommendation from Captain Reynolds...*Uncle Lou* Reynolds, for fuck's sake...had seemed adequate.

"Jenny Edwards," Frank muttered. "Jenny...Wait a minute. Are we talking about *Eddy* Edwards?"

"You know her?" Gabe quit rubbing his head.

"I know *of* her. She's the colonel's kid. Geez, Durrand, where've you been?"

*A little hot spot called Iraq*, he thought but he didn't say the words out loud. "Just tell me what you know about her."

"Well, if she's got her old man's temper, you're not going to want to piss her off. Heard he court-martialed some poor bastard for not removing cover in the mess hall." His fingers tapped away in the background. Frank McManning had taken a desk job years ago and had been happy to do so. "No use risking such a pretty face," he'd said. Frank was, without a doubt, the ugliest toad of a man Gabe had ever met. "And if she looks anything like her old man, you're definitely going to want to… Whoa!"

"What!" Gabe pulled his hand from his forehead and jerked his eyes up…a little too quickly. Tiny stars swam in front of his face. And although he wasn't entirely sure he was right, he *thought* he saw an F-15 zipping between the constellations.

"Holy shit, brother. She's a grade A yam slam."

Gabe scowled. "I don't even know what the hell that means."

"It means she's a hottie. A fox. A babe. A—"

He felt a muscle tick in his jaw. "I don't need a physical description."

McManning chuckled. "No wonder you struck out."

"I didn't…" Gabe gritted his teeth. "Just give me the information."

"Geez, how long has it been since you got laid, man? You sound a little desperate."

Gabe drew a deep breath through his nose and made a bid for patience. "I think I still have the colonel's number on speed dial."

"What?"

"Estevez. He might be interested to know about the life-size photograph you have on your bathroom wall."

"I don't know what you're talking about," McManning said, but his tone had already lost its irritating hilarity. Frank liked to think he was a ladies' man and a computer genius. He was correct about one of the two.

"Where were you stationed during that little photo op?" Gabe asked as if musing to himself.

"What do you want to know, Durrand?" McManning's voice had pitched up a notch.

"Everything you can tell me."

"The CIA doesn't like people poking around in their affairs. I could get in a lot of trouble."

"Yes, you could," he agreed and let the words lie flat.

"Jesus, you're a hardass," McManning said. More keys tapped. "Looks like she graduated with a 4.0 from Cornell."

Gabe scowled, unsurprised.

"She speaks five foreign languages, three fluently. She's got a decent understanding of computers, and...holy shit, Durrand, don't make this chick mad."

*Too late*, Gabe thought wearily and waited for the bomb to drop.

"She could shoot the ass off a grasshopper at five hundred yards."

Or a Ranger from across the latrine. "Is that all?"

"Is that *all*? According to the stats, she's one of the best marksmen in the country."

"What else?"

McManning sighed as if that should be enough. "She's been with the agency for three years and applied for a field position four times."

The first glimmer of hope shone through. If she'd been shot down that often, maybe she'd be willing to take a chance on something else. "Is there anything in there about tendering her resignation?"

"For real?"

Gabe scowled at nothing in particular.

"Is she throwing in the towel?" McManning asked.

"Could be."

"You think she'd want a job with the best hacker in the

northern hemisphere."

Irritation growled in Gabe's gut. "If I get a chance to talk to him I'll ask if he's hiring."

"God, you're funny."

"Yeah, so let's say, theoretically, she turns in her resignation because she feels she's under-utilized."

"You think a sweet little number like that would waste her talents on a field job?"

"Maybe she's not as obsessed with her looks as you are. Will the agency accept her resignation?"

"Would *you*?"

Irritation growled a little louder. "What'll they do?" Gabe asked.

"My guess?" The shrug was implicit even over the phone. "Offer her a shiny new title like analytic methodologist or leadership analyst. Maybe throw in a raise."

"And if she won't accept?"

"From what I see here, she *is* primed to be a full-fledged spook."

Fuck. "They've turned her down before."

"Yeah, but she's gained some seniority since then."

Double fuck. "When will they give her their decision?"

"Who did she give her resignation to?"

Gabe wearily rubbed his forehead. "Do you know anyone called 'Dickhead?'"

"I know a lot of guys called…" There was a moment of silence followed by laughter. "Dickey Mender?"

Gabe jerked his head up. "Maybe."

"Mender *is* a dickhead, but he's a dickhead with clout."

So she *could*, conceivably, receive the promotion she'd been longing for. The promotion that would make dear old dad sit up and notice, which was, undoubtedly, her objective. But where did that leave Shep?

Gabe closed his eyes to the images that invaded his mind.

McManning was still laughing. "Ol' Dickey wouldn't—" he

began, but Gabe didn't wait for the remainder of the sentence.

"Can you stall him?" he asked.

The laughter stopped cold. "What's that?"

"Their offer, if they make one. Can you delay it?"

"Sure. Why not? I could just go shoot Dickey in the head." It didn't take a genius to interrupt the sarcasm in his tone. "That'd slow him down at least."

"I was thinking of something a little less drastic. Maybe waylay his email."

"What makes you think that's how they'd respond?"

That was a pretty good question actually. Gabe scowled, trying to remember the chain of events of the night before through the blur of whiskey. "I think she said she emailed her resignation."

The other end of the line went silent long enough for Gabe to realize a new possibility "Could you get rid of *hers*?"

"What?"

"*Her* email to him. Could you delay that?"

"Absolutely not!" McManning said, but the answer was too quick.

"You could, couldn't you? You could make sure they don't see it."

"No."

"Just for twenty-four hours."

"What makes you think they haven't already read it?"

Shit! Another good point. He gritted his teeth. "If they haven't..." he said. "If they haven't read it yet, can you make it go MIA?"

"Not only would that be immoral, it's—"

"I'll forget the colonel was naked in the pictures."

"Blackmail?" McManning's voice had slipped into the region where only dogs and gerbils could hear him. "You're blackmailing me?"

Gabe rubbed his eyes with his free hand. They felt as dry as dust. "Delay their offer for forty-eight hours and I might even forget you were the one spanking him."

# Chapter Eight

"When will you be flying out?"

"What?" The single word sounded more like a growl than Gabe had intended. He cleared his throat, tried to calm the whiskey demons that pounded the interior of his cranium and tried again. "Who is this?"

"Eddy Edwards."

He sat abruptly, making the room swim a dizzying circuit around him. Planting his right hand on the bed to stop its crazy rotations, he carefully squelched the frenetic hope that soared through him like a hunting eagle. He didn't want to sound too eager. "Is this Jenny with a *y*?"

"Are you hung over?"

"Aren't *you*?"

There was a moment of silence before she spoke again, voice as sober as a monk's. "I will require more information before I can make an informed decision regarding your proposal."

He stood jerkily. Outside, it was fully light. But that was hardly the most surprising part of the morning; he was naked except for one sock. That sock was pink. It was a thinker. "They *are* dickheads," he said.

"What?"

His mind was careening wildly. "I assume the fact that you called means the agency accepted your resignation."

"It's 0700 hours. I doubt they've had an opportunity to consider it."

And he doubted they would for another forty odd hours. Guilt, or something like it, diffused his system, but guilt was a luxury he could ill afford. "What do you want to know?"

"How many operatives will be on this mission?"

"Operatives?" He glanced around the hotel room, searching for God knew what. Maybe the other pink sock? "You really are a spook aren't you?"

"Mr. Durrand, how many—"

"Me," he said and, closing his eyes, abandoned his search. "It's me."

The phone went silent to the count of five, long enough for him to wonder if she had hung up. "Are you suggesting that you are planning a rescue mission into the jungles of one of the most notorious drug countries in the world with no backup?"

"No," he said, "I'm going to have a linguist with me."

She paused a second. "Mr. Durrand..."

"Lieutenant."

"Lieutenant Durrand, I do not think you are fully prepared for this mission."

He refrained from laughing out loud. "That's possible," he said, tone admirably dry.

"In which case, it would not be prudent to involve myself in what could only laughingly be called a—"

"I didn't realize it was your goal in life to be prudent," he said and didn't entirely try to keep the contempt from his voice.

He could almost feel her irritation through the phone. "Neither can I, in good conscience, allow *you* to do something so idiotic."

He did laugh now though he managed to resist asking how she planned to stop him.

"I think it would be much wiser to notify our operatives already in South America about Mr. Shepherd's circumstances."

He drew a deep, steadying breath. "I think you know me better than that, Jenny with a *y*."

"I don't know you at all."

"Are you trying to say you didn't check up on me?"

There was a pause. "I'm not a complete idiot, Mr. Durrand."

He didn't comment. "Then unless your intel is completely worthless, you realize I'm going in whether it's *prudent* or not."

She sighed. The sound was long and slow. He waited in silence. It would have been nice to believe that he wasn't holding his breath.

"Why?" she asked finally.

"Why what?"

He thought he heard her grind her teeth in frustration. It was not an altogether unfamiliar sound. "This could very well be a suicide mission. Why are you going in?"

He thought about the last time he had seen Shep. The bastard's smile had been as cocky as ever. It was the bleak despondency in his eyes that had been new. "He owes me money," he said finally.

"Really?" Her tone was dubious at best. "How much?"

"Ten bucks. We made a bet."

"About what?"

"Whether or not he was going to get his ass kicked in Colombia."

"So, you're going to spend thousands of dollars and possibly forfeit your life so you can extract him from an ass-kicking and collect your ten bucks."

"The Army takes its bets very seriously."

"What do I get out of it?"

He felt his heart rate speed up, but squelched the hope that sailed through him. Hope was for dreamers like Linus Shepherd, who, despite everything life had taught them to the contrary, expected to find the good in people. "I'll split the bet with you."

"Anything else?"

"An all-expensive-paid jungle tour."

"Your generosity is astounding. But I don't think—"

"Plus a good review," he added and let the words lie silently between them. He drew a deep breath and closed his eyes. If he had an ounce of morals, he'd hang up immediately and make damn sure she *didn't* go. Hell, if he had a *soul*, that's what he'd do. But he'd left his soul somewhere near Tehran.

"Like I care what you think about me," she said finally.

He snorted. Pushing the motel's cheap curtain toward the scarred window trim, he glanced outside. He had a dynamite view of the parking lot just a few yards away. A quiet zephyr tossed a plastic bag against a weary Honda's right front tire. "Let's cut the crap, shall we, Edwards? We both know why you joined the agency."

"Do we? Maybe you should enlighten me."

"It's to one-up your old man," he said and let the curtain drop back into place.

He thought she would argue. In fact, he was sure of it, but she drew a soft breath. "All right, let's say your hypothesis is correct. What does that have to do with anything?"

"I'm a decorated Ranger, Edwards. A favorable review from me is as good as pinning a silver star on your chest."

"Sleeping with the right people are you?"

He snorted and glanced to his right. The room looked like a cluster bomb had been detonated under the bed. "Listen, honey, a Ranger doesn't have to sleep with anyone." And rarely did, if he was the norm. "We're gods in the military world." Lonely ass gods with missing pink socks.

"What's the pay?" she asked.

It took him a moment to shift gears. A little longer to forgive her insult to the Army. And how fucked up was that? "Five thousand upon return to the states," he said.

"And if we don't get Shepherd out?"

He stifled a wince. "Either way."

She was silent for an eternity. "All right. I'm in," she said.

For one long moment, he forgot how to breathe. But he forced his lungs to expand, convinced his lips to speak. "Don't you want that in writing?"

"I think I can take your word on it."

Or she wanted to outdo her father so much she really didn't care about the money. Jesus, what had her old man done to her? "Can I take yours?"

"If I say I'll do it, I'll do it."

"And?" His chest felt tight.

A knock on the door surprised him. He scowled and pushed the curtain aside again.

Eddy Edwards stood on the opposite side of the window, eyes steady as a drill sergeant's on his. "I'll do it," she said.

## Chapter Nine

G abe wrapped a stray shirt around his waist and yanked open the door.

Dressed in blue jeans and a short, fitted jacket, Eddy Edwards looked hopelessly fresh and ridiculously young.

"I thought we were in a hurry," she said and stepped forward, ponytail bouncing as she moved past him.

"So you're really in?" he asked.

"You a lightweight drinker *and* hard of hearing?"

Relief flooded him in a tidal wave of gratitude, but he nodded, going for casual. "All right. I still have some loose ends to tie up, though, so you're excused to pack whatever you'll need for the next couple weeks while I—"

"My bag's in the car."

He tried to remember not to blink at her like a stupefied steer. Didn't she need...tampons or hair barrettes or *something?*

She raised a brow at him and broke the silence. "What needs to be done on your end before we leave?"

It occurred to him that her take-no-prisoners attitude shouldn't surprise him. He'd been raised by a woman who could command a squadron of rank recruits while doing one-armed pushups, but

Sarge Ostroot Durrand didn't look like she'd just been plucked off the streets of Disneyland, while this girl... He mentally bumped himself back to the business at hand. "We need airline tickets. I have to pick up some meds, and there are a few people I'm going to interrogate this morning."

Her brows jumped. "Interrogate?"

"Talk to," he corrected. He'd been told on more than one occasion that most of his conversations could be called interrogations. It wasn't necessarily meant as a compliment.

"All right," she said. "I'll purchase the tickets while you get dressed." Dropping her pack from her shoulder, she pulled some sort of unknown electronic device from a side pocket.

He glared at her, but she was already completely focused on the gadget.

"You *are* going to dress, aren't you?" she asked and glanced up.

The quizzical expression on her happy-pixie face almost made him crumble, almost made him admit how damned much he appreciated her taking a chance on him. But he wasn't a dumbass about women like Shep was. And now seemed like a good time to prove just that.

"I think we'd better get something straight first," he said.

"What's that?" she asked, but her lightning-fast fingers never slowed on the miniscule keyboard.

"I'm CO on this mission." He narrowed his eyes. Hers were as round as marbles. "What I say goes. No questions asked, no discussion needed."

Her brows lowered the slightest degree. "Are you afraid of strong women, Durrand?"

He snorted, considered trying to convince her that such a thing was ridiculous, but was pulled irresistibly toward honesty instead. "Damn straight."

She didn't try to hide her surprise, and for reasons entirely unknown that only increased his sense of gratitude. And her appeal.

"If you knew Sarge, you would be, too," he added.

"Sarge?" She shook her head a little. "Your commanding officer?"

"My mother," he corrected.

Her cotton candy lips quirked up just the slightest degree. "Get dressed," she repeated.

He would have liked to argue, but he was getting chilly, and although he admittedly didn't know jack shit about women, he was pretty sure goosebumps weren't considered particularly virile.

"What's with the pink sock?" she asked.

Gabe glanced around the room. Three pairs of jeans and a crumpled dress shirt were laying kittywampus across the arm of a nearby chair. Maybe he should have had housekeeping do their thing, but obviously, he hadn't. It was anybody's guess why he was phobic about people touching his stuff. Shepherd, of course, had all sorts of hypotheses. Generally, Gabe had to threaten him with dismemberment to make him quit guessing.

"Can't seem to find the other one," he said, remembering the topic.

"The other what?"

He skimmed the nightstand where the bright colors of a paperback novel lay waiting and tried not to wince. "Sock," he explained.

"That's probably for the best. From what I hear, they can be a little homophobic south of the border."

"The socks come with me," he said.

Her brows rose slightly, but her fingers never paused. "Whatever you say, Lieutenant."

He nodded. Good job, Durrand, he thought. Make an ass of yourself over a pair of pink socks. He took a step forward, effectively blocking her view of his reading material. And where was he supposed to dress? Scuttling into the bathroom like a blushing debutante seemed a little girly, but he wasn't all that thrilled about baring himself with Miss Ponytail sitting three feet away. Not that he wasn't one hell of a man…but he'd never been terribly fond of pity, and the scar that snaked halfway around his thigh wasn't exactly babe bait.

"You okay with a window seat?"

Her question brought him out of his quandary. He glanced at the back of her head. She didn't turn toward him. Hell, she didn't even seem *tempted* to turn toward him. He dropped his shirt over the book on the nightstand like a challenge.

"Durrand?" she said, fingers still tapping.

"That's fine," he said and snatching up the closest pair of jeans.

She nodded through the exchange then skimmed her gaze down the tiny screen. "You feel comfortable sitting in an exit aisle even in case of an in-air emergency?"

He snorted and hopped a little as he tugged on his jeans, favoring his injured thigh. "You need my birthday?"

"June third, 1982," she said.

He scowled at her knowledge. It wasn't until that moment that she turned around. He zipped his jeans with rapid-fire haste. Not that he had anything to hide. Well…he had a *lot* to hide. But it wasn't as if he were embarrassed or anything.

"I assume you know I have some computer skills," she said.

He lowered his brows. Okay, so her marksmanship was on par with his, her intel was superior, and her memory was disturbingly accurate. Didn't mean he had to challenge her to a wrestling match or anything.

"Can we be ready for the five o'clock flight?" she asked.

"Ready or not…we pop smoke at 0500."

She nodded and tapped a few more keys. "What else do we have to accomplish before we leave?"

He tried not to act impressed even though it generally took him half a day to make flight reservations. He and technology had declared a temporary ceasefire, but they weren't exactly ready to share a foxhole.

"I'll gather info from the remainder of Miller's squad before we leave."

"Names?"

He searched the room again and finally saw a knitted pink toe peeking out from under the bed. "I don't know how many shipped out. But Woody Hilt, Emery Tellman, and Ken Jacobs returned." Pulling off his lone sock, he snagged the other one, stowed them away in a special compartment of his pack and glanced around for more appropriate footwear.

She watched him, brows raised.

But it was best if she learned right now that he didn't owe her any explanations.

The room was as silent as a tomb.

He paced to the far side. She still didn't speak.

"My niece made them," he snapped finally. Finding a crumpled shirt, he yanked it over his head, glared past the ribbed neckline and challenged her to make an issue of it.

"Okay."

"It's important for kids to get validation for their skills. Where the hell are my black socks?"

Without taking her gaze off him, she pulled a pair from under her curvy left butt cheek and handed them over.

"So...Tellman's in the psych ward?" she asked.

Durrand took the socks and tried like hell not to be impressed by her intel. It was bad enough she had sock-finding talents. Computer skills were overkill. "Has been since they got stateside." It was possible, he realized, that he sounded a little petulant.

"You think it's wise to question him?"

"They only gave me a couple minutes with him before. I'm going to try again today."

"It looks like Hilt is still in the hospital. I'll talk to him."

Gabe pulled on his left sock. It wasn't nearly as fuzzy as Zoey's. "You can talk all you want. He won't talk back."

She glanced at him.

"He's still in a coma."

"Oh." She cleared her throat, and goddamn, was she actually embarrassed about her lack of knowledge? "Then I'll take Jacobs and you can—"

"No!" He'd said the word more forcefully than he intended. Zoey would call it his grizzly bear tone. Her mother, Kelsey, wouldn't be quite so pc.

"Why not?" As for Eddy, she was already stiffening with anger, making it seem like a bad idea to tell her the true reason for his refusal. Ken Jacobs was a loose cannon with a bad attitude and a degree of loyalty to Miller that bordered on suicidal. Last time they had spoken, things hadn't gone well, but Gabe was going to try again. A little persuasion might be called for this time.

"I need you to get all the intel you can about Putumayo," he said.

She glanced at him. He could feel her attention like the heat of the sun. Was that a good sign?

"Best guess says that's the area where we'll find Shep. Also, learn everything you can about current kidnappings."

"You think he's been kidnapped?"

Gabe's stomach coiled tightly, but he ignored the gastric gymnastics as best he could. "I think someone else was kidnapped, and they went in to get him out." It was the kind of stunt Linus Shepherd would pull: risking his life for some dumb-ass kid who had skipped into Colombia for a shoebox full of cheap weed. "Get any vaccinations you need: tetanus, malaria. Whatever. Make sure you have clothes that'll stand up to the jungle climate, and take care of any necessary last-minute details on your end."

"Is that all?" If she was being facetious, he couldn't tell it by her tone. Shepherd would have been whining like a lazy hound after half that list.

"That'll do for now."

"Okay," she said and slipping her electronic device back into its hiding spot, rose to her feet. "I'd better get to it. And ahh…" She skimmed her gaze toward the nightstand.

He darkened his scowl. "What is it?"

"You don't have anything to be ashamed of; my grandmother liked those bodice ripper novels, too."

# Chapter Ten

"Hey," Gabe said and pulled out a chair in the common area of Wellington Medical Center. It was as bright as Zoey's Play-Doh and groaned like a ghost when he settled his weight into it.

Emery Tellman glanced up from the jigsaw puzzle at which he'd been poking. He was young, barely past twenty. His hair was blond and short, making his receding hairline seem more advanced than it was. "Hello," he said.

Gabe tried a smile. "How's it going?"

Tellman shrugged, a truncated lift of one skinny shoulder. "It's okay." No recognition showed on his Scandinavian features.

"They treating you all right in here?"

The start of a scowl began to bend the area between the boy's brows. Gabe tensed. The powers that be had insisted that he not disturb their patient's calm, but as far as Gabe could recall, there had never been a single person in his acquaintance that he hadn't disturbed in one way or another.

"Do I know you?" Tellman asked.

"Not really." Even though they had met just two days before. Tellman was one of the lucky few who had made it back from

Colombia. Anger inched into Gabe's system again, fueled by images of Miller's arrogance, and Shep's dim-witted insistence on following the man. "I'm just a friend of a friend."

"Oh." The boy nodded and glanced back down at the cover of the puzzle box. Diamer Face was as pretty as a picture in the glossy photograph. But she could be a bitch when the temperature fell to thirty below zero and al Qaida were hidden behind every damn peak.

Silence fell between them. Impatience gnawed at Gabe like a bad-tempered hound. "You like the mountains?"

Another abbreviated shrug then a sharp glance. "You a shrink?"

"No." Gabe shook his head, trying to look innocuous. "I just came by to talk to you about a few things."

"They already done that."

"They already did what?"

"Talked to me."

"About Colombia?"

"Who?"

Gabe clenched his fist beneath the table and forced a grin. He'd once dated a girl who had compared his smile to that of a Rottweiler, handsome but a little scary. "Colombia. Not a person. A place. A country. You were there, remember?"

The boy's scowl deepened a tad. He shook his head.

"I'm from Texas. Olivia, Texas." Tellman lifted his chin a little with typical Texan pride. Or maybe he was simply pleased with the fact that he had remembered the name of his birthplace.

Gabe's stomach coiled, a product of too much alcohol and too little actual nutrition. He stared across the scratched laminate of the table at Tellman's vacant eyes and reconsidered. Maybe he needed a drink right now.

"You were on a special-ops mission with a man named Miller. Ben Miller. Remember?"

Tellman's expression became increasingly blank for a second, but then he chuckled. The sound was deep and low and hollow, as if it came from the depths of the kind of well they had found in places like Hadidi and Biskra. "Miller time."

"That's right." Excitement scooted through Gabe. "That's right. Miller time. You were in Colombia with Miller and a squad of men. Remember?"

"In Colombia?"

"Yeah. In the jungle. You went there to find someone." He was just guessing now, but it was a pretty good guess.

Tellman nodded, but whether it was because Gabe was correct or simply to be agreeable was uncertain.

"Where were you exactly?" Gabe asked.

Tellman's vague gaze had shifted away, but he spoke in a moment. "Hot there. Steaming. Like shoo fly pie fresh from the oven."

Gabe felt every nerve ending sizzle to wakefulness. Shoo fly pie was one of Shep's weird-ass favorites, a disgusting dessert to be spoken of in hushed and reverent tones. "Can you remember—"

"Mosquitos." Tellman shook his head. "Mosquitos big as aircraft carriers."

"Listen, Emery, I'm just going to take another minute of your time, but you have to concentrate. Okay?"

A shoulder lift.

"There was a cowboy with you. A Ranger. Name of Linus Shepherd. He might have gone by another name. Roy Cherokee maybe. Had about a thousand dumb-ass pickup lines. Do you remember him?"

The man scowled as if deep in thought.

Gabe held his breath.

"I like pie," the other said finally. "But I don't really know if I care for—"

Gabe's patience snapped. "Listen up, soldier!"

The boy jumped, eyes going wide as an infant's. From across the brightly colored room trying too damned hard to be cheerful, a stout woman glared at them. Her cardigan was straining to maintain its station. The name *Irene* teetered on one mountainous breast.

Gabe gave her a smile. She made a face as if she'd just tasted something left too long in the bowels of the fridge.

"Sorry," Gabe said and shifted his attention back to Tellman. "I'm sorry, but Shep's a friend of mine and I really need to—"

"Shep?" Tellman hissed.

Irene was making her way across the scarred linoleum, trundling between the tables toward them with the single-mindedness of a war machine.

"Linus Shepherd." Gabe was holding his breath. "You remember him. He wears a battered old cowboy hat, talks like he just stepped out of a John Wayne movie."

Tellman nodded. Gabe did the same, trying to be supportive, to urge him on.

The boy scowled, thinking hard, then, "I'm hungry."

Gabe did his best to refrain from shaking the kid. "I know you are, buddy. But just focus for one more second. You remember Shep. Tall, dark hair, irritating as a toothache."

"What's going on here?" Irene had arrived at their table. Even more intimidating up close, she could probably match Gabe pound for pound. If he had brought his sidearm, he would have been tempted as hell to draw it.

"Hi," he said and tried another smile, hopefully this one was a little less carnivorous. "I'm Gabriel Durrand."

She narrowed her already narrow eyes.

"Emery and I have a mutual friend," Gabe assured her. He kept his tone as bland as rice pudding.

But she didn't seem to care about his blandness or their mutual acquaintances.

Gabe cleared his throat. "We're just—"

"Shep!" Tellman said suddenly. "I remember."

Gabe slammed his gaze back to the wounded soldier. "Where were you?"

Tellman scowled as if every coherent thought had been suddenly washed from his brain.

"Mr. Tellman," Irene's heavy brows had lowered considerably, a feat Gabe, for one, hadn't considered entirely possible. "It's time for you to return to your room."

"Where?" Gabe repeated, packing every ounce of focus into that one word.

Irene faced him, fists squarely planted on ample hips. "Mr. Durrand, your friend's *friend* has had a traumatic head injury and must not be—" she began, but Gabe reached out and squeezed Tellman's arm. His skin felt warm beneath his fingers.

"It was hot," Gabe said. "There were mosquitos. You were on a mission. Miller gave the orders. Shep cracked the jokes."

Tellman grinned. The expression was lopsided. "What's the difference between a pirate and a goat?"

"Pirate jokes!" Gabe felt his chest squeeze up tight. "Yeah. God, Shep loves his dumb-ass pirate jokes."

Irene reached for Tellman's other arm, drawing him inexorably to his feet while still glaring at Gabe. "We don't allow cursing in this—"

"Good old Shep." Tellman chuckled.

"Where was he?" Gabe rumbled. He rose to his feet but kept his grip on the boy, effectively causing a tug of war with Irene. "Where was he when you last saw him?"

Tellman stared at him, eyes suddenly clear, lips just slightly quirked. "In the pasture," he said and shook his head. "Shep was the best damned cow dog we ever had."

## Chapter Eleven

Eddy rushed through the morning, mentally checking things off her to-do list. She was hell on wheels when it came to lists. Unfortunately, she wasn't nearly as good with people. Especially men. Oh, yeah, she could kick the crap out of Damien—the punching bag she'd christened after her first disappointing crush —but when a real, live, breathing man was in the vicinity, she had a tendency to act like a twittering idiot. And men like Gabriel Bertram Durrand... Well, she'd have to be brain dead not to be unnerved by him. And she wasn't brain dead. She was, in fact, highly intelligent, despite what her current plans suggested to the contrary.

She closed her eyes as her printer regurgitated information regarding the Colombian drug trade, the escalating hostage situation, and civil unrest. There would be time to get sick while reading it later on the plane. As for the vaccinations Durrand had suggested, she'd managed to take care of those at a walk-in clinic not fifteen blocks from the little short-saled Tudor she'd purchased two years before.

She'd notified everyone that needed to be told about her impending departure...namely her mother and her two friends from work. It seemed like a pathetically short list. But it was a good thing there weren't more, because honest to God, she wasn't meant for lying, and yet she had done just that, inventing an unlikely story about vacationing in Aruba then bushing off further explanations by insisting she had to hurry to catch her plane.

She glanced around her personal space. Copper bottom pans hung above her persnickety stove. Small but meaningful memorabilia adorned the walls and furniture in the living area. A wooden mask from Tanzania, a conch from Fiji. As an Army brat, she was rarely in one place for long. Maybe that's why her cozy little home felt so much like a sanctuary. And never more than now. She glanced at the couch where soft blankets and earth-toned pillows were tossed across the cushions. On the north wall, next to the much-used fireplace, hung her mother's first attempt at a patchwork quilt. After fifteen more, Barbara Comfrey-Edwards had become considerably more proficient. Eddy, however, still preferred the blanket with the crooked angles and fraying edges.

But the Tudor was just a building, she reminded herself and glanced out the window. Gray bullets of slush were slashing the pane. Which was just as well; at least the tropical heat of Colombia would seem pleasant by comparison.

"Printing complete," the automated voice announced, making her jump. Embarrassed by her own skittishness, she pulled the printouts from the tray, turned off the machine and stood.

Outside, the slush had turned to hail. Sharp shards of ice struck her window, tapping out a warning. Don't go. Don't go. Don't go, don't go, don't go.

But she shook her head, aligned the papers, slid them into a folder and shoved them into her carry-on. In less than ten hours she would be on a plane to Bogotá. But what was she going to do until then?

———

"I'M NOT SAYING it was Miller's fault," Gabe said.

"You don't *have* to say it, Durrand." Ken Jacobs was short, tan, and wiry. A three-inch laceration had been sutured above his right eye. He had a barbed wire tattoo inked around the biceps of his left arm, and the upright stance of a warrior even when shit-faced, which he currently was. He couldn't have looked more Army if he'd had the United States flag branded on his forehead. "I know you think it's his fault that Shep's gone Elvis."

Gabe gritted his teeth and reminded himself to be civil. "Listen, I just want to find him. I've got nothing against Miller." He was getting better at this lying thing, though he'd never be the virtuoso Shep was...that dumb bastard could make you believe blue was red without breaking a sweat.

Something clouded Jacobs' eyes...but whether it was guilt or worry or embarrassment, Gabe had no idea.

"I can't help you, man," Jacobs said and took a significant slug from a tankard of beer big as a Bradley tank. O'Grady's microbrews tasted like cat piss, but at least the establishment offered a *lot* of cat piss. And O'Grady himself was ex-Army down to the short hairs, so military types tended to frequent his place.

Gabe tightened his fists beneath the table and forced himself to lean back in his chair. Nonchalant as a cobra. "I just want a little information. That's all."

Jacobs took another drink then made a face and shifted his gaze away. "Even if I wanted to stroll down memory lane with you, Durrand, I can't," he said. "I signed a contract. Said the mission was confidential."

Gabe tried to nod, agreeable and easy-going. No one was going to beat the crap out of anybody today. "I appreciate your loyalty," he said. "But a man's life is at stake here, and I can't—"

Jacobs snorted, drained his glass and motioned toward the bartender.

"Something funny?" Gabe asked.

"No. Nothin'," Jacobs said and motioned more emphatically toward O'Grady.

Gabe took a deep breath, calming himself. "I know this is tough, but—"

"Leave me the fuck alone!" Jacobs snarled suddenly and lurched to his feet.

Gabe met him halfway, grabbing him by the shirtfront. "Listen you little—"

"Is this man threatening you, soldier?"

The voice from behind was soft but firm. It seeped into Durrand's frontal lobe, urging him not to do anything unreasonable, like toss Jacobs through the nearest goddamn window. "'Course not," he said and shook his head without turning toward the speaker. "I'm just trying to convince my friend here not to drive drunk."

"Your friend is a hero." The words were said with melodramatic passion. Gabe turned his attention to the speaker. And there, not four feet behind him, stood Jenny with a *y* Edwards. Gabe felt the shock strike him a moment before his brows lowered.

"What the hell are *you*—"

"And I won't stand for you bullying a hero."

Gabe stared at her.

"I don't need your help, lady," Jacobs said.

"I know you don't," she agreed. Her voice was as dulcet as a dove's, completely devoid of that in-your-face attitude she'd demonstrated in a certain woman's restroom not many hours before. "But Daddy'd never forgive me if I just sat over there and let this big oaf badger you." She took a step forward, giving Jacobs his first clear look at her, or as clear as his sight could be through a half gallon of piss-poor beer.

"Christ!" he said, which made Gabe think his vision was pretty damn sharp after all. "Where'd *you* come from?"

She was still wearing the jeans she'd shown up in at Gabe's door that morning, but her jacket was gone. The frilly pink number that now covered her breasts was little more than a red flag to a bull. She drew a deep breath, expanding her lungs and the aforementioned breasts, which weren't big by some standards, but what bull really cares?

"What's your name, soldier?" she asked.

Jacobs straightened, pressing his chest against Gabe's knuckles.

"Jacobs. Lieutenant. First class," he said and quirked a little shit-eating grin.

"Well, Lieutenant, I'd like to buy you a drink. On my daddy. Unless I need to call the cops first," she said and glanced pointedly at Gabe, who forced himself to drop his hands and step back a pace.

Eddy moved seamlessly into the space. "I'm sure you can find some flies to torture or something," she said before turning her attention on Jacobs. Her expression softened.

"Where'd you serve, Lieutenant?"

"What?"

"Your forehead." She blinked, eyes wide and misty, like a fairy-tale pixie about to burst into tears. "Where were you injured?"

"Oh…" He motioned toward the chair Gabe had just vacated. She sat down, movements slow and deliberate, bending forward maybe just a little more than necessary.

Jacobs's gaze dipped irresistibly toward her cleavage. His lips curved up. "I was stationed in Stuttgart for a while."

"You hear that, bully?" she asked, lifting her gaze toward Gabe's. "He's a patriot."

Gabe managed to resist rolling his eyes but couldn't completely contain his snort of disdain.

"Something wrong with Stuttgart?" she asked.

"Not if you're on vacation," Gabe rumbled.

"Listen, you fucking—" Jacobs began and stumbled to his feet, but Eddy grabbed his arm.

"Ignore him," she said. "Tell me about yourself."

Gabe watched the options scuttle like cockroaches through Jacobs' swamped brain: fight with a pissed off Army Ranger, or let the pretty lady stroke his starving ego?

Gabe watched the jaunty lieutenant settle back into his chair and wondered what the hell to do next. Half of O'Grady's sparse patrons were staring at him as if he'd just come down with a critical case of head lice. And Edwards seemed to have things well under control. Maybe she'd even be able to drag some information out of the inebriated little shit. On the other hand, maybe she wasn't there to get info at all. Maybe she really thought he was being unfair by badgering Jacobs.

"We're going to have to ask you to leave."

Gabe glanced to his left then lowered his gaze. O'Grady was an under-sized man with a super-sized belly. "We support our troops here." He jerked a thumb toward a sign half hidden behind a bottle of Absolut. "Says there we have the right to refuse service to anybody we want."

Gabe stared down at the bartender and wondered if he should leave. Although, really, what were the other options? Tell O'Grady Jacobs had left a man behind to die in the jungle? Tell him Eddy Edwards was not as innocent as she seemed, and might, if some dumb fuck were lucky enough, end up in a bathroom stall doing things that violated a couple dozen health codes?

In the end, retreat seemed to be his most dignified option.

# Chapter Twelve

"So, Lieutenant Jacobs—"

"Ken," he corrected. He slurred his name a little and his eyes looked kind of hazy, heavy-lidded and half closed.

Eddy allowed herself a moment to wonder if Durrand had left the building yet, but since Jacobs had the entirety of his dubious attention pinned on *her*, she assumed the intimidating Ranger was no longer present.

"Ken," she agreed. It wasn't difficult keeping her voice soft and empathetic. Colonel Edwards was never going to win father of the year, but he had taught her to respect the military and this poor soldier had obviously gone through hell. "Where are you from?"

He took a sip of his beer. Not his first, obviously. Maybe not his thirty-first, but she wasn't one to throw stones. Not after the debacle of the previous night. "Mansfield."

She smiled a little, charmed that he assumed everyone would know the state his birthplace resided in. "Mansfield?"

"Ohio," he explained.

"Oh." She took a sip of the daiquiri she'd purchased while covertly watching Durrand from the mostly hidden dining area. "I have an uncle from Toledo. He's my favorite of Dad's—"

"What you doing here?" Jacobs interrupted.

She blinked. He might get a little spooked if she told him she'd come to meet *him*. That she'd learned everything regarding his life that she possibly could in an hour and a half. Enough, in fact, to make an extremely accurate guess regarding where to find him at seven o'clock on a cold October evening. "I was supposed to meet a friend here." It was an out and out lie that immediately caused an influx of guilt. Heat diffused her cheeks, a hated corporal betrayal, but he didn't seem to notice.

"Yeah?" He hooked one elbow over the back of his chair and slouched sideways. "Girl friend or guy friend?"

She cleared her throat, refused to squirm and pressed on. "Girlfriend. Mary...Beth. She lives just down the road on—"

"She look like you?"

"What?" She tried to smile again then realized she was still smiling following their previous exchange. Damn her overly cheerful demeanor! Why couldn't she have inherited the colonel's glower or his gravelly speech? Her high school chemistry teacher had once compared Eddy's voice to that of Minnie Mouse. Maybe she was wrong, but she had a feeling it might be difficult for Mickey's girl to be taken seriously in the world of espionage and covert activities.

"'Cause if she does..." Jacobs leaned forward. Perhaps in his mind the movement was suave and suggestive, but for a moment, Eddy feared he might actually topple onto the peanut shells that covered the floor. "Maybe the three of us could do a little something together."

"Something—" She shook her head, unable to imagine what that something could be. It would be a miracle of biblical magnitude if he were still conscious in thirty minutes. In fact, if she had a lick of sympathy, she would tuck him into bed right now and... Oh! Bed! *That's what he's talking about,* she thought and felt her cheeks burn hotter. "No, I'm sorry. She's...Mary Beth's not going to make it tonight."

"Well..." He grinned. Only one side of his face seemed to be fully functional. "Her loss."

"Yes. Yes." She cleared her throat. "So, what happened to your forehead?"

"It's nothing."

"It looks like something," she said and tried to revive her sympathetic expression.

He shrugged.

She softened a little. Okay, so he'd mentioned a threesome... that didn't make him the antichrist. It wasn't her place to find fault with the ways he chose to forget the atrocities he had witnessed. But it *was* her place to learn all she could about his previous mission. "Our country owes you a great debt," she said.

His eyes gleamed for a second but he didn't respond.

"Did I hear the bully say you were in Colombia?"

His brows dipped a little.

She fiddled with her napkin and let her gaze dip shyly in that direction. "Most people think if you're not stationed in a Middle Eastern desert somewhere, you're not in danger. But I know there are brave men like you in all corners of the world."

He shook his head and glanced, narrow-eyed toward the door through which Durrand had exited. "Asshole thinks he's some kind of living legend just 'cause he saved a couple men in...wherever."

"I'm sure your mission was just as dangerous."

His face clouded. He gulped his beer again, draining half the glass.

"Did you lose anyone?"

He swallowed, nodded, drank again. "They didn't have no chance." His face twitched. "Fuckin' sneaky bastards."

She drew a breath and reminded herself that even though she was playing him, she was doing so for a worthy cause. A man's life was at stake. *As is your career*, a cynical voice suggested, but she hushed it. "I'm so sorry for your loss," she said, but he didn't seem to hear her.

"I have myself a drink now and then." He'd slipped a little lower in his chair. "Couple beers, maybe a few shots of whiskey, but them bastards that sell shit to kids..." He shook his head. The movement tilted him precariously toward the floor. "They deserve to be taken down."

It took her a moment to divine the gist of his words. "You didn't..." She shook her head. "You went down there to take out a drug lord?"

He straightened a little. "I didn't say nothing about—" he began, but she was already speaking.

"My cousin overdosed." It was almost painfully pleasant to speak the truth.

His lips remained slightly parted.

"Crack," she added. "Probably from Colombia." She was making assumptions now, but he nodded.

"Beautiful, my ass!" he said and drank again.

"What?"

He exhaled a snort. "Damn bastard is ugly as a turd."

"Who? The drug lord?"

He neither confirmed nor denied. "But we shouldn't a never gone down there. Shoulda stayed home." His eyes welled with tears. Eddy felt honest sympathy bubble up.

"I'm so sorry."

He wiped his nose with the back of his hand. "We couldn't have gotten him out anyhow."

"Who?" she asked, but he no longer seemed to be aware of her presence.

"Fucking river was swollen like a goddamn dick."

"River?" She'd studied Colombian maps until her eyes burned just hours before, and wildly ran through the major waterways in her mind.

"Big as a fucking ocean where it crossed the highway."

"What highway?"

"Was supposed to be so simple." He snorted a laugh. His eyes spilled a couple of sparse tears. "Take him out before he knew what hit him, rendezvous, and head for Alfonzo. Be sipping champagne and munching peanuts by supper time."

"Who were you taking out? The beautiful one? What was his name? Bello? Alano?"

He nodded vaguely, or maybe he was falling asleep. "Bastard was waiting for us with a goddamned army."

"Where were you exactly?"

"I hid." He wiped his mouth with the back of his hand. It shook like a windsock. "Burrowed down in the mud and waited." He was staring into the middle distance, voice little more than a whisper. "Fucking river gets more traffic than the Autobahn. Mostly drug runners. But I thought maybe I could…" He shook his head as if he didn't know what he had hoped for. His breath shook with his exhalation. "I thought sure the others would make it. Miller's a fucking genius. Thought he'd get us all out. But there wasn't no boat, and two miles through the boonies seems like a thousand. Only a few of us made it to the car."

"You think the rest were already dead?"

He was staring sightlessly forward. "Yeah."

"Did you see their bodies?"

"They was dead!" He snarled the words as he jerked across the table toward her.

She juddered involuntarily, but in a moment, he settled back into his chair. "I wanted to wait, but we had to get back. Hilt was floating in and out of consciousness. Tellman and me was both hurt bad." He swallowed and lifted his gaze to her, a dozen aching emotions clear in his eyes. "We didn't have no extra time."

So they had left men behind. She closed her mind to the horror of the situation and wondered if she would have done things differently. "Your friends were lucky you were there for them," she said, but he was lost in another world again.

"Lucky? Took us two fucking days to get to Alfonso. By that time, Tellman was babbling like a damned monkey."

"Alfonso? Is that a person or a—"

"I wasn't doing much better." He closed his eyes for a second, then opened them and focused on her. "Been kinda lonely since I got back."

Her heart stuttered in her chest as she tried to sock away the information she needed to remember. "We owe you a great deal for your sacrifices," she said and rose to her feet.

His lips cranked up. He straightened with her. "You want to thank me proper?"

"What?"

"Wouldn't take too long." He slipped his gaze to her chest.

"I'm afraid I have to go," she said, but he grabbed her arm suddenly.

"You're just like all the rest!"

Fear skittered up her spine. "My father, the colonel, is expecting me to be—"

"All sweetness 'n' smiles. Ooohs and ahhhs. You appreciate our service." He moved in closer. His breath was ripe with fermentation. "But when push comes ta shove...." He pressed up against her. "You ain't willin' to service me 'n return."

She jerked her attention to the bar but no one manned the lengthy expanse. In fact, not a soul was in sight. How had she become oblivious to the fact that the place had emptied out?

"Let me go," she said but her voice quavered.

He shook his head. "All warm and cuddly 'til it's time to pay up, ain't ya?"

"I don't owe you anything."

"But ya said you did. Said ya owe me a whole shitload."

"I just meant...I meant the country at large."

"Well..." He leaned in. "I *am* large." She could feel his erection against her hip. "And here you are."

"I'm sorry if I gave you the wrong impression, Lieutenant—"

"A bit ago I was Ken," he hissed and, suddenly, he was shoving her toward a back room. One hand was fumbling with his belt.

She jerked out of his grasp. But he caught her left arm, leaving her right free.

Her reaction was sharp and instantaneous. He stumbled backward, eyes open wide, hand cradling his bruised trachea.

"I'm sorry," she rasped. "I'm so sorry. Are you—"

"What's going on?" O'Grady appeared from nowhere.

"I…" She snapped her gaze toward the rotund barkeep. "I'm not sure…exactly."

"She 'it me. The 'itch!" Jacobs gasped, but the words were garbled.

The bartender was scowling. "What? What'd he say?"

"He said…he itches!" Eddy rasped and grabbing her jacket from the nearby chair, torpedoed out the door.

# Chapter Thirteen

"**W**here have you been?" Edwards' voice was steady but her tropical eyes looked a little troubled. Gabe tossed his keys onto the television stand near the door of his crappy motel room.

"I picked up a few supplies," he said and turned toward her. "What'd you learn?"

"What?"

"From Jacobs," he said and watched her. Who the hell was this fresh-faced little pixie? And how had she known where to find him and Jacobs? "That's why you wanted to meet the illustrious lieutenant, isn't it?"

Her brows dropped a little toward her watercress eyes. Watercress? Holy fuck, he was losing his mind. "What do you have against him, anyway?"

"Me? Nothing," he said and settled onto the bed to undo his laces. "How about you?"

"What about me?"

He let his first boot fall to the floor. "What'd you think of him?" he asked and propped his right foot onto his opposite knee.

She studied him for a long second before shrugging "I think

he's very..." She paused. He waited, but finally she shook her head as if her opinion wasn't valid. "I think they planned to take out a drug lord."

"What!" He dropped his foot abruptly to the carpet, causing his thigh to throb. But he ignored it. Even Shep wouldn't be dumb enough to waltz into the jungle to overthrow a drug lord whose position would be reassigned moments after the original fucker was gone. "You're wrong."

"Not usually," she said.

He lifted a brow at her. For a fresh-faced pixie, she sounded as confident as a staff sergeant.

"All right." He made himself remain still. Forced himself to refrain from pacing. "What makes you think so?"

"Something Jacobs said."

"So you don't have any hard proof."

"Like a signed affidavit?"

Sarcasm...from a sprite. What next? "What'd he say?"

"That he took a drink now and then but—"

Gabe snorted at the enormity of the understatement then raised an apologetic hand and motioned for her to continue.

She did so after a moment. "He drinks some, he said, but he resented those who sold stuff to kids. He said people should pay for those crimes."

"Resented? That's what he said?"

"I'm giving you the gist."

Gabe scowled. It *did* sound like the type of sanctimonious crap Jacobs could shovel out with both hands. He took a calming breath, careful not to get too hopeful. Optimism could get you killed as quick as a landmine. "Okay. For the sake of argument, let's assume you're right. But there's a drug lord for every acre of coca down there. How are we going to know if—"

"I think his name means beautiful. Or maybe handsome."

He stared at her.

She stared back. "Alano maybe, or Bello, or..." She shook her head. "Maybe Guapo? Or—"

"Guapo Herrera?" A bomb detonated in Gabe's stomach. He winced at the effects but kept himself steady.

"You've heard of him?"

He didn't answer. Everyone had heard of Herrera. "What makes you think he had anything to do with Shep?"

"Jacobs said the guy they were after was supposed to be beautiful, but he's not."

He shook his head.

"Guapo means handsome." Her brows lowered a quarter of an inch over her...What the hell color were her eyes? "You really *don't* know Spanish, do you?"

He barely spoke the King's English, but he didn't see a reason to share that fact with her.

Hurrying toward his bags, he pulled out a map and spread it across his bed. The blankets had gone AWOL some time ago. "From what I've heard, Herrera's territory extends from here"—he stabbed his index finger near Pitalo then dragged it toward San Jose de Frague—"down to here."

"Then he's expanding."

He jerked his attention to her, hiding nothing. "What are you talking about?"

"Herrera. He must be claiming new territory."

"Tell me what you know."

She moved in next to him, tone rife with excitement, warm body vibrant beside his damaged one.

"Jacobs said they were supposed to rendezvous where the river meets the highway, but the waterway was engorged."

He skimmed the map. "That could be anywhere."

She shook her head. "There aren't that many roads that we Americans would consider highways."

He considered that. "And the worst of the drug problems are in the remote regions of the southeast."

She nodded. "Jacobs said that once they rendezvoused, it took them two days to get to Alfonso."

"Alfonso? What's that? A Colombian operative?"

"Maybe. But I don't think so." Her face was flushed. "He said he thought they'd be sipping champagne and munching peanuts by supper

time. Alfonso Bonilla Aragon is Cali's international airport."

Excitement ignited in his gut. "They didn't fly out of Bogotá?"

"I don't think so."

"So we're right. They must have been in the southern region."

"Yeah."

"Far enough away to take two days to reach the airport."

"While wounded."

"Which could increase their travel time considerably," Gabe said and focused every ounce of his attention on the map.

The next two hours were spent in plans and arguments and hypotheses. By the time the conversation wound down, they had pinpointed an area just north of the Ecuador/Peru border. Of course, that region included thousands of square miles of jungle.

Gabe felt drained.

He exhaled and straightened. "We'd better get some cot time. Once we reach Colombia, there won't be much rest until we bring Shepherd home. You sure you have everything you need?"

She didn't answer him immediately. He turned toward her. Her eyes were wide and guileless, her full mouth soft against her ripe-preaches complexion. Worry shone clear as daylight on her face.

Something coiled tight and cautious in Gabe's gut. "You having second thoughts?" he guessed.

She drew a deep breath, giving him a chance to brace himself for her resignation. He'd have to be a world-class ass to try to convince her to risk her neck for someone she'd never even met. But going in alone would considerably reduce Shep's chances. The internal conflict was playing hell with his digestive system.

"I'll make every effort to be sure you get home without—" he began, but she interrupted him.

"Jacobs thinks Shepherd's dead."

The words hit him like a frag grenade, but he took a deep breath and let the impact roll over him. "Did he see his body?"

She shook her head. "I don't think so."

He exhaled slowly, releasing the balled-up tension as best he could while trying to ignore the twist of relief he felt knowing she wasn't planning to abandon the mission. Not yet anyway.

"But he says the others were supposed to meet them at the agreed rendezvous point. I think he believes Shepherd was killed by Herrera," she added. Stark worry clouded her eyes, but he refused to be touched by her concern.

"Yeah, well..." Gabe glanced at the map still stationed on the bed. Where was Shep? Where was the stupid bastard right now? "Jacobs has been wrong before."

"He said he wanted to wait, but they were badly wounded and they couldn't—"

Gabe jerked toward her. "Did he say he was a fucking coward, too?" He growled the words into her face then grimaced when she jolted back a pace. But she rallied in a moment, jerking up her chin and holding his gaze. "What's with you and Jacobs?" she asked.

"Nothing," he said and forced away the guilt he felt for frightening her. Hell, she'd have to be an imbecile *not* to be scared. But she was obviously tougher than she looked. Then again, the same could probably be said of Tinkerbelle. "What's between *you* two?" he asked and wished instantly that he had not allowed the words to leave his lips even though he sure as hell didn't ask out of jealousy. Maybe a niggle of worry for her still existed, which was unfortunate, because in the Durrand family, chivalry could get you an ass-kicking as quickly as stupidity.

"What are you talking about?" she asked. "I just met the man."

"You just met me, too," he said and let the memory of them in a cramped restroom stall float unspoken between them.

She stared at him, nostrils flaring a little. "You didn't seem to have any objections to my moral code twenty-four hours ago."

"I'm not questioning your scruples, sweetheart. It's your lack of caution that worries me."

"I'll keep that in mind." She preened a smile but her eyes looked deadly cold and her tone was equally frosty. Every survival instinct in him suggested he drop the subject, but sometimes his instincts failed him.

"If you're itching to get yourself killed, there should be plenty of opportunity in a couple of days," he added.

She caught her breath. He silently ground his teeth. What the devil was wrong with him? He sure as hell didn't want to scare her off. He needed her. But the thought of her life's blood seeping into the jungle floor made him feel queasy.

"You think Jacobs is dangerous?" she asked.

Gabe scowled. That wasn't the direction he'd planned for this conversation to go. But it was a safer direction. Anything was better than letting her think she might never return from Colombia. But he couldn't stop his next words. "I lied," he said.

She stared at him. "About what?"

"About…" *Shut the fuck up*, he told himself. "About…Shep and me."

She nodded, pixie face solemn. "I thought your feelings for him ran unusually deep."

Maybe it was a testament to his worry that he didn't catch her drift immediately, but finally, he realized what she was saying and snorted. "I'm not gay."

"As I told you, I've got nothing against the homosexual community. In fact—"

"I'm *not*—" he began again then exhaled heavily. "I owe Shepherd my life. That's why I'm going in." He glanced to the left. The world outside the window was as dark as hell. "'Cause I have to. But…" He ground his teeth. His right hand was throbbing. "I don't know if I can keep you safe."

She stared at him.

He glared back. "Did you hear me? I said there's no guarantee you'll—"

"What do you think I am?"

Her voice was low and earnest. Still, he couldn't keep the word *pixie* from popping into his mind again. Luckily, he was a little bit smarter than he had feared and managed to keep from verbalizing the thought.

"Listen," he said. "I've done some research about you, too. I realize you're pretty good with a rifle and—"

"Pretty good?" Her back stiffened. She took a step toward him. "I'm fast. I'm accurate. I'm—"

"And that's terrific," he said, closing the distance between them. "If your assailant is a paper target and *if* you have a rifle, and *if* you have time to sight. And *if*—"

"I've had combat training."

"Fan-fucking-tastic. You can probably handle yourself one-on-one with any instructor who's hoping to get lucky later in the day. But what if he doesn't give a shit if you wind up dead?"

She opened her mouth to respond, but he rolled over her.

"What if there's more than one? What if there're six of the bastards and none of them gives a damn whether you live through multiple rapes?"

He winced. He hadn't meant to be quite that brutal, but she just gritted her teeth.

"What's the matter, Durrand? You scared?" she asked. "You trying to find a reason not to save your best friend, after all?"

He stared at her for a full three seconds then laughed out loud. The sound boomed against the walls like a cannon shot. "Damn right, I'm scared. I'm scared out of my fucking mind, and if you had half a brain in your head, you would be, too. They treat women like pigs down there. And that's their *own* women. Blond American women with emerald eyes and lips that drive men out of their..." He shook his head, searching for the safe, politically correct track that his frantic mind kept jumping. Inhaling deeply, he tried to relax a smidgeon. "Jacobs is a goddamned saint next to half the men in South America."

"Again. What is your problem with him?"

"My problem! Holy shit! My problem?" he snarled and felt the truth slip away from him. "He abandoned his team!"

"He thought they were—"

"Left them in a third world shit hole like fucking old boots." His eyes stung, but dammit, Rangers didn't cry!

"Maybe he's right." Her eyes were solemn, her chin slightly lifted as if she expected a blow, but she didn't back away. "Maybe Shep was already...already...dead when they shipped out."

His stomach threatened treason, but he calmed it then stared at her to the count of five. "Jacobs is never right," he said finally and turned away.

"I've been thinking," she said. "Why don't we take him with us? He knows the terrain. He knows the—"

"Listen, Edwards..." Gabe turned slowly, keeping his temper in check. "If you think he's such a great catch you can hook up with him when we're Stateside again."

"I didn't say he was a great catch. I'm just saying he's not as bad as you paint him, and maybe—"

"Is that why you punched him in the neck?"

Her lips remained slightly parted, but her eyes narrowed. "I thought you left O'Grady's. Thought you were picking up supplies."

He controlled his smile. If fourteen years in the Army had failed to teach him not to underestimate an opponent, life with three opinionated women had not...even if one of those women was only eight years old. "I did leave. But when I got to my car, I realized I'd missed dinner. So I went back and ordered a burger basket in O'Grady's dining area. It wasn't too bad. A little greasy but—"

"You were spying on me!"

"I couldn't even see you from the other room." That much was true, though Gabe had been painfully aware of what was happening inside the bar. "But when Jacobs started gasping and croaking and calling for help..." He shrugged. "It was hard not to notice."

She jerked her chin up a notch and turned toward the door. "I'll see you in the morning."

"You could stay here," he suggested. "Save you the drive."

"No, thank you." Her voice was almost painfully prim.

"Listen…" Guilt or something like it gnawed at him. "I need you well-rested. You can have the bed. I won't sleep more than a couple hours any—" he began, but she swung toward him before he could complete the sentence.

"I'll see you at 0400 and not a minute before. Do you understand me?"

"Yes, ma'am," he said and opened the door for her. She marched through like a cadet on parade, face set, gaze straight ahead.

He exhaled softly, knowing he was lucky as hell she hadn't bailed yet. And knowing, just as surely, that life hadn't taught him that much after all; he was still an idiot where women were concerned.

# Chapter Fourteen

"Get up, pig!" The order was punctuated by a shattering kick to the ribs.

Pain slammed through Shepherd's torso. He grunted and rolled onto his back, knees protecting his internal organs as much as possible. His wrists were tied behind him. His head felt too large for his body. Above him, a man called Treg grinned over the black sights of an AK-47. Beyond their small encampment, the jungle claimed the world.

"What?" Shep squinted, trying to still the gong that banged relentlessly inside his cranium. "Is breakfast finally ready?" Witty. He was always so damned witty, but he was afraid his charm might be somewhat diminished by the fact that his bottom lip was split down the middle, making his enunciation dubious at best. "Hope ya didn't burn the toast. And could I get a side of bacon? I'm a little tired of the swill ya been—"

Treg kicked him again. Fire burned through Shepherd's side and burst like fireworks inside his head. He gritted his teeth and struggled for consciousness. He wasn't going to pass out. Not now. Not when he was alone with this waste of human flesh. Shep had lain, unmoving and silent for the past fifteen minutes, listening as Treg's comrades trudged into the woods.

"Get up!" the man snarled, but Shepherd shook his head. His brain felt numb and every fiber in his body screamed with pain, but he was coherent enough to be intimately aware of every weapon his captor possessed. There was the rifle of course, a serviceable weapon that was practically a third arm to these fucking rebels, but it would be heavy, and in Shep's weakened state might well become a liability. A machete protruded from his captor's drawstring waistband. It had possibilities. But it was the short blade tucked into Treg's boot that Shep most coveted.

"Nope," Shep said. The refusal was no more than a grunt. "If there's no bacon, I'm stayin' in bed."

"Then I shoot you in the goddamned head!"

Shepherd felt sweat wind a shivery course between his shoulder blades, but he'd reached his limit. Death or freedom. One or the other would be his today. "Guess you're not scared of Guapo, then," he said and forced a broken smile.

Treg pulled his lips away from tobacco-stained teeth. "I ain't scared of nothing."

"That must be 'cause you're too stupid to know better."

Shepherd could practically see the insult rumble through his captor's brain. He watched anger bloom into rage on the man's flat features. He leaned forward to grab his captive, and in that instant, Shep yanked his knees to his chest.

Treg jerked up the rifle's muzzle, but Shepherd was already kicking out, slamming his feet forward with all the strength his failing body could muster. His heels connected with the bastard's chest. Treg tumbled to the ground, and in that instant, Shepherd propelled himself onto the other's flailing form. The Latino's eyes were wide, his mouth open for a scream, but Shep jerked his own head forward. Pain exploded inside his cranium as he connected with Treg's brow, but his captor was already going lax and there wasn't a second to lose.

Rolling wildly onto his side, Shep wriggled downward in an

attempt to wrench the blade from Treg's boot. His fingers were numb, his arms practically immobile, but he finally managed to grab the blade's wooden handle.

Laughter boomed off to his right. Shepherd jerked his head up, searching for the source of the noise. The knife tumbled to the ground. He swore quietly, reverently, and tried like hell to find the blade again.

There! Just beside the kidnapper's still-inert body. Grabbing it in his right hand, he knelt and tried to locate the bonds around his ankles...the bonds just long enough to let him shuffle through the woods like a hobbled mule. The blade scraped his boot. Voices echoed off to his left.

He whispered a curse and jerked the knife a quarter inch to the right. It scratched against hemp. He sawed frantically. A few cords snapped. He tried to yank his feet apart, but the attempt was weak. He cut more frantically. A little more rope gave way. Almost there. Almost—

"Hey!"

Shepherd jerked toward the voice. The knife toppled from his numb fingers. Two men were staring at him, identical expressions of surprise stamped on their faces.

They chattered something in Spanish and raised their rifles. Point blank. They had him dead to rights. But death seemed worth the risk when the jungle was only yards away.

"Sit down! Down!" shrieked the nearest guard.

"Okay. Okay!" Shep said but instead he staggered to his feet. The frayed rope snapped, but not before it pitched him forward. He fell. A bullet whistled through his hair.

Beside him, Treg moaned and lifted his rifle. Drawing his knees up, Shep slammed his heels into the man's head. Bullets sprayed around him, but he was already upright, up and racing erratically toward the anonymity of the trees.

Shouts and bullets and curses followed him but he was free. If he were going to die today, he wouldn't die alone.

## Chapter Fifteen

"What do I call you?" Edwards asked.

Gabe gritted his teeth at the question and flicked his gaze to the ear-budded kid sitting in the aisle seat next to her. A heavy rap beat throbbed from the boy's head. Holy shit, every single micro-sized chair on the airplane was filled. If the seating got any tighter, the passengers would have to be shrink-wrapped and hung from the ceiling. But he refused to allow himself to spill over what might laughingly be called an armrest into Edwards' territory. He liked to think he possessed his share of self-control. But she was sex on steroids, at least as far as he was concerned, and the 747's latrine wasn't big enough for round two of the Battle of the Head.

"Kenny Chesney's great isn't he?" Gabe asked and watched the kid's expression. The boy's eyes didn't even flicker. His head never stopped jerking to the irritating beat.

"What?" Edwards asked.

Gabe pulled his gaze from the boy's enraptured face, confident his conversation with Edwards would be private. Ten minutes into the flight, he wasn't sure about much of anything else. Keeping the contents of his stomach where they belonged was generally all he could think about while in the air. "What did you call your last serious boyfriend?"

Edwards' brows jerked toward her hairline.

"We're going to have to make up a cover story," he said and faced forward again. Years of pretending he wasn't prone to motion sickness had taught him it was best to focus on an immobile object straight ahead. "People get nervous when they find out I'm Army, and any yahoo with a cell phone can pry into other people's business." Himself excluded, of course. He was born to be a caveman. "Don't make it too complicated. We're on vacation. My name is Luke Lansky. I'm from Tennessee."

She scowled, thinking. "So that people will underestimate you?"

He chanced a sidelong glance at her.

"I mean, it's assumed that southerners aren't the brightest birds in the branches."

He raised a brow at her. "Sarge's family settled in Cumberland more than a hundred years ago. It's a good place to disappear."

"Oh. I..." Color flushed her cheeks. "You don't have an accent."

"I thought I'd get more respect without it," he said and managed not to laugh at her discomfort, mostly because his gut was trying to toss its contents into his esophagus. "Don't get too fancy with your cover story. The chances of a SNAFU will be considerably reduced if we keep our stories as close to the truth as possible."

She nodded, and for a moment, he thought she might be ready to move past her faux pas but he was wrong. "Listen, I'm so sorry. I didn't mean to disparage... I mean...there's nothing wrong with the south. I just—" Her embarrassment looked physically painful. He watched her expression with interest. "You matriculated from the University of Michigan! The blue and gold with the...the badgers and the—"

"The wolverines," he corrected.

"Yes. Sorry. The wolverines. Aggressive animals I guess with…" Her shook her head, words dwindling.

He watched her, fascinated. If she were any damned cuter, you could use her as a cake-topper. But that non-threatening demeanor might come in handy. It was unlikely anyone would take her too seriously. On the other hand, it made all his as-of-yet-un-quashed macho instincts sing like canaries. He quieted the irritating song-birds and make sure his expression was bland.

"Do you have a name preference?"

"What?" she asked and looked as if she might burst into another apology.

He leaned a little closer, in case the teenager seated next to her wasn't as brain-damaged as he appeared. "What should I call you?"

"Oh. I don't…" She shook her head. "Are we married?"

He had no idea why her question made his intestines crank up another half loop. But it probably wasn't a good sign. "Do you want to be?"

He hadn't thought her cheeks could get any redder. But he'd been wrong.

"I'm just thinking maybe it would be easier to share a room and…things if they thought we were."

He said nothing.

"Colombia is a very…" She paused as if trying hard not to make any more pc blunders. "Moralistic country."

"Except for the drugs and kidnapping and murders."

"Except for that, yes," she said. "They're ninety-two percent Catholic."

"All right." He nodded solemnly. Her eyes were as wide and guileless as an infant's, making him long to roll her in bubble wrap and send her back to the U.S. with *FRAGILE* stamped on her fore-head. "So we're Mr. and Mrs. Lansky. What's your first name?"

"I want to be a doctor."

He stared at her, deadpan. "You probably should have chosen different electives then."

She smirked at him. "You said to keep our stories as close to the truth as possible."

He quirked an eyebrow. It was about all the motion he could manage without tossing his cookies.

"Mom was always sure I could cure cancer if I set my mind to it."

He couldn't help but stare. The world might be headed to hell in a handbasket, but damn she was charming.

"Grand died of liver cancer when I was twelve. So when I graduated from high school, I took all the pre-med courses I could." A shadow of sadness settled over her sunny features. "I think Mom was really disappointed when I didn't continue."

He didn't fail to notice that she didn't say anything about being unqualified for medical school. Shit, what kind of woman would give up being an M.D. to chase down drug lords in the bowels of a foreign country?

"Anyway, I'll be Sarah. *Dr.* Sarah, an oncologist, in Colombia on my honeymoon."

Honeymoon? Holy God! Did she think he was a monk, he wondered and resisted squirming in his undersized seat. "Never work," he said. "If we were just married, they'll expect us to spend all day in our room." Where he would go fucking nuts if she were near. "We'll say we're on one of those wildlife tours."

"An eco-adventure?" she asked then, "Good idea. We're roughing it. We've been married a year and a half."

As if a measly eighteen months would make a difference in his libido. "Okay."

"What do you do for a living?"

"I'm an automotive engineer," he said, and she laughed.

He cocked his head at her, careful not to move so fast as to upset the barfing gods. "Do you find all engineers amusing, or just the automotive kind?"

"Do you even know what a pocket protector *is?*"

He scowled at her. It'd be great if she didn't turn out to be crazy, he thought.

She cleared her throat and explained. "You're never going to pass for an engineer. A fireman maybe or a..." Her gaze swept downward. The blush that had just started fading from her cheeks increased again. "Never mind. You're right, an engineer's fine."

A fireman or a what? he wondered, but before he was stupid enough to ask, she tilted away from him. "I'm going to try to get some sleep," she said and closed her pasture-green eyes.

In profile, she looked like an angel. Not the biblical kind with the sword and the kickass attitude. But the cutesy kind perpetrated by popular culture.

Holy hell, he should be horse-whipped just for thinking about her.

## Chapter Sixteen

E l Dorado was suffering from universal anonymity. It looked similar to every other airport through which Eddy had ever traveled.

She waited on gray carpet near a beige wall beside tan plastic chairs. Their three recently claimed bags lay by her feet. Durrand waited for the fourth, a backpack far too large to be allowed as a carry-on. Boarding and disembarking had gone without a hitch. But then why wouldn't they? Not wanting to raise any red flags, they had left every single weapon they owned in the U.S. Eddy missed her ASP something dreadful.

She had slept for a while on the plane, after which they had expanded their cover story a bit; they'd met online and had immediately been attracted to each other because of their mutual interest in adventure and environmental concerns. But the stranger who waited beside Durrand near the luggage carousel probably would never believe that Eddy's interest had been sparked for such mundane reasons. Creamy skinned and curvaceous, she glanced up at Gabe through dark, forest-thick lashes. Her hair was inky black and a dimple winked in her left cheek when she spoke to him.

He replied.

The woman's lush figure was packed into a dress as snug as a snake's skin, but if Durrand noticed, he didn't seem to care.

*Maybe he really is gay,* Eddy thought. Judging by the few panting minutes they'd shared in the Blue Oyster's restroom, however, that explanation didn't seem very plausible. On the other hand, during the bumpy six-hour flight south, he had kept his considerable brawn within the tight confines of his seat. If not because of differing sexuality, then why? True, Eddy was hardly irresistible. She was too flat, too pale, too apologetic, and too—

"You here for the tour?"

Her self-examination was interrupted by a nearby voice. She turned toward the speaker. He was balding, overweight, and midwinter pale. American, she thought. Possibly from the New England area. Maybe the Midwest.

"I beg your pardon?"

"The coffee tour. You've got the backpack," he said and motioned toward the bean brown bag that lay near her feet. It was, she had to admit, similar to the one suspended from his plump shoulder. "The bus leaves in seven minutes. You want help carrying your packs? My name's Nick, by the way. And yours is —" Eddy watched him bend as if to grab her luggage but Durrand's booted foot stepped onto the nearest strap before he could.

Nick, hand outstretched, straightened slowly, gaze running up Durrand's khaki-clad leg to his face.

"Luke." Durrand's voice was little more than a rumble, his expression about as friendly as a bulldog's. "And this is Sarah." He paused a second, as if to let the meaning of his words sink in. "My wife."

"Oh. Oh!" Nick took a step back. "Well, it's nice to make your acquaintance," he said but his expression suggested it wasn't all *that* great. "So you're here for the coffee tour?"

"No," Gabe said.

"Oh, my mistake. I thought she..." He motioned vaguely

toward Eddy, flighty hand on the approximate level of her breasts. Gabe's brows lowered another notch. Nick cleared his throat. "Well, what are you folks doing in Bogotá?"

Circumventing the backpacks, Eddy curled her fingers around Durrand's arm. It was as hard as granite, tense with distrust and probably about a hundred thousand reps on the bench press. If he planned for anyone to believe he was anything other than military, he should probably learn to smile. Or at least quit growling. "We came to see the cloud forest while there still is one," she said.

"You're not here for the coffee?"

"No. Sorry."

"Oh, well...that's too bad," Nick said, but the glance he gave Durrand suggested he'd probably survive his disappointment. "Nice to meet you anyway."

"Yes, you too," Eddy said.

They watched the little man hurry away.

"You okay?" Durrand's voice was low.

Eddy glanced up in surprise and pulled her hands from his arm. It wasn't the easiest thing she had ever done. "Of course. Why wouldn't I be?"

He stared down at her, expression as hard as his biceps, but maybe there was something a little softer in his eyes. Something he did a pretty fair job of hiding under normal circumstances. "Just be careful."

"Careful of what?"

"Everything," he said and returned to the carousel.

Eddy turned back toward their waiting bags. So...paranoia, she thought. She hadn't expected to see that particular characteristic in such an intimidating man, but sometimes she caught him favoring his right leg or flexing his wounded hand, and maybe one never quite recovered from the kind of trauma he had seen. Physically or emotionally.

Then again, it wasn't her place to psychoanalyze him. It was her place to help get Linus Shepherd back home. And to that end, she'd better get her ducks in a row.

Pulling her tablet from the nearest backpack, she googled Guapo Herrera. A dozen articles popped up relating to a multitude of businesses. He was the president of *Juguetes Nuevos* and the CEO of *Amazon Textiles* but it was his farm that interested her most: six thousand hectares of land just west of San Agustin.

She pulled up images of the area. Judging by the pictures, the hilly region was heavily forested and steeped in mystery. What better place to grow the lucrative coca bush? And for that matter... to hold a prisoner?

Then again, Herrera would have to be a fool to keep an Army Ranger captive. On the other hand, Shepherd would have to be just as idiotic to allow his captors to know he was military, and despite what Gabe had told her, she doubted Shep was any such thing. A showoff maybe. A blowhard and a prankster, but not a fool. Still, would a drug lord run the risk of holding a man like Shepherd hostage? A man with obvious survival skills? It seemed far more likely that he would kill such a man, but... She gave herself a mental shake. She wasn't here to decide his fate. She was here to find him, alive or dead. So—

"Hey, pretty lady..."

She glanced up.

A young man with dreadlocks and amber-tinted sunglasses was grinning at her, one bare, tanned leg cocked, one scrawny arm sporting a bevy of brightly braided bracelets. "If you need a place to crash for the night, you could come on home with Elf."

It took a moment for Eddy to realize he was speaking to her. Longer still to understand that he spoke of himself in the third person.

"Oh. No. Thank you," she said.

He moved closer. His left ear was pierced in five places. His grin was cheery. "Elf has plenty of room," he said.

"Well..." She was beginning to fidget. "That's awfully nice of you...Elf, but I'm..." She felt her cheeks warm even before she forced out the lie. "Married."

He grinned. "Elf don't mind. We can still have us a few laughs. Why don't you—"

"Seriously?" Durrand's voice was desert dry.

Eddy jumped guiltily then zipped her gaze to her employer. He looked peeved, tired, and slightly nauseous. Guilt sluiced through her like a tidal wave, though honest to God, she didn't know why.

"This your old man, pretty lady?"

She zapped her attention back to Elf. "Um, yes, this is Luke."

He had to cock his head back a little to look into Durrand's face. He was grinning when he did so. "You two here on your honeymoon or somethin'?"

"No, we're—" Eddy began, but Durrand interrupted her.

"We're here on behalf of the United States government."

Elf's berry-brown complexion paled immediately.

"Drug enforcement," Durrand added.

"Oh, well, Elf'll let you get to it then. Ciao," he said and disappeared into the crowd, nimble as a wood sprite.

Eddy blinked. "I thought we were going to stick to our cover story."

"Yeah." Bending, Durrand added two more bags to his load. "And I thought you wouldn't get hit on every minute and a half."

Eddy snagged the last piece of luggage from the floor and hurried after him. "That wasn't my fault."

"I didn't say it was."

"Well…" His long-legged stride made it difficult to keep up. And the crowds weren't helping. She skirted an elderly woman carrying a spotted piglet, reevaluated the anonymity of Bogotá's airport, and cruised up beside Durrand. "You're acting like it is."

"Listen…" His voice was very low. A muscle jumped in his salt block jaw. "You want to get funky with Jamaica Joe and American Dad on your own time, that's your business. But right now, I need a linguist, not a supermodel."

"A…" She blinked up at him and laughed. "A supermodel?"

He narrowed his eyes, surveying the crowd as if expecting spies to pop out from behind every coffee bar, but he needn't have bothered. No one cared about two low-budget American tourists. "I should have brought Sims," he said.

"Sims?"

"He's dumb as a post, but at least he's male."

She felt her spine stiffen. "You think I can't do the job because I don't have a penis?"

"I think I don't have time to spend protecting your virtue."

"There's nothing you have to worry about protecting!"

His brows rose a quarter of an inch. She fought off a blush.

"I mean…" She cleared her throat. "I can take care of myself *and* my virtue."

The right corner of his mouth rose a fraction of an inch, but if he was remembering the time they'd spent in the Blue Oyster's latrine, he didn't make mention. "We need to rent a room and a vehicle," he said.

She nodded, pressing those embarrassing memories from her mind.

"Something with four-wheel drive. You think you can handle that without ending up engaged to some obnoxious joker?"

She pursed her lips. "What are *your* plans?"

"I'm going to ask a few questions. See what the locals know."

"That'd be a better job for me," she said.

He stared at her.

"They'd probably be less intimidated by a woman," she explained.

His face was absolutely expressionless as he stared at her. "I like them *more* intimidated," he said.

She considered arguing, but finally shook her head. "Fine. I'll get the car. Do you want the extra insurance?"

Shifting the packs over his shoulder, he turned away. "Every dime you can get," he said.

## Chapter Seventeen

"Edwards?" Durrand's voice sounded strained. Or maybe he was just tired. As far as she knew, he hadn't slept for a minute on the plane and it was dark now. Then again, it was dark twelve hours a day year-round this close to the equator. When accustomed to a world where the days shortened with autumn's falling temperatures, it was oddly discombobulating.

"Yes?" Eddy answered. They had managed to get international cell phone coverage before leaving the U.S..

"What's your location?" Relief or something like it softened his tone.

"I reserved a private room at a hostel in la Candelaria for the night."

"Everything went okay?"

"Without a hitch," she said, which was something of a falsehood. While inquiring about rooms at a questionable motel, a trio of young men had heckled her, calling her *mami* and making kissing noises, but she'd gotten into her vehicle and locked the doors before the situation escalated. Still, it had made her jumpy then subsequently guilty. She was a trained agent and an excellent marksman, for God's sake. There was no reason she should have to hide like a hunted bunny. "I rented a Jeep and purchased a few supplies. How did it go for you?"

"I'll debrief when we meet up," he said, but his tone suggested he was less than jubilant about the afternoon's events. "What's the address of the hostel?" She rattled it off. He repeated it more slowly. A car door slammed. Cabs abounded in Colombia, but there were always caveats issued about those procured on the street. It was advised to only utilize taxis called by a hotel. Then again, if you were built like Thor on steroids it probably mattered less how you obtained your ride. "I'll be there soon," he said, speaking to her again.

"Me, too."

"What's that?" She could hear the strain tighten like a spring in his voice.

"I think we're breaking up," she said. "Get some sleep. I'll talk to you—"

"Where are you?" Strain was heading rapidly toward irritation.

Eddy drew a careful breath through her nose and smiled at the proprietor of El Cerdo. He'd been watching her intermittently from near a bank of multi-faceted bottles. His name was Miguel. He looked tired and bored and maybe a little angry. She'd been sipping Aguardiente, arguably Colombia's national drink, for forty-five minutes, trying to loosen him up. But he didn't seem to be the loose kind. Then again, he didn't *seem* to be the murderous sort that would dump her mutilated body into the odiferous dumpsters behind the building either, so maybe it was a pretty good trade off.

"I'm just getting some supper." It was kind of the truth. She had ordered a quesadilla with her "firewater" and tried to ignore the malevolent stare of the decapitated pig that hung not five feet from her stool. Its left ear was half missing and its tusks broken. The ratty capybara to its right hadn't survived the years much better.

"Where?" he demanded.

"Listen..." She smiled at Miguel again. He was patently unimpressed. It would almost be worth having Durrand looming nearby just to let him see how uninteresting most men found her. "I'm not a child. I'll—"

"Give me your location, Edwards. That's an order."

She debated refusing, but she couldn't afford to lose this job. Not from a financial or a career standpoint, so she rattled off the name of the establishment and the cross streets. He hung up without preamble or explanation but it was a pretty fair bet that he would show up within the next fifteen minutes. Which meant she had run out of time to soften up Miguel. Time for a new tack. She debated which direction to go. He obviously didn't care for her. Then again, perhaps she shouldn't take that personally. Maybe it was Americanos in general he disliked.

She stifled a wince and reminded herself that she probably wasn't solely responsible for his low opinion of her compatriots. Still, her every insecurity itched to change his mind. People Pleasing 101 insisted on it, but she swallowed hard and searched for the tough-as-nails persona she'd pursued for so long. "That was my husband," she said and smoothed a hand down the daisy yellow sundress she had slipped into before coming here. She'd shoved the singular girly garment into her bag at the last minute… in case of emergencies.

Miguel glanced up from where he was washing glasses, dark eyes impassive.

"Ordering me around," she added.

He didn't shrug, but somehow his expression managed to imply that a good wife would be home preparing ajiaco while simultaneously scrubbing floors and swaddling babies.

She felt the people pleaser in her take a cautious step to the rear.

Prodding her shy alpha persona forward, she drained the Aguardiente she'd been sipping and felt the hot effects wash like nitro through her already bubbling system. "This is my vacation, too." The words sounded surprisingly aggressive. Huh. Go alcohol.

"You have another drink?" Miguel's English was broken, but there was something in the inflection of his words that made her think his command of the language might be somewhat better than he admitted.

She shrugged as if to say *why not* and slid the glass toward him. "I didn't want to come here."

He sloshed the vodka lookalike into her cup as if it were water.

"Don't get me wrong, Colombia's very pretty," she said and stifled a burp.

He didn't respond.

"But Nicaragua..." He slid the drink toward her. She tried a scowl. It never felt like she did it quite right. Luis, her second and last serious boyfriend, had once said she had a face made for smiles. That was six hours and seventeen minutes before she found out he was screwing a mutual friend. Their breakup had been quietly amicable. "It hasn't been raped of its natural resources yet."

Miguel narrowed his eyes at her. His was *not* a face made for smiles. She swallowed hard and wished she still had the colonel's ASP firmly thrust into her waistband.

"But my husband thought it was too dangerous. Made me come to this godforsa—" She stopped short as if it took an effort to waylay her insults. "Men are such pansies," she muttered instead.

Miguel's knuckles looked a little white against the washcloth he was squeezing. From behind, she could feel the other patrons' attention settle on the back of her neck.

She tried another scowl. It felt better. Maybe copious amounts of alcohol was the answer. "We might as well have gone trekking in New Jersey for all the excitement we'll find here."

"It is excitement you want, chica?"

She glanced at the bartender from under her lashes and exhaled derisively. "Everyone knows Colombia is as safe as Disneyland since Santos was elected." She made sure her Spanish was broken and uncertain.

"Santos." He snorted the name.

"What about him?"

He shrugged, but there was a light in his eyes. "He has made it safe for the wealthy who hide behind their iron fences. But gringo women…if they are smart…" He shrugged.

"What?" she asked, switching back to English and employing a certain amount of aggressive bravado.

"They should not come to places such as this."

"What about the jungle?"

"The jungle?" He laughed. "Of course, the jungle, it is safe."

"Well, *safer*," she corrected. "Since the U.S. cracked down on FARC activities, the rebels are scared to breathe too loudly."

"*Sí*. Rarely do they any longer *kill* their captives this days." He leaned heavily against the bar. "Not until they learn whether they can get the monies, at least."

"Latin men…" She scoffed and forced herself to drink again.

He stepped a little closer. "What of them?"

She smiled up at him. Her throat felt tight, her face hot. "They've always been uncomfortable with strong women."

"Have they?"

She nodded. "That's why you're trying to scare me now."

He tilted his head a little. "I will leave such things to men like Guapo Herrera."

"I've heard of him," she admitted.

"Indeed?"

"Some people think he's dabbling in cocaine. But I believe he's nothing more than a legitimate businessman."

"Surely, you have an American education, so I am certain you know best."

"You think I'm wrong?"

He shook his head. "No. Guapo will not harm you. But his man, Quinto Castelle…sometimes he likes to take in…guests." He shrugged elaborately. "Still, I am certain he had nothing to do with the chica found near Herrera's rancho. She was naked and gutted."

If he was trying to frighten her, he was doing a bang-up job, but she raised her chin and soldiered on. "You're making that up."

"A tour group, Americanos, in fact, found her body...parts of it, I shall say...at the bottom of Quebrada Verde."

"Quebrada Verde..." she repeated and drank again. It felt like acid in her stomach.

"Not so far from Parque La Paya."

"I guess I'll avoid that particular area then."

"Why ever so? It is a lovely park, and the poor lady probably but met with an unfortunate accident. Though..." He shrugged. "She did have a G branded across the lips."

"He branded her?" She meant to drink, but her stomach coiled, warning her against such foolishly cavalier behavior.

"Your research it did not tell you the beautiful one likes to see his visitors branded?"

She shook her head and found she was barely able to do that much.

"Then it must not be so."

"Or it happened years ago," she suggested.

He snorted.

"It did, didn't it?" she challenged. Pushing herself to her feet, she leaned toward him. "You're just trying to frighten me. It happened long ago, didn't it?"

"*Sí, boca perra inteligente!*" he snarled and smacked both hands on the bar just inches from hers. "If Tuesday was long ago."

"Back away." The voice coming from behind was low and quiet. It took her several seconds to recognize Durrand's feral growl, but try as she might, she was not able to drag her gaze from the Latino's. For a few heart-pounding moments, she was certain Miguel would ignore Durrand, would grab her by the hair and drag her across the bar. But he drew a deep breath through his nostrils finally and backed carefully back.

"*Señor,*" he said, voice barely a whisper in the suddenly silent cantina. "This is your wife?"

Eddy turned woodenly toward Durrand. His brows were low over river-deep eyes, his arms rigid, his right hand thrust into the pocket of his khakis.

"She's mine," he said.

Miguel eased back another half an inch, lifting his palms from the bar and drawing air deep into his lungs. "Then you should teach her when to speak and when it is wise to keep the silence."

Not a soul batted an eye. Everyone with half a brain cell waited for Durrand to pull a stiletto from his pocket, but when he removed his hand, he held nothing more deadly than a sheaf of bills.

"I'll do that," he said and slipping twenty thousand pesos onto the bar, wrapped his big fist around Eddy's arm and tugged her toward the door.

## Chapter Eighteen

Durrand marched Eddy silently from the cantina.

"That our Jeep?" His voice was no more than a husky rasp.

"Listen, I was just—"

"Get in."

"I didn't—"

"Now!" he ordered and propelled her firmly toward the vehicle.

It wasn't until then that she spied the quartet of men who had followed them from the bar.

"*Señora Petardo,*" called the nearest of them and hurried after them. "We will have some fun together. *Sí?*"

"Don't answer," Durrand ordered and prodded her toward the driver's door.

She would have liked to believe there was something in her that rebelled at the rough command, but her shaking hands and quick-fire acquiescence made her think differently.

Despite her uncertain fingers, the locks popped open when she touched the electronic key. She was sliding inside in an instant. Durrand joined her a fraction of a second later.

"Let's go." His voice was tense.

She shoved the Jeep into reverse. The men were still coming, crowding the bumpers, but she shifted into first and roared away, forcing the nearest of the foursome to jump aside.

In the rearview mirror, the cantina looked hunched and vindictive. The Jeep was silent but for the sound of the engine. Durrand stared straight ahead.

Eddy took a deep breath. "I'm a trained operative." She wasn't entirely certain whom she was reminding of that fact, but she shifted a sideways glance at her passenger.

A muscle jumped angrily in his jaw. "Turn here."

"What?"

"Here!" he said and she did as ordered, careening around the corner onto a narrow, rough-cobbled side street.

"What are we doing?"

He didn't speak but kept his gaze on the rearview mirror. There was not a single car visible behind them, but they drove on, bumping over crossroads, rushing past emptied produce stalls and humble houses.

"Take a left."

She did so at the last moment, tires squealing.

"I don't think—" she began, but he interrupted her.

"I noticed. Take a right."

She gritted her teeth and spun the steering wheel.

Silence echoed between them as they sped along, but finally he exhaled and turned toward her.

"I thought we established that I was the lead on this mission."

She wasn't sure when guilt had entered the equation, but there was something in his tone that made her cheeks heat up and her voice turn sulky. "You said I should rest," she reminded him.

He raised one brow the slightest degree.

"I was just having a few drinks. It wasn't like I was running a marathon."

A muscle twitched in his jaw. "Do you always find the company of inebriated men relaxing?"

She tried for a casual shrug, almost succeeded. "My father was stationed at Camp Lejeune for three years."

He gave her a look that asked what the hell a marine station in North Carolina had to do with anything. It was a decent question, and one she would have been hard-pressed to answer, but he didn't pursue it. His inhalation made his chest expand. If he hadn't been acting like such an asshat, she would have been content enough to admit that it was a pretty good chest.

"For the remainder of this operation, you will keep me apprised as to your position."

She tightened her hands on the wheel and hoped to hell he couldn't tell they were still shaking. "This isn't the Army, Durrand."

"Lucky for you it's not, Edwards. If I were your commanding officer, I would have you court martialed for insubordination, and punished to the full extent of the law." He drew in another deep breath. The muscle hopped in his jaw again. "Listen, if you want to get yourself murdered and dismembered on your own time that's your right as an American citizen, but you're going to have to put it on hold. Right now, Shepherd's waiting."

"Yeah?" she asked and found, to her surprise, that her latent sassiness had finally made a surprise appearance, tardy though it was. "Where?"

His glower darkened.

"Where is he?" she asked.

"That's what I'm trying to find out."

"No luck?" Her words were punctuated by a bump in the road that propelled her violently from the seat. It effectively knocked the know-it-all grin from her face, but she felt somewhat better when he was forced to slap a broad palm on the dash and glare at the road ahead instead of at her.

"You want to try your hand with the police, too?"

She glared a question at him.

"Slow down," he ordered. "South American law enforcement makes cantina bartenders look like school children."

She would have liked to defy his command, but one glance at the speedometer convinced her otherwise. She may be methodical and orderly in the rest of her life, but when behind the wheel, her inner demons sometimes took control. Or maybe she simply had to speed to keep the rest of her life on track. She eased up on the accelerator.

He was still gazing out the windshield. "You know how to get back to the hostel?"

"Of course, I…" She paused, glanced at the dashboard, and realized her GPS remained in her bag. "Well, I did until we took those unscheduled turns."

"It's on the east side of town, right?"

She nodded. She'd found it on a map, and she had a good memory. Unfortunately, her sense of direction wasn't quite so stellar. Her mother had once admitted she only baked to help her daughter find her way from the bedroom to the kitchen. The smell of melting chocolate chips would always be due north to Eddy.

"We need to turn right then," he said. She nodded and tried to look intelligent. The fact that he knew which way was east…in the dark…in a foreign country…kind of made her want to poke him in the eye.

She breathed carefully and wheeled around the corner. "What did you learn?" she asked and accelerated again.

He gripped the handle above the passenger door, making the cords in his arm stand out taut and hard. "Not to let you drive."

She shifted her gaze to his face. "Was that a joke?"

"No," he said, but she smiled a little nevertheless and let her body relax an iota.

"I take it the locals weren't too forthcoming with you?"

For a moment, she thought he would argue, but he just deepened his scowl and glanced out the window at the houses rushing past. "Turns out no one in Bogotá has even *heard* of cocaine."

"How about Quinto Castelle?"

"What?" His tone was harsh, his eyes sharp as talons as he turned them toward her.

"Quinto Castelle. The bartender indicated he's one of Herrera's main thugs." She felt her heart trip a little just saying his name. "He also said a woman's mutilated body was recently found in Quebrada Verde. That translates to Green Gulch."

He waited for her to continue.

"The victim's lips had been burned."

His scowl was deep enough to drown in.

She inhaled. It wasn't any easier to say the words than it had been to hear them, but she forced them out. "He said Herrera likes to brand his victims."

The muscles tightened in his left arm, but he took a deep breath and spoke quietly. "You believe him?"

She considered it. She'd been baiting El Cerdo's proprietor. That much was certain, but he'd said the words with conviction. On the other hand, she'd been barely cognizant of the four men who'd been drinking behind her, so maybe she hadn't been as discerning as she had thought. "I don't know," she admitted.

"What does your gut say?"

She glanced at him. "I think—"

"Don't."

She looked back at the street. Three young women with long black hair were laughing together under an overhead light. "I believe him," she said.

He nodded, but not for her benefit. He looked as if his thoughts were miles away. Maybe in the Quebrada Verde.

"Do you know where it is?" he asked.

"The gulch where the woman's body was found?"

"Yeah."

"Southeast, I think. Three...maybe four hundred miles from here?"

"Near where we think Jacobs exited the river."

She nodded, knowing what he was thinking. Despite the less than trustworthy appearance of the men with whom they'd just parted company, Bogotá was as tame as a puppy compared to Putumayo Department, which bordered Peru and Ecuador.

"You sure?"

"I have a good memory for maps." She didn't say the word photographic, though others had.

"How long ago was she found?"

"Tuesday."

"How decomposed?"

She kept her expression impassive though her stomach jittered. "I don't know."

He nodded again. "She probably died fairly recently. Bodies don't last long in the jungle. Especially heads. Insects are most attracted to orifices, so faces deteriorate first."

She managed a stalwart nod. "Sure."

"Of course, we don't know if it really was Herrera's handiwork."

She tightened her grip on the wheel.

"Or that Miller's team had targeted Herrera in the first place. Or that the bartender was telling the truth." He chuckled and stared into the dark distance. "Shit. This is as FUBAR as it gets."

She glanced toward him. In profile, he looked like nothing so much as what he was…a wounded warrior on a life or death mission. "We'll find him." The words left her lips without permission. The trite platitude sounded as silly as a nursery rhyme in the quiet darkness.

She waited for him to blast her for daring to utter such nonsense. He turned toward her, expression ultimately solemn. But maybe in the depths of his eyes there was a pinprick of gratitude. Of hope. "In a billion acres of jungle?"

"You said to listen to my gut."

"And it tells you we're going to find Shep?"

She thought about it for a second then, "I hope so."

"Hope." He breathed the word and faced the darkness outside his window again.

"If you don't have hope, why are you here?"

"Because it's my job."

She waited for him to go on.

"Shep was in my squad."

"So it's duty. That's why you came?"

He shook his head but didn't turn toward her. "No. I'm just a born hero." There was derision in his tone, tension in every line of his body, but she couldn't help but wonder if it was true. If he was simply built to be heroic. If it was in his DNA like his dark hair and intimidating size.

"Is that why you came to El Cerdo?"

He glanced at her, brows lowered.

"The bar," she explained. "Is that why you came after me? Duty?"

"I thought if you were raped it might discourage you from continuing with the mission."

"Rape? Miguel didn't even like me," she scoffed and wished immediately that she could call back the words.

Durrand's brows rose like twin pistons. "You can't honestly be that naïve."

She tried to formulate a scathing response, but he wasn't through with her yet.

"What do you think...that rape's about...affection or something?"

"No. Of course, not. I meant to say, he wasn't even interested in me." Dammit! She refrained from closing her eyes to her own stupidity. "That's not—" she began, but he was already chuckling.

"Holy shit, what the hell was I thinking?"

Anger spurted up, surprising in its ferocity. "Maybe that you'd rather not have your best friend shipped back to you in pieces!"

The words sounded harsh and cruel in the ensuing silence.

"I'm sorry," she said. "I didn't mean that. But I can help you if you'll let me."

The Jeep was silent. "Not if you're dead."

"Well..." Her fingers were beginning to go numb. She eased up on the steering wheel. "I'm going to try my best not to be."

His stare was hard enough to bruise, but finally he turned back to the passenger window. "He's my responsibility."

"What? Shepherd?"

He didn't answer, but she knew that's what he meant. Great. She was learning to read his silences better than she could interrupt his words.

"He's a grown man, Durrand. A soldier. A Ranger, for that matter. Among the best-trained military men in the world."

"He's a jumper." The words were soft, quiet, but she was pretty sure she'd heard him right. She just had no idea what it meant.

"A...what?"

"If someone's in trouble he doesn't think, doesn't..." He drew a deep breath. "He'll just jump right in. So what if he gets his fucking brains sprayed from here to eternity? So what if the poor bastard he's trying to save is already dead. So what if—" His voice broke. He cleared his throat.

She drove in silence, fists tight on the steering wheel, mind churning as fast as the Jeep's tires.

"Just because he was careless, doesn't mean *you* should have been," she said.

"I don't know what the hell you're talking about."

She was tempted to back down, to apologize for being presumptuous, but his eyes were a little too bright. "If you had tried to save Warren, you and Shepherd would both be dead."

He glared at her.

Backing down was looking like a better idea every second. She just couldn't quite manage it. "Ray Warren, better known as Intel to his friends." She'd researched more than Jacobs in her spare time back in her cozy Tudor. Died six months ago in Kabul."

He didn't argue, didn't agree.

"Shepherd tried to save him. You saved Shepherd."

A muscle twitched in one lean, unshaven cheek, but he shifted his attention quickly away. "This is Eldorado."

"What?"

"The highway. Do you know how to get to the hostel from here?"

"Oh. Yeah." Seeing the sign illuminated by the Jeep's headlights, she turned, heading east on the Autopista Eldorado. In less than five minutes, she pulled up to their humble inn, shifted into park and turned off the motor. "*I'm not* your responsibility, Durrand," she said.

He watched her in the dimness for a second. "I'm in charge. That makes me responsible for you. Just like any other soldier in my unit."

She felt her anger fire up again. "So if it was Shep back there in the cantina, you would have dragged him out by his arm?"

"By the time I got there, Shep would have either been shacked up with some black-eyed *señorita* or in a firefight." He snorted a soft chuckle and let his head fall against the cushion behind him. "Possibly both. Dumb bastard never could keep his gun in his holster."

She didn't know if that was supposed to be metaphoric or literal.

"If I had a bullet for every time I bailed his ass out, I'd never have to buy another round of ammo," he said.

"Is that why you think you owe him? Because you saved his life?"

He stared at her, expression bland.

She refused to fidget. "It's a well-known phenomenon," she said.

"We were in Somalia together. Did you know that?"

"I'm afraid I didn't have time to completely research your record."

"It was darker than hell's basement on that beach, but my squad got the hostages out. I stayed behind to hold back the rebels. Fifteen of them. Maybe twenty. No chance really. No hope." He shook his head, turned toward the hostel. "Till Shep came back for me."

"Oh, well..." She cleared her throat. "I guess *that* might be a good reason, too."

"Maybe." His tone was ironic.

Grabbing her backpack, she yanked up the door handle and stepped outside. "Well, that's good news then, isn't it?"

He followed her out, his movements a little slower.

"What is?"

"I haven't saved your life once," she said and jamming her key in the hostel's lock, pushed her way inside. "In fact, for a second back there, I was thinking about killing you myself."

"And how is that good news?"

"You don't owe me a thing," she said then rushed past the tiny kitchenette, made a beeline for the bathroom and vomited as unobtrusively as possible into the porcelain bowl. Damn Aguardiente.

## Chapter Nineteen

"**Y**ou all right?" Gabe didn't glance up when he asked the question. He'd never actually known anyone who was able to upchuck with so much decorum. Impressive. Spooks must have entirely different training than Rangers.

"I'm fine." Her tone was prissy. Also impressive. The guys he knew always sounded a little raspy after tossing their cookies. "I just drank more than I wanted to."

"More than you wanted?" He allowed himself to look up now, but contained the smirk that threatened to follow. He had removed the lamp from the end table and spread a map of the Putumayo area across the rough particleboard.

"It took a while to get the bartender to loosen up," she said. "I figured he would take more kindly to me if I kept drinking."

He didn't mention that she could have ordered something nonalcoholic. Shit. She wasn't a lush was she? Maybe that's how she had become such a proficient vomiter. Practice makes perfect. Or...and maybe this was a worse scenario...perhaps fear had made her vomit. Holy hell, they hadn't even reached the edge of scary yet. Then again, he'd been as nervous as a virgin himself when he'd realized she was alone in a bar. He ground his teeth and knew for a fact that he should have never brought her here. He should never have taken the risk if her presence was going to throw him into a goddamned tizzy every time someone glanced her way. He wasn't normally such a wussy. Hell, while on a mission in Bagdad, Jairo had decided Gabe didn't have any nerves at all. He remembered the pin Shep had used to test the theory. Fucking numb nuts, he thought and felt his eyes water.

"Are *you* okay?" Her voice was quietly sympathetic.

Damnit. He cleared his throat. "I wasn't the one who just barfed up my intestinal tract."

"It's no big deal," she said but she looked pale. Well...*paler*, her fresh-peach complexion practically alabaster. And for a slim second, he was almost tempted to admit that she'd been damn brave, but even *he* wasn't that big of an ass.

"Get some sleep," he said instead and nodded vaguely toward the single bed.

She ignored him completely. They'd hardly known each other for twenty-four hours and she'd already mastered the technique. She must be a quick study. It usually took women at least a couple of days. "Ever heard of technology?" she asked and moved closer.

He scowled at the big ass map in front of them. "Heard of it," he said. "Don't trust it." She was standing beside him, their arms almost touching. He managed to neither move closer nor farther away. Go Army!

"You don't trust it as in you think it's going to fail, or like you believe it's going to betray you?"

For a moment, he wondered if there was a difference between the two, but he wasn't dumb enough to ask. Instead, he considered ordering her to go to bed again. But he thought better of it. What the hell was he going to do if she refused? Wrestle her onto the mattress and tie her to the headboard? The ensuing images were both disturbing and disturbingly erotic. He felt restlessness in his lower regions and increased his attention on Putumayo.

"It's longer than I realized," she said.

He jerked his eyes toward her, but she didn't shift her attention from the map spread beneath his palms.

"The length of the gulch. How long do you think?" she asked. Her eyes were as wide and green as a Tennessee meadow.

"Durrand?" she said and lifted her gaze to his face.

Shit! Was staring at her like she was the Holy Grail? He gritted his teeth and grunted. Hopefully, it sounded more noncommittal than bestial. "Ten miles, I'd say. Did the bartender give you any idea where along the gulch Herrera's men might be?"

"No."

"Have you heard anything on the news about it?"

"I haven't had a chance to check yet," she said and pulled out her tablet.

He waited, studying the lay of the land as he did so. But patience wasn't with him. "Anything?"

She shook her head.

"Maybe the media's no more forthcoming than the locals regarding their little drug problem." He scanned the map. "That's a shitload of jungle to search. Your cantina friend give you any other clues?"

"I didn't want to push him too hard."

"Next time, don't push at all."

"And have no intel whatsoever?"

"Could be he was just stringing you along. See how far he could play the pretty Americano. Fun game. Probably hasn't had that many laughs for months," he said and returned his attention to the maps.

"The tour!"

He raised his eyes at the excitement in her tone. "What?" he asked but she was already tapping away at her keyboard.

"He said the people who found the mutilated body had been on some kind of tour."

He straightened abruptly, heart pumping a little faster. "Private or guided?"

"I'm not sure."

"First thing in the morning, I need you to find out what companies offer trips into that area."

"Why wait?"

"Businesses down here are barely open during regular hours. You'll never find anyone manning the phones this—"

He felt her staring at him and let his words slip to a halt.

"Right…" He refrained from clearing his throat. "Look them up online," he said, but ahe was already lost in technology. Maybe if he were really lucky, she wouldn't realize he'd forgotten about the Internet again. But he wasn't the lucky one. It had been common knowledge in the barracks that Shep had gotten the lion's share of good fortune. The thought almost made Durrand laugh out loud.

"Looks like there are two companies that service that area," she said.

"Any way to know if either of them made a trip last week?"

She was scowling at the screen. Her brow was as smooth as a baby's bottom. Holy shit, he'd probably done his first tour while she was still wearing Pampers and drooling on the colonel's well-decorated shoulder.

"It doesn't say anything on their sites. I suppose finding dead bodies isn't something they'd advertise. Probably not great for tourism. But I can try to hack into their private emails."

He didn't question how that could be done. No use sounding more antiquated than necessary. And maybe he would know how that was possible if he had ever been on the intelligence end of operations. But he had never pretended to be anything other than a warhorse. Intel was the brains of the company, and Intel was dead, just like the others.

His throat felt tight, his muscles wooden, but he managed to pull a topography map from its cardboard tube and press it open.

After a few moments, he shook his head.

"What?" She glanced up, fingers still dancing on the keys.

"There's no way the Jeep's going to make the entire trip."

"How long will it take on foot?"

He narrowed his eyes at the map and calculated. "Looks like

the roads end about eight klicks from the gulch itself. So it'll probably take me..." He shook his head, figuring and feeling a little
sick with the results; Shep may be a colossally stubborn pain in the
ass, and sure as hell, he'd know Gabe was coming for him, but he
couldn't last forever. "A couple hours to reach the gorge?"

"What about *we*?"

He glanced up, worrying over a thousand details at once. What
kind of idiot would bring a woman like her into this tropical slice
of hell? "I'm not sure," he admitted.

"But you think it will take longer with me along."

No one had ever accused him of being a diplomat, but he
didn't like to think he was a complete lackwit. Though more than a
few had suggested as much. "Two *always* takes longer than one,"
he said.

She was staring at him, challenge sharp in her eyes. "I won't
slow you down."

He offered no expression, but seriously, she looked like a damn
fairy princess in her daisy yellow dress, and fairy princesses didn't
seem like they'd be real great at humping a forty-pound pack
through snake-infested jungles.

She was still watching him, maybe waiting for him to make a
total ass of himself. It probably wouldn't take long. "You finding
anything there?" he asked and nodded toward her tablet.

She glanced back down at her tablet, tapped a few more things
on the screen, and inhaled softly. "Here!" Her tone was tight with
excitement, her apple blossom cheeks flushed. "There's an email to
*Emocionante's* employees advising them to steer clear of the Gueppi
vicinity. Isn't that near the gulch?"

He scanned the map and nodded. "Who's the memo from?"

She skimmed lower, lips slightly parted. "Alejdro Garza
sent it."

"You heard of him?"

"No."

"Any way to find out where he lives?"

She tapped away again, paused, and read off an address.

He nodded once then bent. Retrieving the bag of purchases he'd recently made, he tossed it onto the bed and pulled out a twelve-inch hunting knife.

"What are you doing?"

He glanced up at the sound of her voice. Her eyes had gone from Tennessee meadow to Caribbean Sea, but he would be a fool to be influenced by a pair of pastoral eyes.

"I'll be back before dawn," he said and strapped the blade to his hip. "Get some sleep."

# Chapter Twenty

E ddy stumbled to her feet, heart stuttering against her ribs, fingers suddenly cold. "Where are you going?"

Durrand's eyes were dark and hooded. "Lock the door behind me," he ordered and adjusted the sheath that hung against the side of his right thigh.

"Wait a minute." She wasn't sure why her chest felt tight and her hands unsteady. She was a trained operative, she reminded herself for the umpteenth time. But his face looked blank and terrifying. And the knife... She swallowed. There was no one who appreciated a well-oiled handgun more than she did, but there was something intrinsically evil about a knife. "You're going to find Alejdro, aren't you?"

He didn't answer. But he didn't have to; his expression said it all.

"You can't just..." She was breathing hard. "You can't go around terrorizing private citizens," she said but the set of his mouth suggested he could do just that. He turned away.

"Durrand!" She grabbed his arm. "You don't want to get the police involved."

His eyes were flat as glass. "I'll make sure he doesn't call the cops."

Her stomach roiled at the unspoken implications.

"Listen." Her hand was still on his arm. "Let's just think about his for a moment."

Their gazes met.

"Stay here," he said and pulled from her grasp, but there was something in his face, some indefinable regret. Or was she just making that up? Was she just pretending so she could believe he wasn't a monster?

"I'm coming along," she said.

He twisted toward her with the smooth grace of a predator, that indefinable something long gone from his eyes. "You'll do what I say." The words were no more than a growl.

"You're paying me," she said and pressed past him, jaw squared and lifted as if her mind were set, but honest to God, she couldn't look at the knife. Couldn't see that blatant symbol of cruelty without hurling...again. "I'm just earning my keep."

"You'll earn your keep here," he ordered but she was already at the door.

"You'll never find his house in the dark. I've got the GPS," she said and rushed outside.

He cursed and followed her, strides long and quick, but she was in the passenger seat before he reached the Jeep.

Yanking open the driver's door, he glared across the console at her.

"I thought we were in a hurry," she said.

His jaw bunched in irritation, but he slid inside. In a moment, they were backing out of the cobbled parking area.

Eddy's stomach bounced as she programmed the guidance system. A thousand factions warred in her stomach.

Late at night, Bogotá's streetwalkers were hard at work. Transvestites strutted their terrain, wildly flamboyant compared to their born-female counterparts. In these designated 'tolerance zones', prostitution was not only legal but booming.

The le Macarena district looked as bland as white rice by comparison, but Eddy's nerves remained on red alert, making Alejdro Garza's house seem disturbingly malevolent. Its dark door looked like a gaping maw against its white stucco exterior. Its windows were blank eyes, black and staring.

They drove past it once. The street was as dark as death. A scrawny hound trotted through the stream of their headlights, giving them a furtive glance from shifty eyes before disappearing into the blackness.

Durrand took two more rights, then slid the Jeep to a halt a half a block from his quarry's silent adobe.

Eddy tightened her fists and wondered if throwing up again would make her appear less field-ready.

Durrand turned toward her. Half his face looked solemn and resolute. The other half was gone, swallowed by the darkness. She wondered dimly if the same could be said for his soul.

"Lock the doors and slide into the driver's seat when I get out," he ordered. His voice was low and level. "If someone approaches the vehicle, do not speak to them. If there's trouble, honk the horn. Otherwise, wait for me. When you see me exit the residence, come pick me up."

She stared at him.

"Can you do that?"

She nodded.

"I might be in a hurry," he added.

She nodded again.

"Good," he said and opened the driver's door to step outside. His movements were almost entirely silent as he did so. There was something about that predatory stealth that disturbed her more than anything else.

Eddy watched him slip into the shadows.

By some malevolent trick of the light, the stainless steel tang of his knife was the last thing she saw.

## Chapter Twenty-One

The window farthest from the street was narrow and low to the ground. Gabe flattened his back against the wall. The stucco felt cool and rough on his back. He scanned the neighborhood without moving his head. The night was quiet, as if it was safe. But safety was nothing more than an illusion. Perhaps Alejdro felt secure behind his locked doors, but locks could be picked in a heartbeat, windows jimmied just as quickly. Turning toward the building, he slipped the blade of his knife between the sill and the casing.

"Alejdro!" The name was loud and shrill, echoed by a raucous pounding on the front door. "Alejdro Garza, please, I must speak to you."

It seemed to take Gabe a lifetime to recognize Edwards' voice, longer still to grind his teeth and stalk to the corner of the house. But the door opened before he could confront her. An unseen man spoke from the interior of the little hacienda. His words were a jumble of inarticulate Spanish, but the cocking of his shotgun was perfectly clear.

Gabe swore in silence and tightened his grip on the handle of his own modest weapon.

Edwards, just visible past the trailing blossoms of a flowering shrub, lifted her hands and backed away. If she had noticed him, she didn't let on. "Please." Her voice was very soft. "Don't shoot."

"*Abondonar! Dejar o te vas a morir!*"

"American," she said. Her face was midwinter pale in the light that seeped from the open door. Her hands were shaking. If it were an act, she was in the wrong profession. "I'm an American."

Holy shit! Gabe ground his teeth. Why not advertise her nationality, in case Garza hadn't yet decided if he wanted to kidnap her?

An unseen woman spoke rapid fire Spanish from the bowels of the house.

"I'm sorry," Edwards said and fell suddenly to her knees. Gabe jerked at the unexpected movement, but in a moment, he realized she had knelt of her own accord. "Please. I need to know."

"*Abandonar!*" the man ordered again, but Edwards had dropped her face into her hands and was sobbing softly.

What the fuck was going on?

"*Ir!*" Alejdro snapped, but the woman spoke again, her English broken.

"Why is it you are come here?"

Edwards lifted her head. Hair as fine as corn-silk spilled around her face like a veil. "You found a…you found a body." She barely whispered the words, but Alejdro spoke before she could continue.

"Leave!"

She struggled to her feet. "My sister…Trish…she's been missing for thirteen days."

"I know nothing of this." The door creaked closed, but Edwards rushed forward. The sound of wood crashing against the sole of her boot boomed in the darkness.

"Please. Just tell me where she was."

Gabe gritted his teeth. The man had a shotgun, a 12-gauge by the sound of it. And Gabe had never been a fan of showing up at a gunfight with a knife no matter how nice the blade was, but he had little choice in the matter. Tightening his grip on the handle, he gritted his teeth and stepped forward, but the unseen woman spoke again.

"Let her in," she ordered.

There was a moment of heated silence. The night pulsed around them.

"Come," Alejdro said finally, and Edwards stepped inside.

Gabe closed his eyes, gritted his teeth and cursed in silence. He should have tied her to the bed, after all. Should have knocked her unconscious. Should have taken one look at her peaches and cream perfection and run like hell. Or limped, *limped* like hell. He paced the perimeter, peering in every window, but he could see nothing inside the house's dim interior. On the other hand, there were no shots fired either. No screams of pain. No shouts of outrage.

And she was a trained professional. She'd fought like a tiger in the Blue Oyster's latrine. But somehow, that particular memory failed to improve his mood.

A gasp sounded from inside. He jerked toward the door, but barging into the house had a high probability of causing more harm than good. And in a matter of seconds, Edwards was stepping outside, seemingly with all limbs attached and no arterial blood spewing from gaping wounds.

"Thank you." Her voice was soft, barely audible. "Thank you, *señor*," she breathed and stumbled toward the Jeep.

The door closed quietly behind her. Gabe jerked his attention toward it then hurried after her.

She gasped as he curled his hand around her arm.

"Durrand!" Her eyes were as wide as a fawn's when she raised them toward his. "You scared the life out of me."

"I scared *you?*" he rasped.

"Shh," she admonished and glanced toward the modest house behind them before jerking the Jeep's door open and sliding behind the steering wheel.

There didn't seem to be much Gabe could do but hurry around

to the passenger side. By the time his ass hit the seat, she was already pulling away from the crumbling curb.

"What the hell were you thinking?" he growled and tried to work up a good head of steam. Certainly, he deserved to be outraged, but she was already taking the corner at a speed that would have traumatized an Andretti, making it difficult to focus on her past sins.

"I was thinking we wanted to know where the body was found without adding another death to the toll."

He glared at her and tightened his grip on the *oh shit* handle. "I didn't say I was going to kill him."

"You didn't say you *weren't* going to kill him."

He lowered his brows and considered telling her that he wasn't a murderer, but his stomach was already creeping toward his esophagus. In the past, his squad had thought it the funniest thing in the world when he'd toss his cookies after every jump. Or *during*...during his exit from the plane was even more hilarious.

"What'd you find out?" Did his voice sound a little sulky? Shit. Forty-eight hours in her company and he was turning into a toddler.

"She wasn't one of Miller's people."

He shook his head and tried to verbalize a question, but she was already continuing.

"The woman who was killed. She wasn't one of Miller's team."

"That's what you asked?"

"I thought if she were, we would know where—"

He laughed out loud. "Holy shit, Edwards, I could have told you that without risking your damned life."

She shifted her gaze from the street long enough to glare at him. It took every ounce of his self-control to resist screaming that she should watch the damned road. "You said you didn't know who was on his team."

"I said I didn't know *who*. I *did* know Miller would consider a one-legged goat before he'd hired a *woman*."

"Well, maybe you should have shared that information with me."

"Shared that—" He snorted. "You're supposed to be the intel here. Hell! Did you think I brought you along for muscle? Or maybe—"

"The body was found five miles west of where the Tortuga branches into the Putumayo."

He drew a deep breath and tried to marshal his senses. Sometimes, he had a temper. Sometimes, he was just an ass. And sometimes, it was hard as hell to differentiate between the two. "When did she die?"

"I don't know. The bartender said she'd been found on Tuesday. Alejdro agreed. He also said she had a unicorn tattoo on her neck."

"A unicorn?" He scowled into the darkness. She took a left turn like a launched missile, careening around the corner while staring at the GPS. He tightened his grip until his fingers ached. "And he could still identify the tat?"

She nodded.

"So she hadn't been ravaged."

"Even though she was on the banks of a major river, miles from civilization."

"Couldn't have been there long then."

"Probably not more than a few hours. Certainly not overnight."

"What time of day did the tourists find her?"

"Early afternoon, 1500 hours or so."

"Did Alejdro think it was Herrera?"

"He didn't know," she said.

"Didn't know, or wouldn't say?"

"I don't have any reason to believe he was lying about his uncertainty."

"I do," he said and scowled at her naiveté.

"That's because you didn't see Angelique."

He deepened his scowl.

"His daughter. Three years old." She exhaled softly, as if trying to de-stress. Good luck with that. "Eyes like an angel."

He shook his head.

"His wife suggested that he imagine what it would be like if their little girl went missing."

Gabe scowled as Zoey's image popped into his head, snaggle-toothed smile watermelon wide as she razzed him about his inability to whistle. The irritating little monkey had failed to show him a modicum of fear from the moment she was born. He blamed Kelsey. But the thought of his niece being in danger did something deadly to his heart.

In retrospect, making Alejdro imagine his daughter missing might have been a worse fate than threatening his life.

It also might have been cleverer. He glanced out at the night as they careened into their hostel's bumpy parking lot. The Jeep jolted to a halt. His stomach stopped more slowly.

Edwards turned the key and stared across the seat at him. "You okay?"

"Why wouldn't I be?"

"I don't know. You look a little green."

"Let's go," he said. "We've got an early day tomorrow." Opening his door, he took a deep breath, found his equilibrium and stepped onto the gravel.

Yanking the key from the ignition, Edwards popped open the driver's door. "When do you think we'll reach the gulch?"

"Depends how long it takes to get ahold of Javier?"

"Who?"

"Weapons specialist."

They were side by side now, striding toward the hostel. "Where's he located?"

"Don't know yet."

"Then how are you going to find him?"

"He's going to meet us."

"Where?"

"I'll let you know as soon as he tells me."

She stuck the room key in the door and looked over her shoulder in surprise. He glanced away, feeling foolish. It wasn't as if he was thrilled with the system, but Reynolds had warned him that Javier was slippery.

"Paranoid?" she guessed.

He shrugged and studied the area behind him. It was as dark as silt in the lea of the little hostel. "Maybe just Colombian."

"There are good people everywhere," she said. Her tone was a little judgmental. She jiggled the key. Nothing happened.

He glanced to the right, imagining a half dozen men approaching in the darkness. The nearest had a blade clamped between teeth as white as coca powder.

She jiggled the key again, but he pressed her aside. "Holy shit, we'll be dead before morning at this rate," he said and unlocking the door, crowded her inside.

"Speaking of paranoia…" she said.

He could feel her scowl, but he had already moved to the window. Pushing aside a faded curtain, he studied the night. Nothing moved. He let the fabric fall back across the pane.

"What you call paranoia has saved my life a hundred times."

She stared at him a second, brows slightly raised. "Just think what a nice case of psychosis could do for you then."

"I can only dream," he said.

# Chapter Twenty-Two

Two days had passed since Shep had escaped from Treg and his buddies. Two days of scrambling through the undergrowth like a terrified bunny. Of hiding from every scrape of noise. Of eating only what the jungle supplied.

His head was buzzing. Or was it the flies? Those damned insects that circled like vultures. He swept his hand upward, but the movement was slow and disjointed, doing little more than infuriate his tormentors. They hummed louder. Two landed on his neck, one on his cheek. He let them be. Fatigue rode him hard, gouging him like rusty spurs. Sweat rolled between his shoulder blades.

But, it wasn't the heat, it was the humidity. Isn't that what people always said as they sat on their shaded verandas and sipped sweet tea. He grinned as he hurried on. A root, gnarled and bare, caught the toe of his boot. He fell hard, rested a moment then forced himself to stand again.

Something warm spread across his wrist. He lifted his arm to examine it. Blood. His gut wound was oozing again. But it could be worse, though he wasn't sure how. Oh yeah, the bullet could have become lodged in his intestines instead of passing straight through. He *was* the lucky one, he thought and caught himself against the solid trunk of a nearby tree before he fell on his face again. The plant life was ragged here. Small trees were broken and bent. As if some giant beast had plowed its way through. A giant beast or… a bulldozer!

The idea froze in his mind. If there were bulldozers there must be people. Maybe it really was his lucky day. Maybe—

"Fucking jungle." The Spanish words were spoken low but close.

Shep ducked down, half falling, half lunging into the broken flora at his feet.

Foliage scratched against something off to his left. From his right, a twig snapped. Shep gritted his teeth and held his breath.

"When this is over, I'm going to lay in bed for a week."

The man at two o'clock chuckled. "Do that, and Pia will kill you herself."

"Who said I was going to spend that time with my wife?"

There was a snort from the man on the left. "So your niece is visiting again."

"Dulce always comes for All Saint's Day."

"Good Christ, you're a pervert."

The first man chuckled. Close now. So close Shep could smell the onions he'd had for dinner, but he waited, tensed. One step closer. One more step and he would leap. He'd take out the pervert first then—

"*Linus*," his mother said.

He jerked at the sound of her voice, head reeling.

"*Your face is dirty again*," she said and, leaning down, brushed her thumb across his cheek. Her skin felt like magic against his.

"Mama." His voice sounded guttural, but she just smiled. Marjorie Shepherd always smiled, eyes soft beneath the purple scarf she wore to hide her baldness.

"*I swear, you're the messiest boy I've ever seen.*"

"I'm sorry." He wasn't sure why he was apologizing. A dozen things all at once he supposed. His cheeks felt wet.

"*'Course you're the handsomest, too,*" she said and winked, periwinkle eyes shining.

"Where've ya been?" he whispered. His voice sounded whiny.

She shook her head. Her lips were still smiling, but her eyes were moist, shining with a thousand regrets. "*Don't you worry about that, young man. You just take care of yourself,*" she said and turned away.

"Mama!" Whiny had turned to panic. "Don't go!"

"*I'd stay if I could, Saddle Tramp. I'd stay for you,*" she said but she was already fading.

"Mama!"

"Jesus Christ!"

The coarse words snapped him from his trance. The nearest man stood not two yards away, feet braced, AR-15 trained on Shep's chest. "*This* guy got the jump on Treg?"

His friend chuckled. "Looks like the American has had a run-in with our friend the jungle."

The first man cocked up his rifle and switched to English. "You don't look so good, *amigo.*"

Reality leached slowly into Shep's faltering psyche. His mother's image slipped slowly from his mind. So he was delusional. Not surprising, he supposed. And not so bad. Because despite the scores of beautiful women with whom he had spent time, there wasn't one he wouldn't give up for a few more moments with Mama. He chuckled. If that little scrap of truth got around the barracks, he'd never hear the end of it.

"Hey!" The nearest man snarled and kicked him. Pain burned like wildfire through his ribs. Consciousness turned to gray ooze then brightened stubbornly. "What you laugh at?"

Shepherd shook his head slowly. Two days ago, he had been certain death was preferable to bondage. But damned if life wasn't a hard thing to give up. He rolled painfully onto his back. "I'm glad to see ya boys," he said.

The man to his right was scrawny and jittery. A dirty white bandana was tied around his forehead. "Not so happy as we to see you." When he smiled, you could see he was missing a molar. Apparently, hostage-nabbing, drug-running bastards didn't spend a lot of time on dental care. "There will be a pretty reward when we return you to Quinto."

"*Linus,*" Mama called.

Shep closed his eyes and sent his mother back into the shadows, but not without a hard bite of guilt.

"How much?" Shepherd forced the question from between gritted teeth.

They stared at him.

"How big is the reward?" he asked.

"A million pesos."

Five hundred dollars. Shep considered trying a whistle, but there was no point attempting such challenging vocalization. It was fortunate as hell he could even *talk*…but then, he'd always been the lucky one. "That *is* a pretty reward," he said.

The man on the left grinned. He had a moon tattooed on the biceps of his right arm. "The boss, he holds a grudge, *amigo.* Says he want you alive."

Shep tried a casual shrug, but the bruising across his deltoids made that almost impossible. "I suppose it's only fair that he keep the lion's share for himself."

There was a moment of silence then, "What you talk of, *gringo*?"

"*Linus…*"

Shepherd winced at the sound of his mother's voice. She wasn't real. Hadn't been for twenty years. There was no reason to feel guilty for ignoring her now. But his gut felt cramped.

"Quinto told ya about the reward for me from the Americans, didn't he?" Shep asked.

"There is no reward, *amigo.* None wants you."

Shepherd caught the man's gaze and tried the smallest hint of a know-it-all grin. "I'm sure you're right. A guy like Quinto wouldn't cheat his buddies."

The two exchanged a glance. Shepherd could see that much

though his vision had been for shit the last few days. He wiped his knuckles across his eyes.

"There is no reward from the Americans," Bandana repeated.

Shep shrugged. He needed a plan. And he needed it fast, but he wasn't altogether sure he could get his feet under him. And most plans were going to require a little bit of mobility.

"There is no reward!" the man demanded and kicked him again.

"Just ten thousand dollars." They were the first words that came to mind, and were barely audible. His bottom lip, split weeks before, still stung when he was lucky enough to find a sip of water. "Ten thousand American dollars."

"You lie like the pig."

He was slipping again, sliding toward oblivion.

The closest man kicked him hard enough to jolt him back to reality.

"I'm not." Shep's voice was raspy. Blood trickled from his mouth.

"Who's paying?"

"*Gabriel,*" Mama said. "*He's coming for you, Tramp. You know he is.*"

"He doesn't know where I am." The words were whiny.

"*We Shepherds aren't quitters,*" she reminded him.

"But I'm so tired."

"*You answer the man,*" she insisted. "*You answer him.*"

"Gabe." He could barely force out the name. "Gabriel Durrand will pay."

"How much you say he give for you?"

"Ten thousand."

"He lies," Bandana had switched back to Spanish. "Nobody's gonna shell out that kind of cash. Not for a corpse."

The man with the moon tattoo was glowering at him. "He ain't dead, yet."

"As good as. He's not going to make it all the way back to camp. Not on his own anyway."

Moon's expression was getting grimmer.

Bandana slapped a mosquito the size of a train. "*You* want to carry him?"

Moon sighed. "Reward ain't nearly so big if he's dead."

"*I expect you to do what you have to do,*" Mama said.

"What?" Shepherd asked, turning toward her. "What do I gotta do?"

Bandana snorted. "He's loco already."

Shepherd shook his head, though he wasn't altogether sure the man was wrong. "If ya take me to the village, I'll get ya the money. That's a promise."

Bandana grinned. "Think what kind of bauble I could buy Dulce for that kind of money."

Moon chuckled. "You sick bastard."

"You're just jealous 'cause your niece has a face like a capybara."

"You want to get laid, you carry him out of here," Moon said.

"Don't think so," Bandana argued and raised his rifle.

"Quinto must be more forgivin' than I remember," Shep said.

Moon scowled.

"He'll hear the gunshot..." Shep shook his head. It was painful to breathe, almost impossible to speak. A rib, he supposed, was poking into his lung. "He'll know ya killed me. Cost him the ransom."

"Man's got a point," Bandana said and lowered his weapon.

"He does," Moon agreed. Pulling a knife from the sheath at his side, he stepped forward.

Fear seeped through Shep's system, but it was slow, lethargic. Still, Mama didn't raise no quitter. "Let me go. Please." He tried to imbue his voice with pathetic desperation. It wasn't as difficult as it should be. Scrambling backward on his hands and feet was harder. His progress was practically indiscernible. The foliage scraped his hands. "Please," he pleaded again but the moon tattoo kept coming. Closer. Just a little closer. Shepherd dropped his butt to the ground and kicked. His left foot was almost useless, but his right struck true, slamming the man's legs out from under him.

Moon screamed as a severed sapling pierced his eye.

Shep leapt to his feet, but his legs crumbled. He toppled onto his side and froze at the sound of a cocking rifle.

## Chapter Twenty-Three

"Are you sure this is the right road?" Eddy glanced sideways at Durrand. He was holding onto the handle on the dash again, expression dark.

His conversation with Javier, the arms dealer, had been short, quick, and bracketed by thunderous expressions rather like the one that currently occupied his face.

"I'm not sure this goat trail is a road at *all*."

The path they were on wound upward like a vicious snake, writhing and twisting its way toward some uncertain destination. Rocks the size of Halloween pumpkins adorned their route. Eddy swerved to the left to avoid the latest one.

A mile or so back they had passed a boy riding a horse and leading two mules, both of which carried lumpy packs. The scene felt like a slice from the distant past, except that the kid had been punching keys on his cell phone as he rode. Maybe Durrand was right? Maybe any yahoo *could* pry into her business. The idea made her palms sweat.

"He said to take the second right and not the first, correct?" she asked.

"Yeah."

She nodded and glanced at him again. He was scanning the hills. They were endless, impossibly green and desperately lonely. She stifled a shiver.

"You think he's watching us?"

"Probably."

"Maybe it's a setup."

He shifted his gaze toward her without speaking. The look in his eyes suggested that he might have considered that possibility.

"What's the penalty for buying weapons without a permit in South America?" she asked, but he ignored her. She'd never met anyone better at it.

"Slow down." A muscle ticked in his jaw. "Look for a path heading west from the crooked Brazil nut tree."

"Are you kidding me?" There must be a few billion trees in the jungle. And she wouldn't know a Brazil nut from an Argentina monkey.

He scowled at the world ahead. "Do I look like I'm joking?"

At the moment, he didn't even look like he knew *how* to joke.

"There," he said and pointed to an enormous tree that grew at a bent angle across the road.

Eddy swung the Jeep to the left. It bumped over the ruts like a carnival ride gone mad.

"That way." Durrand pointed toward a trail that branched off to their right. But it wasn't really a trail at all, just a few flattened blades of grass and some broken saplings. Still, she turned in. A jagged boulder was perched on a rocky outcropping, almost completely covered in vines. "Stop here," he ordered.

She did so.

"Kill the engine."

Once she turned the key, the morning seemed heavy, pregnant with silence and impending doom. "We walk from here?"

"*I* walk," he said and, lifting a duffle bag from the floor, slipped the strap over his head. "You stay with the Jeep."

She opened her mouth, maybe to argue, but he raised a hand. "Not my decision," he said. "Javier insisted that I go in alone."

She had to admit that he didn't look thrilled with the idea. "Take these." Pulling a small pair of binoculars from one of a half dozen of his pants pockets, he handed them over. "You see anyone coming...anyone at all, call me on my cell. Let it ring twice."

She took the binoculars in one hand, raised them to her face, and wondered if they had any reason to assume their phones would work when they most needed them. "Then what?"

"If I don't show up in two minutes, come in and save my ass."

She lowered the field glasses with a snap.

"*Now* I'm joking," he said and shoved a knife into his boot. She stared at him. His teasing expression was strangely similar to his dour expression. "If I'm not out in fifteen minutes get the hell out of Dodge. I'll meet you back at the hostel."

"How?" she asked.

He was already exiting the Jeep. "Not your problem."

"But—

"Stay out of sight," he ordered. "This should only take a few minutes."

In a matter of seconds, the jungle had swallowed him up. She was not a patient person. Others at the agency would have disagreed with that assessment, but she was not a woman who could sit and wait. Inactivity made her fidgety.

Dragging out her tablet, she tried to do a search on Quebrada Verde. But there was no satellite signal available. Maybe Durrand was right about technology, she thought and opened a conventional map. According to the blog she'd read while online earlier, the Tortuga River was relatively user-friendly. Except for the alligators and...

A noise from behind startled her. She glanced in the rearview mirror and jerked. A lone figure was approaching on foot. He wore the deep green uniform of the Colombian police. Aviator glasses hid his eyes, and his mustache, thick as a raccoon's tail, made him look sinister, like a caricature of a villain. Visions of *Romancing the Stone* stormed through her brain. But she put them aside. She was being foolish, she told herself. Still, she felt sweat bead on her forehead.

Folding the map rapidly, she shoved it under the seat and turned to the window.

"Good morning, officer." She employed her best Spanish and tried to give him the full force of her smile, but her lips quivered with nerves.

He didn't respond, just watched her from behind his mirrored lenses.

"I'm not…" Her mind was galloping. Where was Durrand? "I'm not double parked or something, am I?"

Sadly, that was the best joke she could muster under duress, but he didn't smile back.

"You are American?"

"Is it that obvious?" She upped the wattage of her smile, but there wasn't much left in reserve. "And here I've been so proud of my Spanish."

"Why are you here?"

"*Here?*" She forced a laugh. It sounded painful. "That's the thing. I'm afraid I don't know where *here* is." She gestured toward the maps that Durrand had left on the dash. "I'm totally lost."

He scanned the jungle that surrounded them before returning his gaze to hers.

"Surely you are not in this remote spot alone, chica," he said and removed his shades. His lips curled into a smile for the first time. Neither the sight of his eyes nor his expression made her feel better. His mouth seemed to be entirely disassociated with the rest of her face. Her mind raced along, tumbling over a dozen less than comforting scenarios.

"I'm afraid so," she said. "I wanted to get in some early-morning sightseeing." She shrugged, disarming but confident…or annoying and pee-in-her pants scared.

"Do not tell me you came to our country unchaperoned."

"No!" The word came out too quickly, too forcefully. She smoothed out her tone. "No. My husband…" Durrand's broad, no-

nonsense image filled her mind. She found she desperately longed to convey that image to this less than charming officer. "My husband accompanied me."

He stared meaningfully at the empty seat.

She chuckled. It sounded like gravel on tin. "I mean, he came to your beautiful country with me."

"And his name?"

"I beg your pardon?"

"Your husband…" His gaze dropped to her chest for a moment then rose leisurely. "The lucky man to whom you are wed…what is his name?"

For one frantic moment she failed to recall the fictional name he had chosen, but in a second her mind cleared. "Luke," she said. "Luke Lansky."

His lips twisted knowingly. "Shall I be encouraged by the fact that you could not, at first, recall his name?"

She tried to chuckle. "I didn't forget," she said and forced a shrug. Casual as a heart attack. "It's just that…most people call him…" Her mind was racing along like an out of control locomotion. "Rage." Holy mother of God, what was she talking about?

He raised a brow. She giggled, feeling dizzy. "He's rather…protective."

His smile soured. "Then he obviously was not the man we just spotted slinking through the jungle."

She refrained from closing her eyes, from freezing, from babbling like a lunatic, though all of those things seemed like likely possibilities. "No. If it's who I think it was, my husband is much bigger. That was…Nathan. My brother." She motioned vaguely. "He went to…relieve himself."

"I see." He turned his head again as if scanning the jungle for her fictional kin. Eddy did the same. But Durrand was nowhere in sight. "I hope he did not get lost."

"I'm sure he'll be back in a moment."

"It is easy to become disoriented in the jungle. Perhaps you should return to the village."

"Without Nathan?"

"*Sí*. The sun…" He smiled. "It is hot, and I've no wish for your pretty skin to become burnt."

"Well, that's what SPF 40 is for."

He stared at her blankly.

"Sunblock. See," she said and raised her arm. It was as pale as whipping cream. "Not a hint of color." That much at least was true. Her antecedents, British laborers all, would have known her by her glow-in-the-dark skin.

"Ahhh, you Americans and your many products." He shook his head as if amused. "Still, I fear I must insist that you return to the village. In fact…" Rounding the bumper quickly, he opened the passenger door. "I believe I will accompany you to make certain you arrive safely." He stepped inside.

She swept her gaze desperately toward the jungle where Durrand had disappeared. "I couldn't possibly leave my brother. He'll—" she began, but a small click of noise made her lower her attention. It was then that she saw the pistol resting on his thigh.

The world ground slowly to a halt.

"Please, chica…" He smiled. Absolutely no emotion showed in his eyes. "I must insist."

She swallowed, nodded, and started the engine with fingers numb from fear. "What about my brother?"

"I am certain he will be fine. So long as he does not upset Javier." His smile looked real now. Real and chilling, and frightfully predatory.

She felt gooseflesh prickle her arms. "Who?"

He chuckled. "Turn the car around, *señora*. Or are you not truly married?"

"Why would I lie about that?" Her face felt hot. Her mind was spinning, but she spoke again before he could answer. "My brother is going to be extremely upset if I leave him."

"As is my captain if an Americano ruins his bust…no matter how unspoiled her skin is."

"His bust?" A hundred yards to the right she saw a blur of

movement. Khaki against green. Every terrified instinct in her longed to stare. To convince herself that it was Durrand, but she kept her attention in the rearview mirror as she backed around. The cords in her throat felt as stiff as telephone cables.

"Is that not what you call it in America?" he asked. "A bust?"

She wasn't positive, but she thought there was a fast-moving figure scrambling downhill, skimming through the trees on a trajectory that would intersect the road. She shifted clumsily into first, grinding the gears. "I don't know what you're talking about."

His teeth looked maliciously white against his mustache. "Javier was seen headed toward his little hut by the river."

She shook her head. "Javier?"

"It is where he, at times, meets with his clients to sell them his wares."

"Like..." She shrugged and took her foot off the clutch. The Jeep hiccupped and yanked to a halt. "I'm sorry." Don't look up, don't look, she ordered silently, and kept her gaze on the shifting gear. "I haven't driven a stick in years."

"Start it again," he ordered.

She did so, killing time by studying the tiny diagram on the shifter for a moment and hoping again that she hadn't imagined the khaki-clad figure rushing toward the road.

"Go," he ordered.

"I'm trying," she said and shifted from neutral into first while glancing at the policeman from the corner of her eye. "But what about my brother?"

"With whom you were sightseeing?"

"Yes."

"In Putumayo? Where there is more cocaine than people?"

She opened her eyes wide. "You think we came for drugs?" she asked and let her foot slip off the clutch so that the engine chugged painfully.

"Do you say that you did not come for the coca?"

"Coca? No! Absolutely not. We would never—"

"Then you were meeting Javier for the guns. *Sí?*"

She felt the air leave her lungs.

"Shift," he insisted.

"But the road is so—"

He lifted his pistol. "Shift."

She did so. He smiled. The Jeep began to pick up speed. And try as she might, she could see no more of the khaki-clad figure she hoped she hadn't imagined.

"We must hurry now so that we may take our time later," he said.

She jerked her gaze to his. It was hooded and horrific, shining with a dozen awful thoughts. She felt sick to her stomach. "Take our time with what?"

"Just drive, *señorita.*"

"*Señora,*" she corrected, and he laughed.

"I do not mind if you are married," he said.

She felt the blood leave her face but strove for machismo. "Touch me and I'll turn you in to your commanding officer."

"My captain, he is not the kind to hold this against me. Though he prefers younger chicas, I myself do not mind some...how do you say in your country...some dust on the bottle."

Terror squeezed her lungs tight, but she reminded herself that she was no wilting lily. She'd been trained for such emergencies. She glanced toward him, mind spinning with escape strategies that seemed as unlikely as a miracle.

"Neither do I mind some blood," he said and raised the pistol.

# Chapter Twenty-Four

The passenger door snapped open.

A bullet ripped through the Jeep.

Eddy screamed and jerked. The policeman was yanked out. She opened her mouth to scream again, but Durrand appeared instantaneously beside her.

"Go!" he yelled. Behind him, the officer was already rising to his feet, lifting his gun, firing. "Go!"

Eddy slammed the Jeep into third. They hit a bump and flew. A bullet pinged off their bumper. Up ahead, two men, both afoot, were racing toward the road.

"Get down!" Durrand ordered and, grabbing her head, pressed it toward the seat. She didn't try to resist. Neither did she slow down. A bullet winged through the windshield. Durrand grunted. The Jeep bumped.

Eddy jerked upright. "Are you hit?"

"Drive!" he ordered.

She sliced her attention back to the road and gasped. A vehicle was bearing down on them from up ahead. Three men with rifles peered at them from the bed of a pickup truck, arms braced atop the cab.

"Don't stop!" Durrand ordered and raised a handgun.

Gripping the steering wheel tighter, she stomped on the accelerator. The truck seemed to jump toward them. Bullets sprayed in their direction, pelting the Jeep. The approaching men yelled, or maybe they were her screams she heard as the other vehicle was yanked to the side at the last moment.

They careened past. Metal scraped. The side-view mirror was torn off with a whining protest. Two men were thrown to the ground.

For a moment, every latent instinct she possessed insisted that she stop to ascertain their wellbeing, but terror demanded that she accelerate. Terror won.

Branches ripped at them. Rocks leapt like living beasts at their tires.

"Turn here!" Durrand rasped.

"Where?" There was no break in the jungle.

"Here!" he insisted and reaching for the wheel, yanked them into the trees.

Eddy slammed on the brakes, but momentum carried them through the greenery. They landed with a jolt twenty feet from the road. The engine died.

The silence was absolute.

"Grab your bag!" Durrand ordered.

Eddy blinked, certain they were dead. They must be dead. "We crashed," she said.

"Vines," he grunted and pumped the door handle. Nothing happened. Slamming the door with his shoulder, he managed to wrest it open and stumble outside. "Just vines." Reaching for his backpack, he shoved maps and binoculars inside. "Cover the Jeep."

"What?" Her knee ached. Her mind felt messy.

"Get out! That's an order."

She obeyed without thinking. He was already dragging tattered foliage back into place. She tried to help, but her hands were tingly, her legs unsteady.

"Can you walk?"

"What?" She glanced up at him, barely able to manage that much.

He curled his fingers around her arm. "We've gotta go."

"Where?"

"Down to the highway. We'll hitch a ride from there."

She stumbled once, but he pulled her back to her feet. "We *have* a ride," she said and half turned toward the Jeep, but he steered her away.

"They'll have more forces coming up the road. We were lucky to get past the first truck."

"But we can't..." She felt strangely teary. "We can't just leave it."

He was still steering her downhill. "Would you feel better if I put it out of its misery?"

"I meant it's our only security," she said.

"Security's an illusion." He glanced behind them, expression grim. "Can you run?"

She nodded, though she may have been taking the question in a more existential way. Theoretically she could run. She had run in the past.

"Let's go," he said and picked up a jog.

She followed as best she could, but her legs felt rubbery, her stomach gelatinous. Staggering to a halt, she bent double and threw up beside a towering banyan.

It was several moments before she could straighten.

"You ready?"

She nodded.

After that, it was a nightmare of movement, endurance, and exhaustion.

After what seemed a lifetime, they stumbled onto a road. It stretched before them like a winding viper. Durrand squinted into the distance, breathing hard. The sun was setting. He tugged her firmly back into the shelter of the trees.

"Did we overshoot?"

"What?" She bent double once more, trying to squeeze oxygen into lungs that had threatened to shut down hours ago.

"Which direction to Chaviv?"

"Not sure." In fact, she had no idea. Terror and exhaustion had consumed any hope of differentiating east from west.

"We have to get a new vehicle."

She glanced down the road. It was empty as far as the eye could see. "How?"

"You're going to have to convince someone to stop."

"What?" She jerked toward him. "Why me?"

He grimaced as if his own lungs were complaining. "I don't think anyone's going to care if I show a little leg."

"You want me to show my—" The idea was so absurd she actually laughed. The sound came out on a tortured wheeze. "That's ridiculous."

"Shooting the tires out of a passing car would be counterproductive." He raised the gun and winced at that slight motion. "And we only have one bullet left. We're going to have to depend on your sex appeal."

She blinked down at herself. Her arms were scratched and covered with mud, her clothes tattered. "You're crazy."

He exhaled heavily and glanced into the jungle behind them. "You're overestimating the average male."

She swung toward him. He'd dropped his pack on the ground and removed his shirt. His chest was taut with muscle and smeared with...

She stumbled back. "Is that... Is that blood?"

He glanced up. "Don't faint," he said.

"What?" Her voice sounded hopelessly small to her own ears.

"You're not going to faint are you?"

"No." She shook her head. The world tilted a little, but she hardened her voice. "Of course, not."

"Good," he said and fainted dead away.

# Chapter Twenty-Five

E ddy stared at Gabe. Six feet four inches of solid male lay at her feet. "Durrand?" She said his name softly. There was no answer. Not even a flicker of recognition. "Durrand!" Nothing.

Squashing every fidgety instinct in her, she knelt beside him. She'd been trained to field dress wounds. She'd been *trained*, she reminded herself and found she had forgotten the simplest instructions. Taking a deep breath, she settled back on her heels and forced herself to examine the injury. It was high on his shoulder, well away from his heart. That was something, at least. Still, she'd have to staunch the bleeding, she thought, but realized in a moment that it was far too late for that. He'd probably stopped hemorrhaging hours ago...while they were racing downhill dodging bullets and boulders. She exhaled slowly and dropped her head between her knees. No point in passing out, as well. Not that a trained operative would pass out. She closed her eyes.

Then again, how much worse could it be if she were unconscious? They were alone in the jungle with the police chasing them. They were lost, and the lead on their suicide mission had been wounded, maybe fatally.

She inhaled carefully. Exhaled slowly. No time for that kind of thinking. First things first. She had to get him out of the elements. Get him fluids. Get him medical help.

Which meant that he was right, they needed a car. She'd have to convince someone to stop. Maybe if some Good Samaritan saw him lying there he'd stop to help. More likely, they'd career past and call the police. Colombia was not a wealthy country, but everyone and his sister had a cell phone and...

The sound of an engine stopped her thoughts. Someone was coming. Standing quickly, she dashed toward the road then jerked to a halt. There was no reason to assume the motorists weren't the very same people they'd been running from. But perhaps that was a moot point. If she didn't get medical help, Durrand would die. Stumbling onto the road, she braced her legs and waved both hands.

A white pickup truck raced toward her, swung wide and rushed past, leaving fumes and a raw feeling of panic in its wake. She stared dismally after it then fought to contain her despair. No time for that.

Maybe if she had a flag, something to wave, they would see her early enough to realize she posed no threat.

Hurrying back to Durrand, she retrieved his discarded shirt. Then, noticing his gun, she snatched it from the ground and raced back to the road. Another car was coming. She could hear it. White-hot hope surged inside her. She rushed downhill and fell, sliding five feet before stopping herself. Pain seared her hip, but it was her shin that ached the worst. Gasping, she wobbled to her feet and limped on. A red Volkswagen, far past its prime, was roaring up. Stumbling from the trees, she waved the shirt, but the dilapidated Beetle breezed past.

Shaking, she lurched to the nearest rock and sat down. Her leg throbbed. She pulled up her pants. A stick had pierced the pale skin near her shin bone. She pulled it out with unsteady hands. The wound appeared to be minor. Barely a trickle of blood marred her flesh.

Still, she was so immersed in her own woes, she barely noticed the next car. It was nearly upon her when she glanced up. Thirty feet past by the time she realized it was slowing down. Shoving her weapon into the waistband near her spine, she stood, jittery now that it seemed someone was willing to stop.

The car was aqua blue and angular, harkening from an earlier era. In a moment, a man stepped out of the vintage vehicle. He was young, barely out of his teens, and wore a white suit a little too large for his lanky frame. A cocky fedora shadowed his eyes.

"You're a long way from home," he said.

"Oh!" Relief flooded her. "You're American." It was strange how seeing a compatriot felt tantamount to euphoria.

"Philadelphia originally." He sauntered forward, grin a white slant in his lean face. "Name's Greg Timpany. That's my Thunderbird." He jerked a thumb over his shoulder. "Wanna ride to—"

"I need your help!" Her voice sounded panicked. She tried to smooth it. "My friend's been wounded. We—"

"Wounded!" He stopped dead in his tracks, cocky taking a right turn toward scared.

Seeing it was too late to retract those damning words, she tried to soothe him. "He didn't do anything wrong. We were just—"

"Listen…" He was already backing away. "I'll get you an ambulance. They should be here in…" He shrugged, shook his head. "Shouldn't take more than a couple of—"

"I'm sorry," she said and yanked the gun from her waistband.

He froze.

"Really sorry," she said and winced.

He glanced toward his car, thoughts of escape all but visible as they raced through his brain.

She shook her head. "I can…" She was breathing hard, visibly shaking. "I'm an excellent shot."

He lifted his hands a little then kept them even with his chest. "My wallet's in the Bird. If you'll let me get it, I'll—"

"I don't want your money."

Somehow, those words didn't seem to soothe him at all. He glanced at his car again.

"I don't want to shoot you either," she said and cocked the weapon.

"Okay."

Another vehicle was coming. She could hear it rumbling down the hill toward them. Dammit! "I'm going to lower the gun. If you do anything…" She ran out of words, out of breath, out of ideas, but he shook his head.

"I won't."

"Put your hands down," she ordered.

He did so slowly. She lowered the pistol, letting it fall unseen beside her injured leg.

The motorist slowed to gawk but kept driving.

Eddy breathed a sigh of relief as it rounded the bend and slipped out of sight, swallowed by the jungle. But pain suddenly slashed her arm. She jerked back. Too late. Timpany had knocked the pistol from her fingers. It skittered in the dirt. She dove for it. He grabbed it first.

She rose slowly, heart racing.

He straightened, too. Gone was his convivial grin. "What now, *perra*?" he asked.

She ignored the pejorative as best she could. "I still need help."

He chuckled. The sound was not friendly. "I'm wondering what kind of reward is out on you."

She shook her head, stunned that he had arrived at that conclusion so quickly. "None."

"So your friend was shot for no good reason?"

"I didn't say he was shot." Did she?

He chuckled. "You just happened to be carrying a gun and tromping through the wilderness. Probably for sport. It's all the rage in…" He paused, looking her over. "Wisconsin?"

"Listen, if you'll help me get him to a doctor, I'll pay you."

He tilted back the fedora and raised his brows. "How much?"

"Five hundred dollars."

He shook his head. "You'll have to do better than that 'cause I'm willing to bet that whoever's looking for you will. Who is it, by the way? A jealous lover? *Le policia?*" he asked then shook his head. "But maybe it doesn't matter. A blond-haired beauty in this South American cesspool..." He smiled. The expression was icy. "What would that be worth to the cartel?" He stepped forward. She backed away.

"Don't do this."

"I gotta tell you, babe," he said and jiggled the pistol a little. "These third world bastards don't much care if their women come to them with bullet holes." He shrugged. "They're probably perforated in the end anyhow, but that's not my problem, is—"

"I'm CIA!" she rasped. "Touch me and you'll have the full force of the United States government on you like a pack of wolves."

He stopped in his tracks. "CIA?"

"IOC Division."

"IOC? Really?" His eyes were wide and as round as marbles. She nodded.

"That's fantastic. 'Cause I'm Superman," he said and throwing back his head, laughed out loud.

Maybe it was the raucous sound of his amusement that caused her to break. Maybe it was the pain in her leg or the fact that Durrand lay—possibly dead—in the undergrowth that made her snap.

But whatever the reason, she rushed him.

He jerked up the gun's muzzle and fired.

## Chapter Twenty-Six

E ddy plowed her shoulder into Timpany's belly. He fell backward with her on top. The pistol flew from his hands. She snatched it up, rolled sideways and jolted to her feet, aim dead-center on his chest.

He jerked to his knees then rose more slowly, gaze steady on hers.

"Superman," she rasped. Her voice was shaky, but he didn't look so solid himself. "I guess I didn't recognize you."

He licked his lips. He'd raised his hands near his shoulders. His fingers were spread. His white vest had a streak of green near the waist. He'd lost a button. "Well, I don't..." He swallowed, Adam's apple bobbing. "I don't have my cape."

"You're a jerk," she said and steadied the weapon.

"No, I'm not." Somehow, he managed to sound honestly affronted. "You didn't think I was serious about that stuff did you?"

"What stuff is that? The stuff where you were going to give me to drug runners to be raped and murdered? Or the part where you were going to shoot me first?"

"Both. I was just joking," he said and attempted a smile.

"I gotta tell you..." She was breathing hard and her knees felt noodly. "I don't think you're going to make it in stand-up." She motioned toward the jungle. "Get going."

Sweat had appeared on his forehead but he turned away, walking stiffly. "What are you going to do to me?"

She didn't answer. They'd just entered the edge of the trees. "Turn left."

"This is all just a big misunderstanding. We're going to laugh about it later."

"So you weren't really planning to have me killed?"

"Killed?" He chuckled. "No! I—" He stopped abruptly when he saw Durrand stretched out beneath the shiny leaves of a cork-wood. "Jesus!" His tone was squeaky. "Is that your friend?"

She was almost tempted to ask him how many wounded men could be strewn along the side of Highway 78, but she didn't have the energy required.

"Pick him up," she insisted.

"Are you kidding me?" He turned jerkily toward Durrand. "He weighs like...twice as much as I do."

"Luckily, you're a superhero. Be careful of his wound." She nodded back toward the aqua colored vehicle. "Put him in the backseat."

He opened his mouth as if to argue, but she tightened her fingers on the pistol's grip and widened her stance.

"If you don't quit whining, I'm going to shoot you in the leg."

"I won't be able to carry him if you do that."

She tightened her lips. "It'd be worth it just for the satisfaction. Pick him up."

Squatting, Timpany shoved his arms under Durrand and strug-gled to rise, but his legs were shaking before his burden had cleared the ground. He settled the lax body back down, already puffing. "I can't do it.

Eddy scowled, worry scratching at her soul. Time was running out. "Grab his arm," she said.

"What?" He was still panting.

She repeated the order.

He complied.

Keeping the pistol pointed at Timpany, she picked up Durrand's opposite arm. It was shockingly heavy.

"Okay, we're going to drag him to your car."

"For real?"

"Pull."

Even with the two of them, it was not a simple task. But at least it was downhill. By the time they reached the Thunderbird, Eddy's legs felt shaky. "Open the door."

He glared at her. "If he gets blood on my seat you're going to wish you'd never met me."

"If I shoot you in the leg, you're not going to feel so great about our relationship either."

He opened the door, looking sullen.

"Get him inside."

"Can't do it alone."

"Swear to God, I'm going to pop you just for the fun of it."

In the end, Timpany managed to do as ordered. Durrand lay on his back, legs bent, feet on the floor.

"Okay." Eddy fidgeted, motioning with the handgun. "Now, get out of here."

"Get out of here? Are you kidding?" Timpany shook his head. "I can't leave the Bird. Cesar will kill me if I leave the Bird."

"Who's—"

"My boss!" He looked upset enough to burst into tears. "He owns the auto dealership."

"I thought the car was yours."

"Yeah, well I didn't think you were going to pull a gun on me and make me drag your big ass boyfriend around like a sack of…" He shook his head then set his jaw. "That car isn't going anywhere without me."

"I'm not going to hurt it."

"Are you nuts?" He swung one miserable hand toward the

vehicle. "Your oversized friend is leaking like a sieve. And what if he dies in there? I'll never get that stink out."

She stared at him. "Are you serious? You're worried about the smell?"

"I mean…" For a second, he tried to look empathetic. He barely even managed human. "It'd be the shits if he died." He cocked his head, gazed at Durrand for a second, then raised his brows and examined her. "What is he to you anyway?"

"I'll leave the car where you can find it," she said.

"You two an item or what?" he asked and stepped toward her.

"Stay where you are."

"Listen, I'm not sure how much you know about Colombia, but it's basically a backwater swamp where macho men have pissing wars. It's not safe for a woman alone here. If he dies—"

"He's not going to die!"

"Sure. I know. But if he *does*, things could get rough. Hey, I'll give you my cell phone number." He was pulling a stack of cards from his vest pocket. "Call me if you need to buy a car or something."

"Didn't you threaten to sell me about five minutes ago?"

"I told you I was just kidding," he said and stretching his arm out as far as he could, handed her his card.

She took it for lack of anything better to do then backed away.

"Thank you."

"Yeah. Just… Just be careful with the Bird."

She glanced through the window. A pair of keys hung from the ignition. A topless hula girl danced on the dash. "I'll be—" She began. Just then something stung her eye. She stumbled back as business cards fluttered past, but he was already wrenching the pistol from her hand.

She swung toward the car without thinking. Yanking the door open, she dove inside. A bullet skimmed her arm. She shrieked, slammed down her lock, and turned the key. The engine roared to life as the gun's chambers clicked repeatedly.

"Empty? It's fucking empty! Are you kidding me?" Timpany shrieked, but she was already peeling away, gravel flying in her wake.

# Chapter Twenty-Seven

"I'm out," Jairo said and slapped his cards down beside the kitty on the table...table being a euphemism for the upturned wooden crate that had once been used to transport poultry...kitty being an almost unidentifiable pile of oddball objects that might have had a modicum of value at some point in history.

"He's bluffin'," Shepherd said and kept his eyes on Gabe. "You can always tell 'cause he gets that dumb-ass innocent look on his face." Shep coveted the plastic rat Intel had bet. Gabe was sure of it. It would go nicely with his rubber chicken and flying bat. "I'll raise you one slightly used wool sock and—"

Ten feet away, Abdul Wakil Ghafoor burst through the door.

Instincts sharpened like stilettos had Gabe grabbing the bastard by the throat. His fingers tightened.

"Don't!" someone begged, but he was sworn to protect his squad, to—

"Durrand!" It took him a moment to realize Ghafoor's voice was a little feminine. Longer still to notice he sounded like Edwards. By the time he was fully conscious, her face was a frightening shade of gray.

He loosened his fingers with an effort. She coughed and stumbled backward.

His surroundings came into focus by slow increments. The room was small, dim, curtains pulled. They were in their humble hostel in la Candelaria. Not a single assailant was in sight.

Holy hell! His hands were shaking. "Sorry. I'm sorry."

It wasn't until then that he realized a plastic tube was protruding from the cephalic vein in his left forearm. An IV bag hung from the headboard, and his left shoulder was bandaged.

Guilt flared through him like a guided missile. "You okay?"

"Lie down." Her voice was raspy.

He shook his head and twisted to stand, but she pushed against his chest.

"Lie back before you screw up your fluids."

He eased onto the pillow. Not because she told him to. And certainly not because he was too weak to resist.

"How long was I out?"

She rubbed her throat and cleared it. Her expression was kind of pissed. Maybe she wasn't the kind of woman who liked to be strangled after saving some jerk-off's life. "Three, maybe four hours."

Holy shit! he thought but kept his expression bland, his tone neutral. He'd learned long ago to put his emotions in another compartment. The Army was top flight on teaching stoicism. "How'd you get me here?"

"Stole a car," she said and shaking two tablets from a plastic bottle, handed them over. He wondered if the tremor in her hands was merely to remove the tablets or if perhaps she was a little disturbed that he'd tried to off her. "Take these."

"What?"

"Ampicillin. I found them in your duffle. Along with everything else known to mankind." She shook her head at his excess. She wasn't the first to think he took the Boy Scout maxim too far. "Do you really think we need firecrackers? And what's with the chloro—"

"You stole a car?" He wasn't sure if she had misunderstood his question, or if she was avoiding the subject intentionally.

"Yeah, well, I was going to carry you here but I thought someone might get suspicious if they saw me piggybacking you down the Central Trunk Highway." She lifted an open can of 7-Up. She'd lucked out finding a store that sold American beverages. "Drink this. It'll help restore your pH."

He took the soda but didn't lift it to his lips. "Where's the car now?"

"Anyone ever tell you you're a crappy patient?"

"My sister," he admitted. "Sarge." He scowled. "And every nurse I've ever met."

"You strangle them, too?"

"I usually try to refrain."

She laughed. He was pretty sure the sound shouldn't make his heart flip over. Especially since she looked like hell. If he didn't know better, he would think that someone had taken an eggbeater to her strawberry shortcake hair. There was a streak of blood across her hand, and a stripe of mud traversed a jagged course from her cheek to her opposite eyebrow. But that was nothing compared to her clothes.

"What happened to your shirt?" he asked.

She glanced down, lifting her brows when she spied the left sleeve hanging precariously from her shoulder. "Tough day at the office."

"What happened?" he asked again and noticed for the first time that a scratch marred the creamy skin of her upper arm.

"Take your meds and I'll tell you."

He nodded. Strangling her, hadn't made her more cooperative, after all. Maybe compliance would.

He popped the pills into his mouth. The soda felt strangely soothing and abrasive at the same time. He drained the can in a matter of seconds and set it on the cheap laminated bedstead.

She nodded, looking impressive. "I bet you were a big hit at frat parties."

"Your shirt," he reminded her.

"I met a guy. Greg Timpany. American, actually."

He waited.

"Turns out he didn't really want to give up his car. Or…" She wobbled her head a little, juggling semantics. "His *boss's* car, actually."

Gabe's gut cramped up. He should have never brought her here. Not when he wasn't one hundred percent. Maybe not even then. But he drew in a deep breath. "Where's the vehicle now?"

"My guess? A bordello. Maybe on Carrero 16."

He stared at her.

She cleared her throat. "Timpany has probably retrieved it and gone looking for entertainment."

It took him a minute to absorb her words, longer still to surmise the implications. He managed to gain his feet a split second later. "How did he know where to find it?"

"I called him."

A couple hundred questions stormed through his mind, but there was no time to voice them. "We ruck up in five minutes," he said.

"What?"

"We're leaving." He glanced around. "Get your stuff together. All the medical supplies. Ditch the water. We'll sterilize what we need on the way. But don't—"

"We're not going until your blood pressure's back up."

He narrowed his eyes at her, heart beating like a drum in his overtaxed chest. "Mission accomplished."

"Listen…" she said and spread her hands in front of him as if she were warding off an angry bull. Her fingers looked ridiculously dainty. Goddamnit, he should never have brought someone here with such ludicrously tiny fingers. "He's not going to turn us in."

He inhaled slowly. He was a patient man. There was an entire platoon of men who would attest to that fact. "You said you stole his car."

"Well…technically, yes."

"Then you told him where to find it."

"Yes."

So many goddamn questions! "How'd you know how to contact him?" he asked and tossed a pair of khakis into his duffel. A spasm contracted his back at the movement.

"He gave me his card."

He turned toward her, wasting precious seconds as his eyebrows jerked toward his hairline. "Planning to have drinks later on?"

Her cheeks flushed, making him wonder if he was near the mark. Holy fuck. He tossed a map at his bag.

"Listen, I don't know why he gave me his card."

He stared at her guileless eyes, her Barbie doll body. "Probably a mystery that'll never be solved," he said and turned toward the items that remained strewn across the lone chair.

He could feel her frown on the back of his neck.

"What's that supposed to mean?" she asked.

He drew a deep breath and glanced over his shoulder at her. "What makes you think he won't tell the authorities?"

"He promised he wouldn't."

His gut cramped up as he scanned her tattered clothes again. "Was this before or after he attacked you?"

She pursed her cherry blossom lips. "He doesn't know our location."

"Where'd you leave the car?"

"I parked it by la Parque Independencia."

He thought about the map he had poured over two nights before and shook his head, bemused. "How far away?"

She shrugged and checked his fluids. They were two-thirds gone. "Three miles. Maybe four. Sit down."

He sank slowly onto the bed, mind churning. "You ditched the car and walked here?"

"Ran mostly. But no one saw me. It was dark. Lie back."

He did as ordered. The mattress felt ridiculously lovely beneath his achy muscles, lumps notwithstanding. But he felt as rigid as a rifle. "This Timpany guy…was he—"

"Just be quiet. Relax."

Relax? Was she kidding? He hadn't relaxed since 2001. "Sure," he said. "I'm just a little fuzzy about the chain of events."

"You can defuzz later."

"Humor me," he said.

She gave him a peeved look. If she were any cuter, she'd be a carny prize. Three direct hits and you win a Jenny with a *y* Edwards doll. "Take these and I'll give you a rundown," she said and held up a trio of multi-colored capsules.

"What are they?"

"Pain meds."

"I don't need 'em."

"Oh. You don't like drugs, GI Joe? Okay." She nodded. "I guess Shepherd will just have to work out his own problems then."

She looked too sweet to be so manipulative. Huh. Wrong again. He held out his hand. She dropped the pills onto his palm. A glass of water followed. He drained that too then set it beside the empty soda can before starting to list off the order of events. "We reached our rendezvous at 1400 hours."

"Thereabouts," she agreed.

"The police arrived minutes later."

"Or they were already waiting."

He nodded, thinking as he spoke. "Or they were already waiting.

One of the officers approached the Jeep. What did he say?"

Her expression looked pinched, her only concession to an ordeal that would have bested half the men in his unit. "He said he saw you leave our vehicle. Knew you were going to get drugs or weapons."

"So either they were watching Javier or someone tipped them off." Guilt struck him, so sharp it stung, but he ignored it, still wending his way through the shady hours in his mind. "I saw them coming and returned to the Jeep at a tangent to the road."

"You were wounded," she reminded him and looked a little shaky.

"Yeah." The pain was beginning to slip away like water through terry cloth, leaving him drained and limp.

"When did it happen?" she asked.

"Your passenger got off a shot before I could get my hands on him."

"You should have told me you were hurt."

He ignored that. "How long do you think it took us to reach the highway?"

She shook her head. "Seemed like days."

True. He remembered the bitching pain with tense breathlessness. "Three hours maybe?"

"Could have been more."

"So we reached the road at approximately 1700 hours."

"Sounds about right."

"Then I passed out."

"Swooned like a debutante."

He snapped his gaze to hers. Did she find this amusing? No. Nobody would think being run down like rodents was entertaining. Except Linus Shepherd, of course. But not a girl with apple dumpling cheeks and too skinny fingers. Still, the light in her eyes fascinated him.

"I passed out," he repeated, watching her carefully. "In a very manly fashion."

She grinned, just a flash of humor so enchanting it made his chest hurt. But he forced himself to go on. Timelines were important.

"Then you..." Good God. "Jacked a car and..." He frowned. The world was getting a little mushy around the edges. "How the hell did you get me inside it?"

"We dragged you."

He raised his brows, beginning to understand his myriad aches.

She darted her eyes away and fiddled with the bed sheet.

"Sorry about that but…" She shrugged, looking peeved and apologetic at the same time. How the hell did she manage that? "Turns out, you're really heavy," she said, and he chuckled.

When he glanced at her again, she was gazing at him. Was there tenderness in her eyes, or was he losing his mind? It did seem to be slipping away. He tried to soldier his thoughts.

"You must have had the gun on him."

"Sure," she said but her expression seemed strange. Sheepish almost.

"We still have the one bullet left?" he asked.

She glanced away. "I don't think so."

He managed to raise his brows.

"I'm pretty sure it's empty."

"Did you wound him?"

"No," she said and fidgeted some more. "Not to speak of."

"What does that mean? Not to speak of?"

"We had a bit of…" she shook her head. "Fisticuffs."

His heart rate was picking up again, making his chest feel heavy, his head light. "Fisticuffs?"

"We fought over the gun."

He stared at her. "And not a restroom in sight?"

"Go to sleep, Durrand."

Not on her life, he thought, but his limbs felt like wet cement, his tongue like glue. "Where's the gun now?"

Turning slightly, she adjusted the dial for the IV and murmured something.

"What's that?"

She cleared her throat. "Timpany's got it."

He felt his stomach freefall. "He shot at *you*?"

She shrugged, but he managed to grab her arm and tug her toward him. The scrape along her biceps took on new, red-hot meaning.

"That's from a bullet?"

"Could be. Things happened kind of fast."

He nodded. "So Timpany probably knows our location within a

three mile radius, the police are after us, and we have no weapons. Is that about it?"

She pulled her arm out of his grip, scowl hard on his face. He would have laughed at the expression if he weren't so damned tired. "Listen, I did the best—"

"No, *you* listen." He managed to snatch her fingers before she was out of range. But darkness was coming for him, rolling him under. He tried to marshal his senses, to impress on her the seriousness of the situation. "You...did...hell..." he mumbled and dropped weightlessly into the abyss.

## Chapter Twenty-Eight

G abe awoke with a start. Beside him, Edwards' eyes were wide, her body motionless.

They were still in the hostel, but someone was at the door. Somehow he knew that, though he'd been unconscious moments before.

He lifted his finger to his lips to signal for silence, yanked the IV from his forearm and slipped silently up beside the door. Dragging the knife out of his boot, he motioned for her to stay behind him, but she stepped around him and turned the knob.

"Come in," she said.

Gabe straightened with a snap.

A skinny man with dark skin and an ingratiating smile stepped inside.

"What the hell's going on?" Gabe's voice was little more than a rumble. His mind felt like woolen batting. He hated drugs.

"Thanks for coming," Edwards said.

The scrawny guy nodded briskly and raised his hand.

Gabe lifted his knife in unison, but the other waved his fingers as if warding off a fly. "No need. We friends."

It wasn't until that moment that he noticed the man was carrying a duffle bag. A very large very red duffle bag."

"Edwards, who is this man?"

"I don't know his name."

Gabe kept his attention dead center on the Colombian. "I usually know the names of my friends."

The little man shrugged, smiled and unzipped the bag. An armory lay inside. From where he stood, Gabe could see an AK-47, a Beretta, a SIG, and a pair of grenades. He shifted his attention to Edwards.

"I called in a favor," she said.

To whom, he wondered. God himself didn't have that much artillery readily available. So maybe the *devil* owed her a little something. Still… "How do we know we can trust you?" he asked. To which the little man simply shrugged, set the bag on the bed and moved toward the door. In a moment, he was gone.

The room went silent.

"What the hell just happened?" Gabe asked, but Edwards was already pulling an assault rifle from its mates.

He actually caught his breath at the sight of it. She grinned. "Pretty, isn't it?"

He tried to remain aloof but… "You got a Light Fifty?" he asked and lifted the weapon from the depths of the goody bag.

"Plus scopes and flash suppressors."

He caressed the barrel. "How did this happen?"

"I called a friend of a friend."

"Your friend's friends make gun deliveries?" He pulled out a Smith and Wesson. "Like Dominos Pizza?" It was too good to be true. "How do you know we can trust him?"

"Well…" She was slipping rounds into the double stack magazine of a G21. "For starters, he just gave us enough weapons to break into Fort Knox."

She had a pretty good point there. But he was born and bred to be distrustful. Hell, he didn't even trust his mother. Then again, no one with a lick of sense trusted Sarge. "Who's your contact?"

"I'd tell you," she said. "But then I'd have to kill you." She glanced up. "Literally."

She was standing with her feet braced wide. Her hair was wet, framing her heart-shaped face and her t-shirt clung to her body like overzealous cellophane. Special-Ops Barbie, he thought and put his hormones on lockdown.

"You think he's trustworthy?"

She nodded. "As does the CIA."

He drew a deep breath. It was entirely possible he didn't really know this girl. "All right," he said. "Let's—" he began and paused. Lifting his nose slightly, he sniffed the air. "What's that smell?"

"Oh..." She glanced almost guiltily toward the tiny kitchenette. "I made soup."

He stared at her, sure for a moment that she couldn't be serious. But she had already set the Glock aside and was dishing up a bowl.

It smelled like braised beef and something else. Contentment maybe.

How the hell had she managed this, he wondered as she pushed the dish toward him.

"It's just a can of soup."

He raised his brows at her. He may have been catatonic, but he wasn't entirely stupid.

"With a little meat added. And some onions. A couple tomatoes."

He still stared at her. Was she blushing?

"You have to build up your strength, and I...I like to cook." She sounded strangely defensive as she forced the bowl into his hand and turned stiffly away.

He tasted it as she tested the weight of a semi-automatic, but it was difficult to focus. The soup sucked him in. In a minute, it was gone. He glanced toward the pot that remained on the stove and refrained from mimicking Oliver Twist.

"I already ate," she said. "Finish it up. There's bread by the sink."

She didn't have to tell him twice.

Finally full, he set the bowl aside and wiped his hands on a towel.

"Thank you."

She glanced up from where she was tucking away the last of the medical supplies. It wasn't until that moment that he realized she had organized every article in the room. Holy shit, Action Barbie had just busted her hump while Sleepy Ken took a twelve-hour siesta.

"No problem," she said.

Really? He wondered and refrained from kissing her feet. "You didn't happen to secure a Humvee and an armed escort, did you?"

"Just the guns," she said and raising the Glock again, sighted down the sleek, black barrel.

It was the sexiest thing he had ever seen. And what the hell did that say about him?

"You okay?" she asked.

"Yeah." He pulled himself from his dumb-ass trance. Not only had he taken an unscheduled nap, he was now acting like a prepubescent redneck in the throes of his first crush.

"Are you feeling faint again? Maybe you should lie down."

"Good idea," he said and felt his molars grind as he pushed the curtain aside a scant inch and glanced outside. The sun was just painting its first blush on the morning. "How about I hit the rack again while you go rustle up another vehicle."

"I think I liked you better when you were comatose."

"Everyone does," he admitted, and shoving the SIG into an oversized pocket of his khakis, put his hand on the doorknob. "Get some sleep. This might take a while."

"What are you doing?" Her tone was already tight with worry.

"Going to buy a car."

"*Buy* one?"

"Untraditional, I know, but having one irate motorist out for our blood might be enough." He glanced at her. She was still holding the Glock in both hands but had let it drop to arms' length so that it was perfectly positioned between her thighs. Holy fuck.

"Are you sure you're okay?"

"Yeah," he said and managed to raise his gaze to her face. "If you see even a hint of trouble, call me on my..." He touched his pocket. "Where's my phone?"

"Oh." She hustled into the bathroom and returned in a moment, removing the cell's cord as she reached him. "I charged it. Didn't know when we'd have access to electricity again."

Shit! It was like having a sharpshooter and a wife all rolled into one. Except, of course, for that little omission of conjugal rights. Which wasn't such a tiny omission if you thought about it too hard...or saw her when she was holding a firearm.

But maybe she was as disappointed by those lack of rights as he was. After all, she must have been digging around in his pocket, so perhaps...and fuck he was acting like a retarded ass-wipe again.

"Stay out of sight," he ordered and stepped outside.

# Chapter Twenty-Nine

E ddy's gear was already damp from her dash through the rain by the time she shoved her pack into the backseat of Durrand's newly purchased vehicle.

It was putrid green, rusted through at both bumpers and missing one headlight.

The passenger door moaned like a ghost as she closed it behind her. Water sloshed from the hood of her jacket. When Durrand swung in beside her and shifted into first, they jolted away from the hostel like a buckboard pulling out of Dodge.

"Nice ride," she said. She felt pretty good considering the circumstances. She'd always been a power sleeper and hadn't needed the recommended nine hours. On the other hand, one and a half seemed a little short. "You get a good deal?"

He glanced at her out of the corner of his eye. "I didn't want to look conspicuous."

"So you actually *prefer* the post-apocalyptic look?"

He breathed a snort. "If I had known you were so fussy, I would have had you give your new boyfriend a call."

She chuckled a little and pulled out her GPS. "I figure it'll take six to eight hours to reach the west end of the gulch."

"How far from there to Herrera's plantation?"

She jerked her gaze to him. "We don't know that he's got Shepherd."

"And we won't until we take a look around."

"So we're just going to waltz in and ask."

"I–" he began, but she stopped him before he could leave her out of the equation again.

"Don't speak the language worth crap."

He gritted his teeth and returned his gaze to the road ahead.

"And every day Shepherd is missing decreases his chances of survival," she added. "So, are *we* just going to waltz in and ask about him?"

Something sparked in his eyes but he didn't argue. "We'll have to ditch the car."

"Really? This little gem?"

"And go in on foot."

"Pretending to be lost?"

He nodded. "If we have to. I'm hoping to find Shep and get him the hell out of there without ever being noticed. But if we are spotted, we're back to our original plan."

"Where we're Sarah and Luke Lansky?"

"Just two Americans on an eco-adventure."

"I've always wanted to see the cloud forests," she said and did her best to keep her tone light. But her stomach had done a hard roll. She had a feeling drug dealers might not appreciate unexpected visitors.

"We'll be on the road for a while," he said. "You might as well get some more sleep."

"What about you?"

"What about me?"

"You were shot, remember? Maybe that means you should rest."

"The bullet went straight through."

"Oh, right. So you're fine?"

"Yeah."

"Great," she said and, shrugging out of her rain jacket, stuck it against the window for a pillow. If macho man wanted to play superhero, that was fine with her. She probably wouldn't be able to sleep. *But I am more than willing to ignore him,* Eddy thought. Unfortunately, memories of the previous day nagged her, forcing her to speak. "Listen...I..." She drew a hard breath, expanding her ribs. "Thanks."

"For what?" His tone was bland, but his expression showed surprise and more than a little worry, as if she'd lost her last functioning brain cell.

She didn't glance his way. "Military men aren't really known for their affirmations."

"I don't know what you're talking about."

"And my father..."

"The colonel."

"Yeah. He wasn't the easiest man to please." She wished now that she hadn't started down this road, but it was too late to turn back. She cleared her throat. "I appreciate your praise."

His brows were low over storm warning eyes. "I didn't praise you."

She watched him. He was all but wiggling with discomfort. "You said I did a hell of a job."

His scowl darkened, and for a moment she thought he'd argue but finally he said, "I'd been shot, Edwards. My mental capacity had been compromised. Don't make too much of it."

She stared at him. Maybe she should be insulted that he couldn't even admit he had complimented her. But somehow the idea that he had praised her against his will was doubly flattering. And the sight of him squirming with discomfort made her want to laugh out loud. But she wasn't sleep deprived enough to think that was a good idea.

Turning her face toward the window, she smiled into her raincoat.

---

SHE WOKE to the soft snick of a door. It took her a moment to remember where she was, longer still to realize the putrid little car had stopped and Durrand had stepped outside. Scooting up in her seat, she gazed ahead. But her vision was blurry with sleep. Or... No, she realized belatedly. It was rain that made it difficult to see. Still, she could make out the river. The river that washed across the entire road. She straightened abruptly.

Outside, in the deluge, Durrand bent, lifted a rock from the middle of the rushing stream and tossed it aside. Water sprayed up like a geyser. He made a slow circuit through the river before striding back to the car and scowled at her through the windshield. His hair was plastered to his head. A rivulet made a winding course down the broad width of his neck. "Get your raingear on," he ordered.

She rolled down the window, but it got stuck half way. "What?"

"It'll be safer if you stay on this side while I drive across."

She frowned, feminist instincts unfurling rapidly. "I learned to swim as an infant."

"Yeah?" They were virtually shouting at each other through the rain.

"Became a certified lifeguard at age fifteen."

He shrugged, a single lift of heavy shoulders. "Then you drive," he said.

"All right."

She didn't notice until that moment that he had a coil of nylon rope in his hand.

"I'm going to tie this to the bumper and run it around that tree," he said.

She nodded, wondering muzzily if she had been outmaneuvered.

"The ground's giving way near the edges, so stay to the left of midline. But not too far. And goose it a little."

She nodded again and scrambled over the console.

He attached the rope to the bumper then strode through the

river to the opposite side. Choosing a substantial deciduous, he wrapped the rope around the trunk twice and gave her nod.

Eddy took a deep breath, shifted into first and stepped on the gas. Water sprayed up as she hit the edge of the river. She struck a bump. Something scraped the bottom of the car. Spray peppered the windshield. The backend fishtailed, but she accelerated, heart pumping. Nearly there, nearly… And then the hind wheels sank. There was a clank. The engine stalled.

Eddy cursed fervently, but Durrand was already striding toward her.

"Start it up again," he ordered. "I'll push."

She touched the key, but before she turned it, a battered pickup truck rounded the curve behind them. A man wearing a bright blue raincoat and a slouch hat stepped out, leaving what appeared to be his family behind the foggy windshield. His expression was solemn.

"*¿Tiene problemas*"

Eddy exchanged a glance with Durrand then stepped quickly out of the Pinto. "*Sí. Parece que estamos estancados,*" she said and motioned toward the vehicle.

He nodded at her obvious statement and made one of his own, his Spanish lightning fast. "You should not try to cross in such a small car."

Durrand stood beside her now. "What did he say?"

She repeated his words.

"I think they can get around us."

"Or they could help us," Eddy said and glanced up at his impassive face, but he was already shaking his head. "That's not a good idea."

"Don't you trust anyone?"

"No."

"We can help you," the Colombian said.

Eddy repeated the words in English, but Durrand responded before she finished speaking. "No."

"I am Claudio. These are my daughters…" The little Colombian waved toward the battered vehicle behind them. Two girls stepped out. "Bianca and Noa."

Both looked as shy as fawns, black hair loose around their faces, eyes as bright as agates.

Eddy gave Durrand a look. He scowled, looking a little sheepish.

"All right," he said.

"If it's okay with you, Bianca will drive," Claudio said. "The rest of us will push."

Eddy nodded, but Durrand spoke again, keeping his voice low. "Tell him you have to drive."

"What? I'm not—"

"We don't know these people from Satan."

"What are you talking about? They're little girls."

"Bonnie Parker was a teenager when her crime spree began."

"Who—" Eddy began, then recognizing the reference to Bonnie and Clyde, barely resisted rolling her eyes.

"Tell them," he repeated.

She brightened her smile a notch and switched back to Spanish. "I'm sorry. I injured my shoulder while hiking. Do you mind if I drive?"

Claudio shrugged. "No. Of course, not. I have raised my daughters to be strong."

"Thank you," she said and headed for the driver's seat.

The others lined up behind the vehicle. Eddy sank into the Pinto and started the engine.

"When I count to three," the Colombian said, "you drive forward."

She did so. The car squiggled on the uncertain surface but in less than a full minute, the little vehicle was idling irregularly on the far side of the river.

Eddy stepped onto the road just a few yards from the others. "We'd like to pay you for your trouble," she said and managed to refrain from throwing Durrand an I-told-you-so smirk.

"Pay?" The little man shook his head. "It hurts me that you Americans think my people are only after the pesos."

Guilt flooded her. "I'm sorry. I didn't mean to insult you," she said and glanced meaningfully at Durrand. It wasn't until that moment that she realized little Noa had a 9 mm Walther tipped beneath the Ranger's right ear.

"Your hands," the girl said, eyes hard as granite. "Put them up."

Durrand raised them slowly. "Paranoia," he said. "You should get some."

"What's going on?" Eddy jerked her gaze from him to Claudio. Her voice sounded hollow to her own ears.

The Colombian shrugged. "My darling Noa..." he said and shrugged. "As deadly as she is lovely, yes?"

## Chapter Thirty

The man with the moon tattoo screamed and thrashed. Blood gushed from his eye as Shepherd swung wildly toward the one remaining kidnapper. But he was too far away, already lifting the rifle's muzzle, already squeezing the trigger.

Shepherd sucked in his breath and breathed a prayer.

And then the shooter fell, toppling over backward, eyes wide, white bandana blooming red at the center.

Shepherd froze, heart pounding, but someone was already approaching. He twisted toward the footfalls, head spinning crazily.

"*Amigo.*" The man who spoke wore a canvas hat and a vest over a loose-fitting white shirt, but it was his rifle that held Shepherd's attention. "You are not hurt?"

He shook his head. The movement cast him off balance, but he braced his feet in the uneven foliage and remained as he was. Beside him Moon thrashed weakly.

"Ahh, but you have been in the inhospitable jungle for too long, have you not?"

Shepherd's gaze crept toward the felled man beside him. His screams had turned to whimpers.

"Would you like a call girl?"

Shep blinked. The sun felt as fierce as a branding iron against his back. "What?"

"I asked what I shall call you."

"*Por favor...*"

The little man scowled as he glanced at the man who whimpered on the ground. "Ruben, Jorge, help that poor fellow will you?"

Two men appeared from out of the blue. Bending, they lifted Moon and carried him away. Or, maybe they flew. Though even in Shep's current condition, that seemed a little unlikely.

"I am a doctor and can help you once we reach my property. But until then, we have a little something to make you comfortable."

There was a rustle behind him. Shepherd tried to turn to look, but he was already falling, slipping weightlessly into the soft abyss.

# Chapter Thirty-One

E ddy remained immobile, staring in confusion. Durrand stood just as still, eyes as steady as an osprey's on the girl with the gun.

The little Latino behind Durrand laughed. "I have tried to raise them right, but times are hard, yes? And there is so much they want: American jeans, American music, American cars, although..." He glanced sadly at the Pinto. "This, it is a piece of shit. Still..." He shrugged. "We are *thieves* not automobile connoisseurs. Is that not so, girls?"

"*Aléjese del coche,*" Bianca said.

Eddy shifted her gaze to the elder daughter. The pistol she now sported was trained with deadly accuracy on Durrand.

"What did she say?" he intoned.

Eddy's throat felt tight. "They seem to want the car."

His eyes narrowed slightly. "Tell them we'll give up our money and our bags if they'll let us keep the Pinto."

She almost argued; everything they needed was in those bags: their passports, their weapons, their medical supplies, but in a moment, she understood his line of thinking. Gabe Durrand might be more devious than she had realized. She nodded. The movement felt jerky. "Please don't leave us stranded," she said and shifted her attention to Claudio.

The little Latino raised his brows with interest.

Eddy swallowed and hurried on. "If you let us keep the car we won't turn you in to the authorities. You can have our money and whatever's in our bags."

"Do you hear that, my daughters? They wish to keep that pile of shit. Why do you suppose?"

Bianca smiled. Noa chuckled.

"It's not what you think," Eddy hurried to add. "We don't have anything valuable hidden in it or anything. We just...we don't know our way around. We could die if left afoot. But we've got cash," she said suddenly and jerked open the Pinto's back door. A bullet pinged a few inches from her foot.

Eddy spun about with a shriek.

Noa smiled. "Make my day." She said the words in Spanish, attesting to her familiarity with Hollywood if not with the English language.

"I'm sorry!" Eddy breathed and jerked her hands higher. The trio stared at her, unspeaking. The father, too, now held a gun in one short-fingered hand. Eddy swallowed her bile and wished she had shared Durrand's cynicism early on. "We don't have a lot of money. A thousand... Wait. No. Not quite. I paid for the hostel and—"

"Get the bag," Claudio ordered.

Eddy nodded. Her legs felt stiff, her arms heavy. But she kept them above her head. "Can I..." She paused, swallowed. "Can I put my hands down?"

"Unless you can lift the bag out with your teeth," he said and chuckled. "That would be amusing, would it not, if she—" he began, but in that instant she grabbed the SIG from the pocket of her pack and swung it toward the youngest girl.

His chuckle stopped abruptly. The world went silent. He had lost his jovial expression. "I knew Americans were silly bastards," he said, "but I did not think they were suicidal."

"Take out their old man first," Durrand said. His tone was absolutely even, but Eddy didn't bother to shift either her gaze or her aim to the man who covered her.

"I'm an expert marksman," she said, gaze glued on the girl. If she wasn't mistaken, she had heard honest pride in Claudio's voice when he spoke of his youngest. "This is a SIG Sauer 1911. It's got a muzzle velocity of 950 fps. I can put five rounds into Noa's lovely forehead before you can squeeze off a single shot."

"Edwards..." Durrand's voice was low. "Take out the old man."

"But you are outnumbered." Claudio smiled. "And I am certain one of us can shoot you before you take out all of us. Although we have not had your wonderful American training, so perhaps you will not be dead. But..." The smile fell from his face. "It is possible you will wish you were."

"Edwards—" Durrand said again but she was already pulling the trigger. Noa stumbled backward with a shriek of pain as Eddy dropped to one knee and fired again.

It was over in less than a second. Noa cradled her wounded hand against her chest. Blood seeped between Bianca's spread fingers, dripping down her arm. Their father lay on the ground, moaning as he clasped his thigh in both hands.

The youngest girl snarled something and reached for her pistol with bloody fingers, but Eddy sent it skittering through the mud with an additional bullet.

"Get your father on his feet." Her command was almost unrecognizable to her own ears.

The girls stared at her for an instant then seeming to realize their good fortune, hurried through the rain to retrieve their diminutive father.

"Now get the hell out of here," Eddy ordered.

The trio struggled toward their pickup truck, Claudio hopping miserably between his daughters. In a matter of minutes, they were gone.

Gabe stared after them. "Didn't they train you to go for the body shot?"

"What?" Eddy turned toward him. Her vision was bleary, her legs unsure.

He glanced at her. "Are you—" he began, but she jerked away, stumbled off a few steps then bent double and vomited silently onto the riverbank.

# Chapter Thirty-Two

E ddy was asleep, curled up in the passenger seat, knees tucked nearly to her chest, downy lashes soft against her apple dumpling cheeks. She really did look like an elf, or a fairy. Shit! What had he been thinking?

Gabe ground his teeth and faced the road ahead. It was still raining. The roads were deteriorating by the second, which meant they would have to hoof it soon; the fairy was going to have to get wet. Soaked, in fact. Drenched. And maybe killed. Or tortured.

God, he wished he had her gift for silent vomiting.

Seeing a break in the jungle on his left, he goosed the Pinto's pathetic engine. They bumped off the so-called road and into the vines, but they didn't make it twenty feet up the mud-slick hill before the engine failed.

Beside him, Edwards woke, dewy-eyed as a bottle-fed lamb as she yanked a hand toward the dash with a gasp.

The world seemed silent after the clatter of the engine. Dusk was just falling, though the dark, low-slung clouds made it seem later.

"What's going on?" Her voice cracked a little.

"We'll have to leave the car here."

She took a second to digest that information. A second longer to absorb the abysmal conditions outside their questionable refuge. "Are we going to try to hide it?"

He gave that some thought. "The jungle might do the job itself. I'll take the keys and hope we can come back for it. But it's not registered in our names, so it shouldn't come back to haunt us."

On the other hand, she already looked a little haunted. But that wasn't his concern. She'd signed up for this little slice of perdition of her own volition and she was a big girl.

She glanced over at him as she laced up her boots. "What's wrong?"

For a big girl, she had seriously tiny feet.

"Nothing," he said and shoved Noa's Walther into his pack. If they acquired any more weapons, they'd have to rent a U-Haul.

Edwards pulled her pant legs down over her laces and straightened, lips pursed. Lifting the GPS from the dash, she tapped a couple of buttons and scowled at the screen. "Looks like it's about ten kilometers to Angels Falls. Just a little farther to the gulch."

Ten klicks. How far was that on fairy feet?

She shoved the GPS into her pack. "That'll take what? Four, maybe five hours?"

He was tempted to call the whole thing off, to get back onto the road and return to Bogotá, but the putrid Pinto probably wasn't going to start, and that dumbass Shepherd was still MIA.

"Durrand?" she said.

He bumped his mind back into gear and took a chug from his camelback. It wouldn't be long before they had to filter any water they found. They wouldn't do Shep much good if they were puking up their guts from giardia or whatever creepy little organisms were found in these parts. Of course, Tinkerbelle had already ralphed twice with nary a giardia to be found.

"Depends on the terrain," he said, happy as hell he could remember what she'd been talking about. "We'll probably be lucky to get there before dawn."

"Then we'd better get at it," she said and stepped out of the car.

He didn't have much choice but to follow suit.

———

THE REST of the night was like a quaint little version of hell. The rain was nonstop. The footing was horrendous, slick as petroleum jelly with roots and rocks protruding at bone-jarring intervals. It was as dark as pitch inside the bowels of the jungle, but they kept going, creeping forward with nothing but their pale headlamps to light their way.

"Durrand." Edwards' voice was raspy and faint. She stopped, bending slightly to catch her breath. They'd been climbing steadily for over an hour. His right thigh pulsed with pain and his latest gunshot wound wasn't attributing to his comfort. "Do you hear that?"

He held his breath and gripped his sidearm. "What?"

"Water."

He stared at her and let his hand relax on the butt of his pistol. "It's raining," he said.

She might have given him a peeved look, but who the hell could be sure in these damned nightmare conditions. "It sounds like a waterfall. I think we're getting close."

He took a moment to concentrate, and maybe...maybe she was right. Then again, maybe it was Guapo Herrera pissing on their boots.

Optimism...it scared the shit out of him. "We'll set up camp once we reach the other side," he said.

They trudged on, tripping, gasping, moving at a snail's pace. But finally they stood at the edge of the falls. The rain had stopped, but the wind had picked up, chilling their damp bodies and chasing the clouds over the moon and beyond.

"Look at that," she breathed.

"What?" he asked and found his pistol again, but she remained absolutely still for a moment, suggesting they weren't about to die...at least not in the next few seconds.

He glanced to the left where the cliff arced away. Here, beyond the canopy of the trees, it was brighter. Plump droplets sprayed into the darkness like diamonds on black velvet, and below them, the river wound away like a chain of silver to some unknown destination.

"That's the most beautiful thing I've ever seen." Her tone was awed, her back unbowed.

His bitched like a bleeding ulcer.

"Maybe we should pitch the tent here." She turned toward him. Her eyes were bright, and her shirt was plastered to her body, showing every delicate curve.

He hauled his gaze away. What the hell was the matter with him? It was bad enough he'd dragged her to this godforsaken piece of nowhere without treating her like she was a damned sex object. "No," he said. It sounded like his throat had been cleaned with battery acid. "We'll stay on schedule. Cross now. Get a couple hours of sleep and do reconnaissance in the morning."

She nodded, humped her pack like a good little soldier, and gazed into the fast-flowing stream a few feet in front of them. "It doesn't look like it's more than a few inches deep here," she said and stepped toward the water.

He caught her by a strap. "Me first."

She glanced back at him.

"We don't want to risk our gear," he said and tried not to groan as he dropped his pack on the ground. "You stay here while I check the depth."

She didn't argue.

There was no point in trying to cross on the rocks. A single slip could cause disaster. Besides, he was wet anyway. Still, as the water soaked into his boots, he shivered. It was mid-winter cold and probably crawling with creepy things. He didn't like creepy things. But overall, the news was good. The water never rose above his knees. The stream wasn't more than thirty feet wide, and no one seemed to be waiting on the far side to shoot them dead. Turning carefully, he returned to Edwards and retrieved his pack.

"There are potholes off to the right," he said, bouncing a little to settle his straps against the blisters on his shoulders. "But if we inch a little closer to the edge, the bottom's relatively smooth and the water's not too deep."

She nodded.

"Stay behind me," he added.

The current tugged at his pant legs, but he kept his footing and she followed behind.

"It shouldn't be more than two—" she began and then there was a splash.

Durrand spun toward her, but she was already falling. Lunging forward, he caught her by the sleeve and dragged her close. She flailed, trying to get her footing. It seemed to take a lifetime for her to rise again, but finally she stood.

"You okay?" His voice was raspy.

Hers sounded atypically subdued. "Yeah," she said but she looked small and frail in the moonlight. "I'm fine."

He stared down at her and squelched the despicable desire to lift her into his arms. "Hang on," he said.

"What?"

"Hang on to my pack."

He didn't know if he should be alarmed that she didn't argue. But he turned away and felt her grip the strap up high near his shoulder. They plodded through the water in unison until they finally stood on the opposite shore. The bank sloped up from the river.

A sliver of relief sliced through him. "All right. Let's find some-where fairly level to catch some –" he began but suddenly his feet slid out from under him. He crashed into her. She was down in an instant and gathering speed as she shot toward the falls. For a second, her face was a perfect oval in the moonlight and then she was gone, torpedoing over the edge and into the black void beyond.

## Chapter Thirty-Three

"How do you feel, my friend?" The words were spoken in accented English.

Shep opened his eyes slowly, assessing. His right leg throbbed. His head felt tight, and his left hand was immobilized, but overall, the pain had receded to a dull hum. He glanced to the side.

The speaker was a small man. He wore loose, clay-toned trousers and a vest with a half dozen oversized pockets, as if he were ready to return to fly fishing at any given moment.

Pieces of the past fell slowly together in Shep's uncertain brain.

"Like I've been run over by a draft horse. But I think I owe ya my thanks, Mr...."

The little man smiled. His eyeglasses were wire-rimmed, his mustache sparse. He shrugged. "My name, it is difficult for Americans. You may simply call me Doc."

"Doc..." Shep settled his head gingerly back against the pillows. "Where am I?"

"You are on my rancho."

"I'm on a ranch?"

He smiled modestly. "It is a grand word for a little plot of land.

Not so impressive as the spectacular spread you are accustomed to, I am certain, Mr. Cherokee."

Shep frowned, and Doc smiled.

"You talk in your sleep," he explained.

*Apparently, I also* lie *in my sleep,* Shep thought and groggily wondered if it was worth setting the record straight. An alias had come in handy on a hundred occasions…as often in love as in war.

He glanced to the right where an IV bag was suspended from a metal stand. A tube was attached to the fluids and inserted into his hand.

"You were badly dehydrated. Indeed, it will take some time for you to return to full health. I am sorry for the welcome you received at the hands of my countrymen."

"Ya don't have nothin' to apologize for," Shep assured him. "My corpse would probably be rottin' in the jungle if ya hadn't come along when ya did."

"I must remember that sometimes difficulties are blessings in disguise."

Shep blinked. The movement felt slow, lethargic. His body was getting heavier. "What?"

"Daphne disappeared. We were looking for her when we stumbled upon you."

Shep tried to lift his head, but it hardly seemed worth the effort. "Daphne?"

"My best milking goat. We searched for many hours."

The pain was ebbing quietly away. He was dry and sheltered, safe and warm. He felt his shoulders drop. "With AK-47s?" he asked.

"I beg your pardon?"

He rolled his head against the pillow to glance at his host again. "Do ya usually carry assault rifles when roundin' up your…" It was becoming harder to speak. "…livestock?"

Doc sighed. "I fear my country is not always so peaceful. Indeed, it is, perhaps, more like the wild west of your past. Which makes me curious; why did you leave your own fine rancho to come here at the start?"

Shep's mind stuttered slowly. Memories crowded in: his mother's smile, Durrand's low chuckle, a slow-winding creek through long, rolling hills. But he wasn't quite sure how to separate one image from another. He saw himself on a tall sorrel. Its mane was flaxen, its socks white and evenly matched. "Doc Bar Jones," he said.

The little man scowled. "Your pardon?"

"Orneriest horse I ever rode." He was beginning to slur his consonants. His tongue had grown thick.

"Why are you here?" the doctor asked.

Light flashed in Shep's mind. He jerked with remembered pain. Someone screamed. Another man moaned.

"Go the hell to sleep," Durrand ordered from Shep's mixed up psyche.

And for once Linus Shepherd was not too stubborn to obey.

# Chapter Thirty-Four

"Eddy!" Gabe yelled and reached for her, but she was already gone, snatched into the nothingness.

Grabbing an overhanging branch, he lurched toward the edge.

"Edwards!" He skimmed the darkness with frantic eyes. "Edwards!"

A squeak of noise reached him. He glanced down, and she was there. Wasn't she? Somehow suspended a couple dozen feet above the river?

"Hang on! Edwards, can you hear me?"

He thought she answered, but the words were washed away by the rush of the falls. Straddling a submerged log, he hooked a foot behind a slippery branch and peeled off his pack. It was all but impossible to find the coil of rope stashed away inside. His fingers felt numb, his heart rapped like a hammer against his ribs.

"I'm coming," he yelled, but if she heard him, there was no discernible response. He fell trying to tie the rope around the log. Water splashed, cold as death in his face. He didn't attempt to stand again but crawled through the rushing river toward the edge. "Edwards?" He thought he saw her lift her face toward him, a pale oval in the darkness. "I'm throwing you a rope," he said and hooked the toe of his boot between two submerged rocks closer to the edge.

There was no response from below. Holy shit, was that even her? It was as dark as death in the shadow of the cliff.

"Edwards!"

"Durrand?"

His lungs burst back into action at the sound of her voice. He fed the nylon through fingers clumsy with cold and fear. "Can you see it? Can you see the rope?"

"No. I... Wait! There it is! It's there! But I can't...I don't think I can reach it."

Lying flat against the bedrock, water sweeping over his back, he squinted into the darkness. Moonlight shone off her outstretched hand, but it was several inches from the rope.

She teetered toward the wall and gasped in panic.

"Don't!" he yelled.

She drew back, grappling for purchase on the slick timber where she'd landed.

"Don't try to get it," he ordered. Twisting around, he searched the darkness overhead. A bare branch shot into the sky not five feet away. Scrambling toward it, he broke it off, then shimmied back to the edge and glanced down, squinting through the cold spray. "Edwards!" For an endless second, he thought she was gone, but then she stirred. His heart bumped back to life. "I'm going to push the rope out toward you."

Maybe she nodded. Catching the rope in the fork of the branch, he prodded it forward. His foot slipped on the rocks between which it was wedged and he was swept toward the brink. He rolled frantically. His right knee struck something immoveable, shaking him to the core, but he snagged an unseen log with his right hand and hauled himself away from the edge. Jamming his boot back into a rocky crevice, he caught the rope with the branch and prodded it forward once more.

"Do you see it?" His voice sounded empty and lost in the rush of the waves. Hers was almost unheard.

"Yes! It's there."

"Can you reach it?"

There was an interminable wait. "Edwards—"

"I got it."

He closed his eyes in relief. "Tie it around your body. Under your arms."

Another age passed, but finally she spoke again. "It's not long enough. I'd have to…" Her voice broke. "I'll have to stand up."

"Don't! God dammit. Don't stand up. We'll think of another way." He glanced frantically about but nothing came to his stumbling mind.

"No time."

"What?" He jerked his attention back to her. Had she risen? Was she crouched on the log? He swore again but silently now, scared to disturb her. Terrified that she'd topple into the long darkness.

He waited, fear gnawing at his nerves as he strained to see into the blackness below him but finally she spoke, voice breathy, barely audible.

"Okay."

"You're ready?"

"I think so. Yeah."

"All right." He wrapped his fingers in the nylon. Pain seared his hand, but he gritted his teeth against it, challenging it. "I'm going to pull you up." How? His demons demanded. How the hell was he going to do that with a wounded hand and compromised strength? "You're going to swing into the waterfall." If his hand didn't give out. If the rope didn't slip. If she didn't fall to her death because of him. "And then the cliff. You'll hit the rock with your body if you're not ready for it. Bend your knees as soon as your feet leave the log."

Silence.

"Edwards. Can you hear me?"

"Yes. I've got it. I'm ready."

But was *he*? "All right," he said and pulled. The rope tightened.

His shoulder popped. She swung toward him, nearly yanking the rope from his fingers. He gritted his teeth against the agony. Fire burned his upper arms. He reached out with his left hand, drawing her up by inches. Then feet. He could see her now, but his foot was slipping. He paused, trying to wedge his boot back into the crevice.

"Durrand?"

"Yeah. Just a minute. I'm almost—"

"The knot's slipping."

Dammit! "Hold on tight. Don't let go. No matter what. Don't let go. You hear me?"

Her body was nothing more than a black mass, but her eyes were visible now, wide with terror, bright with the fragility of life.

"I'm going to pull again."

"Hurry!" Her voice was raspy. From pain or lack of oxygen or nerves. It was impossible to tell.

He hauled her up. The rock edge peeled skin from his arm. Only a few feet separated them now, but suddenly her body jerked as the knot loosened.

"Durrand!" she rasped.

Straining to hold the rope in fingers that were perfectly numb, he reached past the edge.

"Grab my hand."

"I can't!"

"Do it!"

The rope gave away again. She shrieked as she dropped another inch. Her knuckles were white as bone against the nylon. "Durrand–"

"Now!" he barked.

Her hand shot up. Their fingers met, wet on wet, slippery as seals, but they caught. He hauled her up then seized her arm with his left hand and pulled until she finally lay beside him on her belly. Water washed over them, between them, around them.

"You okay?" He could barely force out the words.

"Yeah. I think... Yeah."

He closed his eyes, trying to catch his breath, trying to quiet the gallop of his heart. She was safe now. He hadn't failed again. Not yet.

"I lost my pack." She paused, breath still coming hard, eyes bright in the moonlight.

"The GPS?"

"Gone."

He nodded, practical matters marching inexorably through his well-trained brain. "The Light Fifty?"

"All my weapons." Her voice sounded shaky, like she might cry. She was sitting in the river with her legs curled under herself like a goddamn water imp. The urge to pull her into his arms, to soothe her, was almost more than he could resist. Instead, he spoke, voice as soothing as a jackhammer.

"Nothing we can do about it now. Let's get humping," he said and pushed himself to his feet. Or rather, he tried, but for a second his legs, numb from the icy water and bitching strain, refused to do his bidding. He remained in a crouching position as she stood.

"Are *you* okay?" Her voice was very small, making him want to cuddle her against his chest, but instead, he forced himself to rise, to turn, to retrieve his pack. His legs shook but whether from fatigue or the residue of terror, it was impossible to tell.

"Hurry up," he said and managed to step toward shore. "It's almost daylight."

"Durrand?"

He swung back toward her. Her face was picture perfect in the moonlight. Her eyes lipid and stunning and haunting.

"I'm sorry."

## Chapter Thirty-Five

She was sorry.

The thought exploded in Gabe's mind, burning a little deeper with every jarring step he took. He had fucked up...again. Made mistakes that nearly cost both their lives. And *she* was sorry. The idea was damn near hilarious. But he wasn't laughing. Instead, he trudged on, watching her as she moved ahead of him through the receding darkness.

They didn't hike far before finding a little haven a couple hundred yards from the river. Sheltered on the south by an over-hanging bluff, from the east and west by almost impenetrable vines, it was relatively dry and utterly hidden.

"We'll rest here for a while," he said.

She nodded but remained silent.

He didn't ask if she was all right, didn't offer platitudes, didn't coddle her. She'd volunteered for this mission, he reminded himself again. She was a trained agent, for God's sake, not some half drowned fairy goddess, no matter how she looked. "I'll see what I can find for kindling."

"I'm fine," she said.

He glanced over his shoulder at her. She lifted her chin a little.

"I don't need a fire," she added but didn't quite manage to suppress the full body shudder that shook her.

Holy shit. "Well, I do," he said and stepped back into the elements. But in the end, he had to admit defeat. Every inch of jungle was as wet as a first kiss.

He turned toward the cave in defeat, a little more tired, a little more angry, a little more fucked up.

And *she* was sorry.

It took him a few minutes to get his bearings after turning back, but he finally ducked through the wall of vines to find her digging through his pack. He stopped. Had there really been a time when he resented others touching his gear? It seemed unlikely, since the sight of her pale, delicate fingers against his bag made him feel strangely... He didn't have a word for how he felt. Nostalgic maybe. Or homesick.

She glanced up. "I'm sorry. I can't find the matches. They were in *your* pack, weren't they?" Her voice was hopeful, but her lips were blue.

"It doesn't matter," he said. "I couldn't find any dry wood."

"Oh." Though she tried to hold on, the hope had slipped from her voice.

"Take your shirt off," he said.

She blinked.

"Hurry up," he ordered.

She rose reluctantly to her feet, skin ashen, as if she'd rather face a firing squad.

He scowled at her. It wasn't like he was the devil or something. There were women who actually found him attractive. None he could name right off the top of his head, but oh...fuck, she was taking off her shirt.

He dropped his attention to his pack with a concerted effort and fumbled with the ties that held their one remaining sleeping bag. Rising, he prepared to hand it over, but she was just pulling her bra over her head and suddenly his mouth couldn't quite remember how to formulate articulate speech.

He blinked at her, heart pounding. Who would have guessed her breasts looked like…well, like that! "Pants, too," he managed.

She stared at him as if unsure whether he had spoken. But, hell yeah, he wasn't a complete moron.

"What?" she asked.

"Listen…" He tried to keep his tone deadpan, but while his heart was doing some kind of weird happy dance in his dumb-ass chest, his head was reminding him that it was hard enough making it through the jungle with a healing shoulder, an achy hand and a bitching leg wound. A full-blown hard-on wasn't going to make things any easier. "You don't need to worry. I don't have enough energy to bother you anyway."

"I'm not…worried," she said.

"Then get out of those pants before you catch your death." *Catch your death?* Holy crap, he sounded like some antiquated school marm. He might as well have said she was going to catch the ague. What was the hell *was* the ague anyway? Something the super-hot women in historical novels always seemed in danger of contracting.

"I'm fine. Really," she said, but just as the words left her mouth, she shuddered.

"You're not fine," he said. "You're freezing. Take off your pants. We'll get you as dry as we can."

She pursed her lips and bent to untie her boots. But her fingers were sluggish.

Crouching, he nudged her hands away and undid her laces. She straightened self-consciously, taking her breasts with her. He tugged off her footwear and tossed them aside. In a moment, she was easing out of her pants.

Holy ever-loving hell, her legs were almost as spectacular as her breasts. And who the hell would have thought that was possible? They were pale, smooth, and as long as a thoroughbred's. Her belly was flat, her panties red, and her sweetly rounded bottom almost entirely visible beneath the wet fabric.

Sweat popped out on his forehead like dew on a lily. He jerked his gaze away and fiddled with the zipper on the sleeping bag, but it was stuck tight.

"Could I have that?" she asked and reached toward him.

He blinked.

"Durrand?"

"What? Oh!" he said, realizing belatedly that she was reaching for the sleeping bag.

He handed it off and she wrapped it around her body. Still zipped, it left spare pieces and parts disturbing visible: her left shoulder, her right thigh. Jesus God, was she trying to drive him crazy?

Visions of the night they'd first met flashed through his discombobulated brain. Maybe she wouldn't be completely adverse to the idea of sex. In fact, hey! It would warm her up. Practical, really. And, at one time, she hadn't seemed entirely repulsed by him. Some women found him mildly appealing. True, that was generally before he opened his mouth. And he'd pretty much done everything wrong from the moment he'd laid eyes on this particular woman. He had, at one point, threatened her life, and past experience with women, though admittedly sparse, suggested that the fairer sex didn't usually appreciate that sort of thing. But she was standing very close, making his gut cramp up and his cock—

"Does it hurt?"

He stared at her.

"Your hand," she said. "Let me see it."

He didn't know how long it should have taken him to respond. But he was pretty damned sure his silence shouldn't last a full thirty seconds. "My hand's fine."

"It's bleeding."

He glanced at it. Yup, it *was* bleeding. "You should take off your..." He shook his head. For reasons entirely unknown, he couldn't seem to say the word *underwear* in her presence. He considered *undergarments* but that seemed ridiculous, like some fastidious blue-haired woman in a PBS special. *Unmentionables* might make her wonder about his literary choices, and the term *panties* remained stuck in his throat like a goddamn cocklebur. "—the rest of your clothes," he finished badly and squatting, untied his own boots. His fingers felt like chilled sausages.

"Aren't *you* cold?" she asked.

He straightened, toed off the wet leather then pulled off his saturated t-shirt. "No." The air felt like shards of ice against his bare chest. "I'm naturally hot-blooded." Hot-blooded? Really? Shit.

She stared at him, eyes bright as emeralds in the slow-waking sun. "What if you run a fever again?"

"Not going to happen. I'm still on antibiotics and I have dry clothes," he said then tugged a shirt from his pack. If he weren't mistaken, at least part of one sleeve wasn't entirely soaked.

She drew a deep breath before speaking. "I'll do better."

"What?" He glanced up sharply.

"I won't mess up again," she murmured and something in her melancholy expression made his mind explode.

"What the hell are you talking about?" His voice growled like a cantankerous bear, but she didn't back down.

"That pack was my responsibility. I should have been more careful crossing the river. I compromised the mission and for that I apologize."

He ground his teeth at her. "Listen, Edwards, this is my operation. I ordered you to cross the river knowing the risk factor was escalated due to fatigue and darkness." Goddammit, he sounded like a fucking robot. Not to mention the fact that he was the one who had knocked her over. "Culpability is mine."

She drew a deep breath through her nostrils. Her nose was slightly upturned, and damned if he couldn't make out her freckles even in the shit poor light. You know who shouldn't be on deadly mission in the middle of a fucking jungle? Fairies with freckles.

"Maybe I can find the GPS," she said.

He turned his head slightly, certain he had heard her wrong. "What?"

"The guidance system," she said. She was standing ramrod straight. "I dropped it when I fell, but it may not have hit the river. If you let me use your headlamp, I can check the east bank and be back before it's fully light."

*Is she fucking kidding?* he wondered, but one glance into her ridiculously serious face assured him she was not. "Listen, Edwards," he said, "mistakes were made. Things went south. Let's not make the situation worse than it is. Try to get some sleep." He pulled the half-soaked jersey over his head and glared at her over the top of the ribbed neck only to find that she was just jerking her gaze up to meet his.

He froze. Holy shit! Was she checking him out?

She lifted her chin. "I understand that you feel it's your duty to keep me safe," she said. Her gaze was as steady as granite on his now, and her cheeks had gained a little color. "But I'm a trained agent. I can look after myself." She took another stuttering step toward him. "And I would appreciate the opportunity to remedy my mistakes." Her tone was as stiff as her posture; her knuckles white where they clutched the edge of the sleeping bag, which brushed her thighs. Her bare thighs. Her long, smooth, hopelessly perfect bare thighs.

His cock did a little check in, but he checked it back out.

"Just get some sleep," he said and forced himself to turn away before there was no hope whatsoever of doing something so painfully sensible. "That's an order."

# Chapter Thirty-Six

H e was being drugged. Linus Shepherd was certain of
that much.

The room where he lay was windowless, but the mist in his
mind had cleared a bit and his internal clock told him it was night.
Approximately three hours had passed since he realized he was
handcuffed to the bedrail, nearly that long since he had exchanged
the original IV for another. Though an extra bag was hanging from
the stand, he had no reason to believe it was untainted. Thus, he
had searched until he'd found a still-sealed liter in a cabinet
beneath his bed. Reaching that cabinet had not been an easy task.
But he had managed. Eventually, the bag he'd stashed below the
others would be found, but for now, a simple solution of elec-
trolytes flowed into his veins.

Fatigue still pulled at him, but he fought it, needing to think.
He had tried to pick the lock on his cuffs, but his fingers were
unwieldy. And even if he succeeded, what of the lock on the door?
Surely there was one, not to mention a possible guard outside.

It was clear that he would have to wait until he was more
coherent to attempt an escape. His memories of the past few days
were uncertain, vague, and undependable. Some suggested he had

been roping steers from a fire-breathing dragon. Others involved conversations with his mother. In one, he had been sword fighting with Durrand. Then there was the affable gentleman who repeatedly asked why he had come to Colombia but had a strange habit of morphing into a catfish. All these scenarios seemed less than likely. Durrand, for instance, had been dueling with ambidextrous fluidity when everyone knew he couldn't do shit with his left hand.

A noise sounded outside the close walls of his room. Voices! Forcing himself to relax, he dropped his head back against the pillows and closed his eyes.

The door opened a second later.

Shepherd lay perfectly still, keeping his breathing shallow, his eyes shut.

"What do you say, Curro?" The voice spoke in Spanish. Shep was fairly certain it was Doc, but was he also the man who questioned him about his reasons for being there? And what had Shepherd's answers been to those queries? Everything was uncertain. But, apparently, he had not yet said anything damning enough to get him executed. Did that mean that his inquisitor was no friend of Herrerra, the drug lord Miller's detail had been hired to displace? Or did it indicate that Shep had managed to avoid giving the real reason for his visit to this little piece of tropical hell?

"Have you seen this man before?"

Footsteps paced closer. The second voice was low and confident. "He does not look familiar."

"No?"

"No."

"You're certain? That is to say, he is distinctive, yes?"

"American, isn't he?"

"Judging from his speech patterns and rather garbled statements I have surmised that he comes from the southern regions of the United States. An area known for its cowboys."

No response.

"Do you know how cowboys are perceived, Curro? They are

applauded for their toughness. Their…resilience."

"He does not look so very tough."

"Not to a man of your prowess perhaps." The doctor chuckled. "But looks can, at times, be deceiving. For instance, sometimes a man can seem as if he is in your country for no purpose other than entertainment. When truly he has come for more nefarious reasons. But you say that none of the men Herrera hired to kill me have survived, is that not so, Curro?"

There was the slightest shuffling of feet. "I watched each one die with my own eyes."

"Then who do you suppose this fellow is?"

The shrug was implicit in Curro's answer. "Someone foolish enough to stumble into Herrera's hands, I suppose."

"Just another of Guapo's hostages then? Some poor unfortunate tourist who was in the wrong place at the wrong time? A naturalist perhaps come to see the wonders of our humble country?"

"Perhaps."

"We do indeed have a vast array of beauty. Do we not? Did I tell you I saw an oropendola just yesterday morning?"

"No *señor*, you did not."

"Fascinating birds. There is so much we can learn from the wild. So many ways we as human beings can benefit from the amazing abundance around us. Ours is a country of vast diversity. There are means to cure illnesses, as well as ways to create poisons, right in our own backyard."

"Yes, *señor*."

"So perhaps this cowboy…" There was a pause as if they turned toward him again. "Perhaps he has come here to learn what he can of our world."

"That must be it, *señor*."

"I wonder, though…" The footsteps paced closer still.

It took all of Shep's self-control to remain as he was. Unmoving, unseeing.

"Where would he get these wounds?" The doctor shifted the

sheet aside. Shepherd stayed absolutely still as cool air touched his bare skin, perfectly immobile as the other tugged the bandage from the wound on his abdomen.

There was a moment of silence then, "Herrera is not known for his kindness," Curro said.

The older man chuckled again. "Not like me, isn't that so?"

"You are indeed forgiving, señor."

"While Herrera is a bloody barbarian!" There was sudden passion in his voice, but it dissipated quickly. "Still, there are other wounds. Older wounds, long ago healed." He slipped the sheet lower. Shepherd stifled a shiver. "This, for instance, just beside his hip." He touched the aging bullet wound so disturbingly close to areas he had shared with only a few dozen affectionate women. "How would he sustain such an injury, do you suppose?"

"I do not know."

"And this." His finger trailed up Shep's body to the ridge of scar tissue just below his bottom rib--the place where an unhappy jihadist had had the misfortune of just missing Shep's internal organs. "What of this?"

"You said cowboys were known for their toughness. Perhaps he fell from a horse. Or was gorged by a bull."

"An interesting supposition, Curro. But you see, they are bullet wounds." Doc's voice was very soft.

"These cowboys..." There was a shrug in his voice. "Do they not carry guns?"

"Oh, Curro..." The chuckle again, good-natured and paternal. "Sometimes your childishness delights me."

"I am glad to entertain you, señor," said the other but his tone suggested the opposite.

Shep steeled himself. He had learned long ago to read the nuances of tone, to decipher body language. The playground had not always been kind to the son of a drunken womanizer.

"I should not laugh at your naiveté, I suppose," Doc said.

"No, señor. You should not."

The older man chuckled again. "But you see, you have been

watching too many…what are they called? Spaghetti westerns. The cowboys of today do not become involved in shootouts at the OK Corral or challenge the bad hombres to duels at high noon. Hence, they do not often sustain injuries such as these."

"I shall remember that."

"You know who does, though?" The elder man's paternal tone had returned. It would grate on the nerves of a saint. Curro was no saint. That much was abundantly clear.

"I should get back to the compound. We're making a shipment today. I am to relieve Raul at the—"

"The coca will wait. We'll be done here in a moment. You know who does get shot with disturbing regularity?"

No response.

"Hired killers."

"You don't think—"

"Yes, I *do* think!" the doctor said and, suddenly, there was a hiss of noise. Footsteps stumbled backward.

Shepherd snapped his eyes open. His gaze met Curro's frantic stare. A syringe protruded from the side of his neck. He opened his mouth to speak, but he was already falling.

"I think a great deal," the doctor added. "Something I wish you had done a bit more of. Then I'd have no need to hire a new head of security. But, you see, I do not pay you to allow Guapo's thugs to trespass on my land. Neither should I be forced to deal with those thugs on my own. I am a doctor. A gentleman." A chair toppled over as Curro crashed to the floor. "A healer. I cannot be seen killing another human being. But neither can I allow them to live. But what of this poor fellow? Was he one of the men I paid to see Guapo dead? The men who failed miserably! Was he nothing more than Guapo's victim? Or could he be part of an intricate trap? What is his name? Where did he come from? And might he somehow yet be used to destroy that barbaric bastard? So many questions."

Curro lifted a frantic arm to point at Shepherd, who dropped his eyes closed before the doctor turned toward him.

"A little late for you to worry about our guest," Doc said. "Now is the time to catalog the effects of the golden frog on the central nervous system of an adult male of our species."

A gagging sound issued from the corner of the room. Metal clashed as Curro thrashed about.

"Is it not amazing that such a tiny animal can bring down a bull elephant?"

"Please…"

"I have no proof that this is true, of course, but I see that it can cause my former head of security to plead for his life."

Heavy breathing filled the room.

"There is the possibility, of course, that the antidote I have been tinkering with would revive you. And, truly, I wish you no harm, Curro."

"*Señor…*"

"I will make you a deal, my boy…if you can crawl to me, I will forgive your shortcomings. If not…" The shrug was in his voice.

There was a lifetime of labored breathing followed by the sound of someone laboriously dragging himself across the floor.

"Well done. That's it, son," the doctor said but Shepherd could hear him backing away. After an eternity, the dragging noise stopped. The gasping halted. "So close. If only you had put as much effort into eliminating my assassins. Or, at the least, confessed your failings." He exhaled softly as he turned toward the bed.

"And what of you, young man?" he asked and placing a cool hand against Shep's skin gently traced a line from one injury to the next. "Such a handsome lad you are. And strong. I can see it in you. You are a fighter. But do you lie to me, too? If I allow you to awaken, will you share the truth of your reasons for coming here?" He sighed quietly, like a long-suffering father. "I believe it is time to find out," he said and tugging the tube from the needle in Shep's hand, inserted another in its place. "Time to learn if you will be honest or if I must employ other means of ascertaining the truth."

# Chapter Thirty-Seven

"Stay down." Durrand's voice was low and quiet, barely a rumble in the pre-dusk dimness, but Eddy heard him. They were lying on their bellies, hidden...she hoped to God...on a bank overlooking a coffee farm. According to their best intel and Durrand's disturbingly accurate sense of direction, this was one of Herrera's plantations.

She skimmed the area two hundred yards below them. It was a tranquil scene. Coffee trees grew in rows ten feet high, shiny leaves bright in the late afternoon sun. The pickers chatted and joked as they dropped cherry-red beans into plastic buckets suspended at their waists, but it was the three men who dismounted from a nearby Jeep that held Eddy's interest. Although they were dressed in loose fitting shirts and trousers similar to the others, there was something about them that didn't quite mesh.

"Overseers?" Eddy guessed quietly.

"I doubt the coffee beans put up that much of a fight," Durrand said.

She scowled but didn't shift her gaze from the scene below.

Moving slowly, attention still glued on the workers, he handed over the binoculars he had remembered to stash back into his pack after the debacle with Javier. "Notice Red Shirt's back."

Eddy carefully focused the glasses on the man he indicated. He was laughing as he spoke. His *compadre* chuckled in return, their attention caught on the third member of their party.

"Looks a little lumpy around the middle," Durrand added.

Eddy zeroed in on the man's midsection. Sure enough, the lay of his loose, button-up shirt suggested he had something stuck into the waistband of his pants. Something that was about the size of a 9 mm Beretta. She stifled a wince.

"And Hat Man's left pocket," Durrand added.

Eddy shifted her attention to Red Shirt's friend. A couple of inches of hard, black plastic were just visible between the dark fabric of his pants and the edge of his rucked up shirt. The polymer handle of a Smith and Wesson would look just about like that.

"What about Don Juan?" she asked and shifted the glasses slightly to the left where a potbellied man with a crooked smile was flirting with a woman half his age.

Durrand paused for a second as he studied him. "Maybe he prefers knives."

She felt the hair on the back of her neck stand up a little though it made no sense. It wasn't as if being shot was any more civilized than being stabbed.

"No gun?" she asked.

"Could be the *señorita* doesn't care to be courted by a guy who carries a semi-automatic. There was a shrug in his tone. She tried to sound equally cavalier. As if she spent every day of her life debating the relative merits of various means of being murdered.

"Stranger things have happened I suppose," she said and felt Durrand's gaze slip to her face. Had she put the wrong inflection on the statement? Or maybe he knew she was scared out of her mind, but she refrained from long-winded explanations, swallowed any apologies that might be tempted to bubble to the surface and asked, "What do we do now?"

He remained silent. She turned toward him. He was still watching her, expression unreadable. "Durrand?"

He pulled himself from her gaze with a start and shifted his attention to the scene below. "We wait," he said.

"For...?"

"Dark." Crab-walking a few feet down the hill, he turned onto his back, rested his head against the slope behind him and stared at the vines above. "I don't want to get us into a firefight."

Firefight. The word made her feel a little woozy but she put her game face on. "What happens after dark?"

"We check out the buildings, try to avoid the hired guns, and search for signs of hostages."

She nodded, slid down beside him, and hoped, just this once that dusk would fail to come.

---

BUT SHE WAS FOILED AGAIN. At 1800 hours, the sun was settling into the high branches of the jungle just as it did every day of the year.

An hour later, they had checked the compound and come up empty.

"Looks like it really is nothing more than a coffee farm," Eddy said. She kept her voice low. They stood alone in a long, dark shed that housed machinery she could neither fully see nor identify.

Durrand's face was grim in the uncertain light. His voice was barely a rumble. "Why the weapons then?"

She shrugged. "Colombia isn't exactly known for its tranquility, and caution doesn't make them guilty. Maybe this is just one of Herrera's legitimate holdings."

"Or maybe we haven't looked in the right corners," Durrand argued and stepped between two rows of shelves that housed burlap bags full of what appeared to be coffee beans.

Suddenly, light exploded around them.

Eddy swung sideways, half squatting as if she could disappear into the dirt beneath her feet.

But the man in the red shirt was already aiming his handgun at her heart. The Beretta looked polished and well cared for. He spoke in Spanish.

"Hello." His grin was cocky. His teeth were the color of tobacco. Behind him, the man she'd called Don Juan looked less certain. The fellow in the hat had pulled out a pistol. She had misjudged. It was a Ruger, not a Smith and Wesson. *I should have known*, she thought, foggily aware that now was not the time to worry about such things. "Welcome to El Rojo Del Amanecer. But I am curious. What do you do here?"

For a second, Eddy failed to speak, failed to verbalize so much as a salutation. Without glancing sideways, she knew that Durrand had disappeared. What would he do now? What should *she* do? And how much did these men know? She swallowed her fear, pressed her damp palms against her thighs, and punted. "I'm so sorry I'm trespassing." Her English was quick with undisguised panic and almost inarticulate to her *own* ears. "I was—" she began and stepped forward, but Red Shirt raised the muzzle of his gun a fraction of an inch.

"Stay as you are, *señorita*." His Spanish was low and smooth. "I have no wish to kill someone so pretty as you. Not before you answer a few questions, at least."

She stopped, fear racing through her.

"Firstly…" He smiled, tobacco teeth winking. "What is it that you are doing on Señor Herrera's private property?"

She shook her head. Maybe it would be best to pretend she didn't speak Spanish. Or maybe she was screwed either way.

"I didn't mean to cause any trouble." She was using a disjointed mix of languages, letting her words roll together like tumbling stones. "But I'm lost and…and…alone."

"Lost? Well, I am certain we can help her find her way, don't you agree, Jax?"

"*Sí*." Hat man smiled. "I have a compass right here," he said and grabbed his crotch.

Don Juan scowled.

Red Shirt chuckled, never shifting his attention from her. "But first we must be rid of your friend." He shrugged. "For you see, I fear two of you were seen entering this building."

She shook her head as if confused by the language barrier.

"Maybe she will understand this," Jax said and tipped up his Ruger.

But Don Juan grabbed his sleeve. "What are you doing?"

Jax jerked his arm free. "My job."

"That does not involve harming women."

The man in the hat snorted and turned toward Eddy just as the nearest shelves toppled sideways. The metal rack struck Red Shirt's head. A filled bag caught Jax across the shoulders, bearing him to the ground. Don Juan jumped aside.

Eddy yanked her pistol from her waistband just as Durrand appeared around the rubble, rifle in hand. His eyes were narrowed above the polished black muzzle he trained on Don Juan.

"I got him," Eddy said. Durrand glanced at her, jerked a nod and strode toward the downed individuals. Red Shirt was motionless, but Jax was moaning. His eyelids fluttered. He grabbed for his gun, but Durrand rapped him sharply beside the ear with the butt of his rifle. His hat tumbled off as he slumped into a stupor.

Retrieving the fallen weapons, Durrand tossed them aside and approached Don Juan. The Latino raised his chin, defiance and fear blending quixotically in his eyes.

Silence filled the space like darkness. Eddy could hear her own heartbeat.

"Tell him I'm going to kill him," Durrand said into the quiet.

Eddy jerked her gaze toward him. "Wh-what?"

"Tell him he'll be dead in ten minutes unless he tells me what I want to know."

She shook her head. The motion felt frantic and out of synch. "He wasn't the one who threatened…" She exhaled heavily, trying to find her equilibrium. "We don't even know if he's armed."

Durrand didn't glance toward her but kept his gaze perfectly level on their captive. "Tell him, Edwards."

She swallowed, turned toward the Latino and spoke in Spanish. "We need information."

The man's lips curled up angrily. "You may kill me if you wish, *chica*. I will tell the hulking *gringo* nothing."

Durrand stepped up closer. His eyes were deadly, his voice low. "What did he say?"

Eddy swallowed hard but kept her gaze steady on the Colombian. "He said if you'll move back a little, he'll consider your request."

Durrand scowled, remained absolutely still for a moment, then took two steps to the rear, spread his feet, and let his hands fall beside his thighs. A warrior at the ready. "Ask him if he's seen an American matching Shep's description. My height but rangy, brown hair, blue eyes."

Eddy nodded then addressed the Latino again. "What's your name?"

He narrowed his eyes a little. "I am Alvaro Esteban Gallo."

"Alvaro." She said his name softly. "Do you have a brother...or perhaps a son?"

He gritted his teeth and narrowed Spanish black eyes. "If he so much as breathes my boy's name he will curse the day he was born."

"We won't harm him." She rushed the words out, seeing she had taken the wrong tack. "My husband...Luke...would never hurt your son." She glanced at Durrand. He looked as formidable as a warship, as unforgiving as an Uzi. "He's just looking for his brother."

Alvaro watched her in silence.

"The brother of his heart," she said and placed her free hand over her chest. "His name is Linus Shepherd. Perhaps you knew him by a different name, but he came to your country five weeks ago and has not been seen since."

"Then perhaps he should have stayed in the land of the pale and not bothered the innocent people of my homeland."

Eddy nodded. "We hope to take him back there. To return him to his loved ones and leave you and yours in peace."

"Why do you tell me this?" He deepened his scowl. "Do you think me a kidnapper?"

"No!" Eddy said. "Of course, not."

"What's going on?" Durrand asked.

Eddy ignored him, her full attention focused on Alvaro. "I think you're a compassionate human being. That's why I'm talking to you instead of your companions."

He flickered his attention to the men at their feet but didn't bother to mention the fact that their unconscious state might make such a conversation difficult.

"Perhaps you've heard talk," Eddy said. "Women like you, Alvaro. Maybe they've mentioned seeing an American. They would remember him. He's handsome, like you. Tall, with dark hair and blue eyes."

He shook his head.

"Shep's got a tattoo. A horseshoe on his left arm." Durrand said.

Eddy translated and watched the man wince.

Durrand lowered his head and stepped forward. "Where is he?" he growled, but Eddy grabbed his arm. He stopped, body still, gaze never leaving the other man's. "Tell me or I'll break your fucking neck."

"What did he say?" The Colombian's voice was no warmer than Durrand's.

Eddy felt the situation spin toward hopeless. "Alvaro," she said, tone teetering dangerously on panic. He shifted his dark gaze to hers. "We're willing to pay for information."

He snorted. "You think we Colombians want nothing so much as your money."

And so far, there had been little evidence to the contrary. "What *do* you want?" she asked.

He raised his brows at her. Seconds ticked away. "The women of my country, they are beautiful," he said finally.

"Has he seen him or not?" Durrand demanded.

They both ignored him, but in Eddy's case, it was because she couldn't force herself to look away.

Alvaro grinned. "But we do not see so many like you."

She felt her fingers go numb as the gist of his words sunk into her soul. So this was, she realized, the moment of truth. The tipping point when she would learn how far she would go for a mission. For Durrand. To save another human being. The answer was disappointing. "I won't have sex with you," she breathed.

Alvaro opened his eyes wide then shook his head as if disappointed and a little disturbed. "I did not say anything about"—he paused—"such a thing."

She wasn't sure it was appropriate to feel embarrassed. She certainly shouldn't feel chagrined. And yet she did. "What *were* you thinking?"

He shrugged then grinned a little, just a peek of the charm he had shown in the field on the previous evening. "I just want... What do you *gringos* call it? A flash."

She blinked at him, feeling as if she was floating outside of her body, leaving this surreal world behind. "You want to see my... you want me to open my shirt?"

He smiled and shifted his attention to Durrand. There was challenge in his stance, anger in his gaze. "I'm a simple man."

"What the hell's going on?" Durrand asked, but Eddy didn't dare look at him.

"I think he's seen Shepherd," she said. Her voice was breathless.

Durrand's was taut with emotion. "Where?"

"Just...wait!" she said and exhaled carefully. "And don't interrupt."

He remained silent as she spoke to Alvaro again. "And if I...if I do as you ask... you'll tell me what you know?"

He glanced at Durrand and grinned. "*Sí.*"

"Why?" she asked.

"Because I do not like this man," Alvaro said, glaring at

Durrand. "Yet…" He shrugged. "I do not wish him dead. I think, perhaps, sharing his woman's charms will be punishment enough."

She didn't dispute his foolish assumptions. Instead, she reached down with her left hand and yanked her shirt, sports bra and all, up over her clavicle.

Durrand started as if shot.

Alvaro stared then grinned.

Eddy pulled her shirt back into place with a hand that shook. "Where is he?"

The man in the red shirt moaned. Eddy glanced at him, gut pitching. Surely Alvaro couldn't afford for his companions to know he was spreading their secrets. But he shrugged, seeming unconcerned. "Guapo Herrera does not have him."

Excitement punched up. "But he did?"

"*Sí.*"

"So you've seen him."

He shook his head. "But I know that Quinto sent men to find him."

"Find him?"

"I am told he escaped."

"When?"

"Five days ago perhaps?"

"But they didn't return with him?"

He glanced at Durrand as if assessing the danger there and wondering if Shepherd may have posed the same degree of threat. "Neither did they come back themselves." His expression suggested it was no great loss.

"What happened?"

"One man was found dead. The other has not been heard from."

"So they're still searching for Shepherd?"

He shook his head. "I am told his tracks led onto Timoteo Santiago's land."

She shook her head, not understanding.

"Even Herrera's worst bastards do not venture there," he said and nodded with almost random boredom at the twosome beneath the shelves.

"Edwards—" Durrand growled, but the sound of an approaching engine interrupted his next words.

Alvaro shrugged. "On the other hand...they do sometimes come *here* in the small hours of the night."

Durrand turned, shifting his gaze toward the door through which they had entered, but Eddy kept her attention on the Latino.

"Who is Santiago?"

"A man with many faces. A man you have no wish to meet."

"Where does he live?"

"He has several homes, but his coca fields are to the east and south. I do not recommend you go there."

She wouldn't recommend any of the things she had done recently.

Footsteps sounded outside.

"Is there another way out of here?" she asked.

Alvaro stared at her for several long seconds, as if doing nothing more dangerous than assessing his next chess move. "A chica as lovely as you might find a door beneath the tarp at the back of this shed."

"Where does the door lead to?"

"The jungle."

She stared at him, heart pounding, mind spinning at the idea of a trap.

"Behind the shelves," Durrand ordered quietly, gun muzzle steady on the Latino's chest. "Both of you. Tell him if he yells I'll—"

"Come on!" Eddy ordered and grabbing Durrand's arm, pulled him toward the rear of the building.

"What are you doing?"

"Hurry!" she rasped and releasing his sleeve, ran between the shelves. In a second, he turned and followed.

The tarp was canvas, the trap door narrow. The tunnel beneath it was as dark as sin. But they made their way through it as quickly as possible and finally rose, hurrying up wooden rungs to emerge in the dim warmth of the jungle.

The insects were singing. The air smelled of hope and rain.

"What the hell just happened?" Durrand asked. His breath was coming hard. His eyes were fierce.

She turned away, stumbling through the darkness. "Herrera had Shepherd, but he escaped."

"Where is he now?"

"Alvaro wasn't sure."

"Yeah?" He was breathing hard as he hurried after her. "Is that why he had to look under your shirt?"

# Chapter Thirty-Eight

S hepherd lay awake. He wasn't at full strength. That much was certain. Twelve hours had passed since Curro had died, and Shep could wait no longer. Tonight, he would leave. The doctor usually visited him sometime before dawn, came to ask questions and when he did....

A noise outside stopped his thoughts. He dropped his head onto the pillow and lay still.

"I don't know what I can do for him?" The voice was soft and feminine, immediately conjuring up a dozen sultry memories. Shepherd felt his breath catch in his throat. How long had it been since he'd heard a woman's voice?

"Possibly nothing, my dear. But I thought perhaps just your presence would revive him. As I said..." Doc's voice, though hardly a whisper, sounded as rough as a blow horn next to hers. "He is rarely awake, and when he is, he is barely coherent. Perhaps there is trauma to the head of which I know nothing. But I'm a simple country doctor and lack the appropriate tests. Therefore, there is little else I can do for him."

Footsteps approached Shep's bed. It took every bit of his flagging self-control to remain as he was. But he would wait until the doctor was within striking distance. He would wait, and then he would act.

"But…*señor*, he is he handcuffed."

The doctor sighed. "I so hated to do it. But in all honesty, I know little of him."

"Did you not say that Herrera's henchmen had him?" There was a shudder in her voice.

"Yes, but was he merely an unfortunate passerby? Or was he, perhaps, in Guapo's employ? As you know, that animal treats his own no better than he treats others."

"You believe him to be one of Herrera's men?"

"I think it possible," Doc said. "But my vows as a physician insist that I do what I can to return him to full health. You understand that, don't you?"

"Of course."

"I am sorry to bring back hard memories, Carlotta. But I thought just the sight of you might give him hope. Knowing you survived your time at that animal's hands…" He paused as if it were difficult to go on. "But perhaps it was selfish of me. I should not have—"

"No," she said and stepped closer. "It is fine. I will do as you ask."

"You are a saint, Carlotta."

"I owe you much."

"Nonsense. It is I who owe you. You have been like an angel since the passing of my dearest Dalia."

So she was important to this man…this personification of evil, Shep thought. Therefore, she was evil by association. And she was close. So close. Maybe this would be his only opportunity. He could grab her and use her as leverage. Barring that, she would serve as a shield of sorts.

He felt the bed dip as she sat upon it. He tensed, prepared to do what he must to be free.

"*Señor*," she said.

Shep snapped his eyes open, ready to seize her, to use her, but in that second, her gaze caught his.

Wide as forever, her eyes were the color of river stones. They shone with humor and worry and a thousand regrets.

His hand stopped in midair. His breath clogged like dredge in his chest. Some kind of strangled noise issued from his throat, but even he had no idea what it meant.

She raised narrow eyebrows at him. Her hair, dark as a gypsy's, fell around her face like a midnight waterfall. And that face... As long as he lived, he would never forget her face, for it was life personified, light after a thousand nights, rain in the midst of a drought.

"How you feel?" Her voice was heartbreaking. A melodic mix of little girl sweetness and carnal sexuality.

"What are you doing here?" He didn't mean to say those words. Didn't mean to imply that he knew anything of Doc's nature other than the benevolence he revealed to the world. But her beauty shocked him, confused him.

She smiled. His heart cracked open a little wider, though Shep himself couldn't have said why. He had known his share of beautiful women. Hell, he had slept with most of them, but she was... well...she was an angel.

"You give my friend the nasty fright," she said.

For a moment, he was so enmeshed in the sound of her voice that he forgot to respond. But he caught himself.

"I'm sorry." He cleared his scratchy throat and shifted his gaze to the doctor's. "I didn't mean to worry y'."

The man stepped a little closer, though he was still out of reach, even if Shepherd had been coherent enough to attack. "I feared you were slipping away from us. But my ploy worked, did it not? A beautiful *señorita* and...voila. Life is not so easily thrown aside, is it?"

Shepherd held the other man's gaze. Was there a double meaning there? Was there a threat? Or had he imagined the entire episode with the man called Curro. The man who had died pleading for his life just three feet from Shep's bed.

# Chapter Thirty-Nine

"**D**o not move."

The voice behind them was low and quiet. Eddy's breath jammed tight in her throat. Beside her, Durrand, too, was frozen. He cut his eyes to hers. They raised their hands in slow unison. Alvaro had warned them not to cross Santiago's borders, but what choice did they have? They stood now, surrounded by miles of misty hills, countless acres of nearly impenetrable forest. Alone. Or so they had thought.

"Do not move!" The words were a hissed warning followed by a click. Eddy jerked, anticipating a bullet. But the sound was only accompanied by a flash of light. Something shuffled in the foliage behind them. "Wait. Just one more. Oh, never mind. He is gone."

Every muscle taut, Eddy twisted slightly. Behind her stood a small man in loose fitting khakis and a pocketed vest. In his hands, he held a boxy looking camera. He smiled as he lifted it.

"I know the world has moved on to newer ways of capturing images, but they cannot compete with the resolution you get with an old Hasselblad."

Eddy turned slowly, heart thrumming hard against her ribs. Durrand's elbow brushed hers as he, too, swiveled about.

"Not when trying to capture such beautiful camouflage."

They stared at him.

"The horned marsupial frog," he said. "There are so few left these days." He shook his head as if saddened. "Deforestation has cost us much.

"But I am forgetting my manners." Shuffling his antiquated camera into his left hand, he thrust out his right. "My name is Tevio Ortez."

Eddy calmed her heart and kept her expression benign as she reached for his hand. "I'm Sarah and this is my husband, Luke."

"Americans, I assume."

"Yes," she said.

"Hiking. It is good to see. So often people come roaring through in motorized vehicles or zipping through on those silly lines." He sighed. "They miss out on much. How are you enjoying our beautiful country?"

"It's amazing," Eddy said.

"Is it not?" He smiled like a doting father. "I have lived here all my life except for a few years at university, and I could not wait to return. There is nothing like it. Do you not agree?"

"Absolutely," Eddy said.

"And what of you, sir?" Tevio asked. "Are you enjoying the adventure, or are you here simply to appease your sweet wife?"

"You have a very beautiful country," Durrand said. "In fact, we were supposed to meet a buddy of mine here, to enjoy it with us."

"Really? He is interested in Colombia's natural bounties also?"

"Maybe the beer was more of an incentive," Durrand said and Tevio laughed.

"Ah, yes, some of the locals are quite unforgettable. The beer and the *señoritas*, *sí*? Well... I cannot blame him for that. My humble country is famous for both. And I must admit there was a time I was more interested in them than in silly amphibians." He smiled. "Even those that can produce enough poison to incapacitate an elephant." He shrugged, seamlessly switching gears. "Where are you to meet this friend?"

Durrand didn't miss a beat. "The plan was to hook up two days ago in Cali but he didn't show."

Tevio tsked and wrinkled his brow. "What do you suppose could have happened to him?"

"Knowing Shep, he met one of your *señoritas* and forgot all about our agreement. We've only been friends for twenty years."

Tevio chuckled. "Does Shep not have a cellular phone?"

Durrand shrugged. "We tried calling it, but he didn't answer."

"Well, I do not think you need to be concerned. But…" He shifted his gaze to Eddy. "I would consider it an honor if you would spend the night at my hacienda. I can ask about to see if anyone has seen this friend of yours."

"We'd better keep moving," Durrand said. "If we didn't meet in Cali as planned, we were supposed to wait in Esperanza."

"But, honey…" Eddy said, "Mr. Ortez is a native naturalist. And isn't that why we came here? To learn more about the flora and fauna of the region?"

Durrand scowled at her.

"I'd love to discuss with him what can be done to slow the degradation of the rainforest," she said. "And maybe…you know…" She grinned. "If we *have* to, we could sleep on a real bed tonight." She shifted her smile to Tevio, who laughed.

"*Sí, señora,* I could indeed offer you a bed. Since my children have grown and moved away, I have several empty rooms in *mi casa*. Come, *señor*, listen to the wisdom of your lovely wife. And I will do all I can to locate your friend."

"Please, honey," Eddy said and looked up at Durrand with all the adoration she could muster.

"All right," he agreed. "If it'll make you happy."

She grinned and tipped up on her toes. "Thank you," she said and kissed him on the mouth. Her lips were warm and supple, her eyes the color of spring.

It was impossible to tell if they were walking into a trap, but for a moment, Gabriel Durrand didn't give a shit.

## Chapter Forty

"Welcome to my humble home," Tevio said and lifted a hand toward a clearing in the jungle. Eddy followed Durrand who paused momentarily to hold back a banana leaf for her to pass.

The house was a simple, rectangular design. A deck of sorts encircled the top floor. The exterior was made of cool, pale stucco. The roof was red tile, the doors blue. Not fifty feet away, a fence contained hump-backed cattle and a smattering of horses.

"Oh," Eddy exhaled at the homey beauty of the place.

Tevio shrugged. "I am certain it is as nothing compared to what you have in the United States of America, but it is where I first brought my young bride."

"You're married?" Eddy asked. They were making their way toward the house. Natural wood railing twisted its way about the long upper deck.

"For most of four decades," he said. "But I fear she passed some eighteen months ago."

"I'm so sorry."

He sighed. "Dalia and I had many happy years together. She gave me seven wonderful children."

"Seven!" Eddy said and noticed that Durrand was studying the farmyard with narrowed eyes, as if expecting commandos to jump out from behind every frond. But she could feel only serenity here. The sun was just setting, turning every droplet to diamonds on a million serrated leaves.

"Five sons and two fine daughters. I am a blessed man," he said. "But enough of me. Come in. We will get you dry and fed.

Opening the sky blue door, he motioned them inside. "Luisa, we have guests," he called.

A plump woman hurried from the cool bowels of the house. She bobbed a greeting, and as Tevio spoke in rapid-fire Spanish, her weathered face turned grim. Then she turned briskly and hurried away.

The little man chuckled quietly.

"We don't want to put you out," Eddy said.

But their host shook his head. "Do not let Luisa fool you. She adores company. It is simply that she is vain."

"Vain?" Eddy asked.

"My housekeeper, she is an exquisite cook. She but worries that her skills will not be shown in the best light since she was not expecting you."

"We brought our own supplies. We'd be happy to make do with what we have," Durrand said, but Tevio waved away his protests.

"Luisa would never forgive such an affront to Colombian hospitality. No. I will show you to your rooms. When you have rested, the meal will be served."

They tried again to dissuade him from going out of his way for them, but he shushed them.

"Please allow me to share my humble home. And do not judge us simple Colombians too harshly."

"What do you mean?" Eddy asked and glanced about. Crystal clear photographs graced the walls. Bright snakes and exotic birds watched them from a dozen wooden frames. "You have a beautiful house, and the pictures are amazing. Are these yours?"

"An old man's silly hobby," he said. "Dalia sometimes suggested that if I put my skills to something more useful we could have indoor plumbing. But as it is, I fear you will be forced to shower outside. So if you spy a stray gecko or anole do not be concerned. Most are perfectly harmless."

For a moment, his gaze rested on Eddy's and then he waved them into a dim room. "Please, make yourself at home. You will find towels in the drawers there and a wash basin through that doorway." He motioned toward an open archway at the end of the room. "Luisa will call you when the meal is served."

In a moment, they were alone. Eddy dropped her shoulders and sighed. The room was small and cool. An old armoire stood near the corner. A picture of the Madonna stared at them from beside the window. The bed lacked a headboard. The mattress was narrow, bowed in the center, and boasted a single blanket; she'd never seen anything more beautiful in her life. It begged her to tip onto it, to test its softness, to fall into its dreams. But she had no desire to dampen the coverlet and spoke before her will weakened. "Do you want to get cleaned up first or should—" she began, but in that second Durrand kissed her.

She gasped, then caught her breath as his fingers slid into her hair. Surprise torched through her, followed by something else, something warmer and heavier. His tongue touched her lips. She opened her mouth to the onslaught and in that moment, he pulled back a quarter of an inch, still cupping the back of her head with his strong fingers.

"We're tourists," he whispered. "And lovers."

She stared at him in stunned silence, but the meaning of his words seeped slowly into her fatigued brain. "You don't think—" she began, but he leaned in again. His kiss was slower this time, weightier.

"Grab a shower," he ordered finally, voice louder now and husky with meaning. "I'll meet you back here in ten minutes."

She would have argued...probably, but her lips seemed incapable of formulating any kind of articulate phrases. In fact, nodding was almost out of her range of possibility. Still, she tried to speak, cleared her throat and tried again. "Where did he say the shower was?"

He nodded his approval, then glanced around the room, eyes sharp as he peered into every corner. "Outside. Just around the corner, I think. But hurry. I miss you already."

"All...all right." She tried to think what she would say at that point if they truly were newly married, but it was out of her realm of expertise. "I'll just...get cleaned up." Sexy. Very sexy, she thought and found a towel with unsteady hands before turning away, but he stopped her.

"Undress in here," he said.

Her mouth dropped open. He smiled. Good God, how had she forgotten what his smile did to her gut? How it grabbed her from the first moment? It wasn't as if she attacked men in restrooms every day of the week...or ever...until he had come along. Until he had grinned, showing that spark of humor, that small, almost uncertain glimpse of hopefulness.

"Where I can watch," he added.

"I just... Okay."

She dropped the towel on the bed and reached for the buttons on her blouse. Her heart felt funny and her throat dry. Holy crap. Maybe she should find it amusing that his presence unnerved her more than the drug runners and carjackers and would-be rapists she'd encountered. Then again, she wasn't throwing up...yet.

Her fingers felt cold against her skin as she slipped out of her shirt. Then, holding her breath, she pulled off her bra and managed to glance up. It wasn't until that moment that she realized he wasn't even watching her. She turned to the right, feeling an odd niggle of anger shoot through her. Holy shit. He wasn't even in the *room!*

She shook her head and reminded herself it was all a ruse. A deadly game played in an attempt to keep them both alive. Which was a good thing. A valiant thing. So why the hell was she *mad?*

"You're as beautiful as the day we met."

She jerked her head to the left where he had just stepped out of the little wash area at the back of the room.

Their gazes met. He remained absolutely still, as if waiting.

She stared at him, face hot. It took her half an eternity to realize she was expected to play along. She swallowed hard and gave it a try.

"I could say the same for you." She tightened her hands to fists. Holy smokes, what was wrong with her? It wasn't as if she'd never had a lover. Well, maybe the word *lover* was kind of a presumptuous word. But she had had sex. And more than once. She raised her chin, already angry at the need to defend her sexual maturity and fighting for some clarity as to the kind of dialogue that normal couples might exchange. "...*if* you'd get out of those clothes."

He raised his brows at her, eyes alight. "You know what happens when I get naked."

Holy crap! "No," she said and managed, though she would never know how, to put a little purr in her voice. "It's been so long I think I've forgotten."

The hint of a smile lifted his lips. A mesmerizing mix between mischievous boy and wounded warrior. "I guess I'll have to refresh your memory then," he said and pulled off his shirt.

Unlike him, she couldn't help but stare as he peeled the garment from his chest. Couldn't help the punch of desire that hit her solar plexus as he dropped it on the floor. She knew the sight shouldn't affect her. They were just playing a game, after all. And it was just a chest. A male chest. A very male chest with muscles bunched in all the right places and small flat nipples set high on bulging pectorals. Then there were his abs, rolling moguls that...

But hold the phone...he was unbuckling his belt.

"You next," he said and slowed his motions as he nodded toward her. For a moment, she was absolutely frozen, but finally she managed to blink and forced herself to sit on the edge of the bed. Unlacing her boots, she toed them off.

"Now you," she breathed.

He chuckled. The sound was low and as sexy as hell. In less than fifteen seconds he was entirely naked.

And God Almighty, he was pretty, his chest hard, his belly flat, his legs long. Nestled between his powerful thighs, his balls were pulled tight against his upended cock.

She tried to think of something to say. Somewhere to look. Something to do. Absolutely nothing came to mind. Her brain had wilted.

"Your turn," he said.

Her face felt hot. Her hands cold.

"Sarah?" he said.

She wrestled her mind into submission. Pushing herself to her feet, she put unsteady hands on the button of her khakis. With some effort, she was able to get it undone, managed to pull down the zipper and slide her pants, panties and all, to the floor.

When she tossed them aside, he was no longer smiling. They stared at each other. And then he stalked toward her. She felt her head fall back, felt her heart gather speed, like a deer about to bound away.

He touched her arms, smoothing slowly downward. His lips landed on hers again, softly now, as sensual as a dream.

"Be careful," he mouthed.

She opened her eyes. His face was only inches from hers, his mouth a slant of desire so near she could feel his breath. His body so close his taut desire pressed against her belly.

She nodded and turned away on shaky legs.

"Sarah?" he said. She pivoted back, barely able to manage that much and watched as he raised his gaze back to her face. "Much as I enjoy the view, I don't care to have others do the same."

She blinked, entirely unable to guess if they were still playing the game. His eyes were dark, his lips tilted, his throaty tone as sexy as a forbidden dream.

"You might want this," he suggested and raised the threadbare towel she'd dropped on the bed.

She reached for the terrycloth. Their fingers brushed. Sparks soared between them like skittish fireflies.

She jerked her gaze to the side then forced herself away, knowing he watched her as she turned, wishing her butt were rounder, her hair thicker, her...

"And sweetheart?"

She turned again, breath held.

"You might want to lose the socks."

"Oh..." Her voice sounded hopelessly breathy, but she managed a nod and tugged them off under his perusal.

Entirely uncertain where to look, she jerked her gaze away, wrapped the towel around herself with the speed of light and all but sprinted toward the dubious safety offered outdoors.

## Chapter Forty-One

E ddy stepped cautiously into the shower. It was a little U made of stucco built into the side of the house. The cement beneath her feet felt rough, and the view over top of the curved wall was stunning, rolling away in varying shades of green so bright it all but hurt her eyes. Overhead, a macaw the color of butterscotch winged its way into a nearby coffee tree. But Eddy barely noticed any of these things.

Embarrassment consumed. True, Durrand was probably showing the depths of his paranoia by suspecting Tevio was guilty of anything more egregious than lusting after his housekeeper's *quesadillas*. But perhaps he was right. And…

She shook her head as she washed her hair. The point wasn't whether Tevio was as pure as a saint or as guilty as sin, the point was, she had acted like a moron in there. Worse than a moron— like a tongue-tied teenager, awed by her first kiss. It was bad enough that she had jumped Durrand in a seedy restroom and tumbled off a waterfall like a wayward toddler. At least she could rise to the occasion when a little faux chemistry was called for. But she'd been blindsided. One moment he was all business, the next he was kissing her, fully clothed then entirely naked. None of those mind-warping scenarios was as discombobulating as his smile, however.

But she was ready for it now. It was, after all, just a smile. True, his little boy grin juxtaposed against his blatant masculinity had initially stunned her, but she would do better in the future.

Scrubbing vigorously, she finished her shower as she gave herself a pep talk: She wasn't a child. She was a woman full grown, a trained CIA agent, an expert marksman. More to the point...*two can play this damn game*, she thought. Fluffing her ultra-fine hair, she wrapped herself in the towel and returned to their shared room.

Durrand had turned a light on in the little alcove, but the sleeping area was still dim, and for that she was grateful. He stood near the bed, face in shadow. He'd twisted a towel around his washboard waist. The cloth looked ridiculously small and maybe a little giddy.

"What's this?" Nodding toward the fabric that hid his assets, she let her own fall to the floor in a show of newfound confidence. She paused for a moment, letting him take in the sights before sauntering toward him. "I thought you were in a hurry."

His brows rose. If she weren't mistaken, other things did, too. But she wasn't absolutely positive. Still, she reached for his towel, untucking it in one quick move. "Or were you all talk?" she asked and lifting her face to his, kissed him.

For a moment, he didn't respond. It was the longest second of her life. But suddenly, he was bending into her, kissing her back, pressing against her, cock straining against her stomach. She thrust her tongue into his mouth. He moaned, slipped his hands over her ass and hauled her up against him. She wrapped her legs around his rock-hard waist. He kissed her neck and she arched away, nipples thrust against the formidable strength of his chest. His buttocks bunched beneath her heels. His breathing was hard and fast. He turned, pressing her against the wall. Need, too long suppressed, screamed through her, but the desire to impress him was stronger still.

She dropped her head toward his, letting her hair fall around them and her lips slide along his ear. "Shouldn't we be…" He was doing something delectable to her derriere. "…in bed?"

His breathing was heavy. "I don't think there are any hard and fast rules."

"I mean…" she whispered. Good Lord, he was throbbing like a heartbeat against her belly. "If there are cameras…" The rest of her sentence was lost as he blazed a trail of kisses toward her left breast. But his caresses slowed. He lifted his head. His breathing seemed shallow.

She forced herself to ease back a little, to find his eyes through the forest of his lashes.

"The room's clean," he said.

She stared at him from inches away. Heat pulsed between them. "What?"

"No cameras," he said and clearing his throat, loosened his grip a little on her bottom. "No bugs."

Oh God. She felt herself stiffen. Felt her breath clog in her chest. "Are you…" She shook her head a little, though she had no idea why. "Are you sure?"

"Yeah."

She nodded. Her legs remained wrapped around him as if he were a knight's white steed, and she couldn't quite figure out how to dismount.

"Well…" She unhooked her heels finally. Somewhere deep inside her, a shrill voice suggested that she refrain from being a moron, but she exhaled shakily and continued on her chosen course. "I guess…"

"Yeah," he said and slid his hands over her waist and up to her ribs.

The shrill voice gasped with hope, but he was just helping her stand. She loosened her grip on his neck, dropped her feet to the floor and turned away, hip brushing his erection.

"Sorry," she rasped and sprinted her gaze to his. His teeth were gritted, but he shook his head.

"No. No, it's… Well…" Did his voice sound a little shaky? He ran splayed fingers through his hair. "I guess I'll take a shower, too."

"Yeah, good idea. Not that you…" She felt like dying. Honest to God, death didn't look like a horrible option. "Not that you stink or anything. You just probably… Actually you smell pretty good. Like…"

She raised her gaze painfully back to his. Was she honestly trying to describe his scent?

"Like…um…woods, or earth or…something."

He was staring at her as if she'd lost her mind. And honestly, it was a distinct possibility.

# Chapter Forty-Two

"This is wonderful." Edwards' voice was quiet. Gabe didn't look at her. Across the table from them, Tevio beamed.

"Did I not tell you Luisa was the best cook in all of this great country?"

"You did." There was a smile in Edwards' voice. "What kind of meat is this? Mutton?"

Gabe forked rice into his mouth and wondered what the fuck was wrong with him? There wasn't a reason in the world he couldn't have waited to tell her there were no hidden cameras in their bedroom. No reason he couldn't have pretended he didn't understand why she was throwing herself at him. True, that would have made him a world-class, grade-A bastard, but at least he wouldn't be a bastard with a hard-on the size of Texas. He shifted uncomfortably in his chair, but stopped himself when Tevio's gaze settled on him. A newly married man wouldn't be as horny as a hop toad after just spending two hours with his bride. Unless his bride had a Victoria Secret body and a girl-next-door smile. Unless his bride periodically, and without provocation, he might add, suddenly jumped his bones like he was the hero on one of those ridiculous bodice rippers that sometimes had some pretty good plots and could, on occasion, help a guy forget all the shit…

He stopped his thoughts abruptly, quit chewing, and realized with some consternation that the room was absolutely silent. And he was staring at Edwards like she was a porterhouse and he a slavering hound.

"Honey?" she said. Her tone was a little pointed.

Oh, fuck, she must be waiting for an answer. He swallowed, cleared his throat and jumped in. "What?"

"I said we can never thank Señor Tevio enough for his hospitality. Isn't that right?"

Was it right? Why had their host taken them in? Hospitality? It was possible, he supposed. But he wasn't a huge believer in people's innate goodness. Shep had once suggested Gabe might be lactose intolerant when it came to the milk of human kindness. Maybe his line of work had something to do with that. Perhaps men in his occupation didn't always see the best side of humanity. "Right," he said.

Did her eyes show the slightest bit of anger? Was it because of his monosyllabic responses, or because he had made her believe they were being videoed when they were not. Or hell… maybe she was mad because he'd confessed they *weren't* being filmed, removing her excuse to continue on the course they had jumped onto way back in the Blue Oyster. He had no idea what she was thinking…though, granted, the idea that Action Barbie would need an excuse to do anything seemed a little preposterous.

"And this *empanada*…" she enthused, "it's the best I've ever tasted. Don't you think?"

"Absolutely," Gabe agreed and wondered what the hell *empanadas* were and if he liked them.

"I'll admit," she continued, "the jungle is a little more than I had bargained for. I mean…it's so easy to become disoriented, and the rain…" She shook her head and took another bite of whatever the hell she had called it. "It's incessant."

Tevio shrugged. "I *have* been a bit curious about why you would come to our fair country during this time of year."

"Well…" Somehow, she managed to look chagrined and amused at the same time, as if regretting her own naiveté. But she wasn't naïve. *She knows what she does to a man,* Gabe thought. Knew that nobody in his right mind would be able to think straight once she so much as glanced in his direction. "It was the only time Luke and I could get away. And we never really had a honeymoon."

Gabe stared at her, and damned if she didn't have the decency to blush.

Tevio smiled at her girlishness. "But surely there were other places you could have gone. Places where they do not get three hundred centimeters of rain during the wet season."

"Well, yes. You're right, of course. Luke's mother has been wanting us to visit her forever, but we've been dreaming of the Amazon for so long." She sighed. It sounded wistful. Who the hell was this chick? "The mountain tapir, the spider monkey…their habitat keeps shrinking. We were afraid if we didn't come soon, there would be no giant anteaters left to see. But…" She paused, scowling a little and making Gabe hope he wasn't supposed to jump in here somewhere. He had jumped back in the room and didn't feel up to doing so again soon without some kind of satisfactory outcome. "I confess to being a bit unnerved."

"Unnerved?" Tevio said and set his fork, tines up, on his brightly colored plate.

"Don't get me wrong," she rushed to add. "We know that some of the stories we hear are just that. But there's been a rash of crimes attributed to drug lords lately."

The old man nodded. "Sadly, these are…" He tilted his head back with a scowl. "What is the word? Legitimate. These are legitimate concerns. But most of my countrymen are like myself," he said and spread short, brown fingers across his chest. Each nail held a tiny crescent of soil tucked against the cuticle. Gabe wondered vaguely if Edwards found it repulsive or charmingly earthy. "Simple folk just trying to make a living."

"We know that, don't we, honey?" Edwards asked and reached across the table to take Gabe's hand in hers. Her fingers were warm and ridiculously soft, making him think of other places even softer. "But I was worrying we had gone too far south." Gabe *had* been moving south. Hell, he'd been heading toward the fucking Promised Land when his stupid ass mouth had to chime in with the truth. "I was scared we'd come too close to Santiago's territory."

He'd been so close to... Wait a minute! Shit. Gabe refrained from grinding his teeth in frustration. While he'd been fantasizing about his imaginary sex life like a pimply-faced teenager, she'd been setting the stage to learn more about Shepherd's captors.

He swore in silence and tried to tune in to the conversation.

"So you know of Santiago?" Tevio asked.

She shook her head and shivered a little. "Rumors, you know. Innuendos. Wild tales."

Tevio scowled. "It is men such as he that give us all a black name. But you needn't worry. So long as you remain between the branches of the rivers all will be well."

"The rivers?" She blinked.

"The Putumayo and the Tortuga," their host explained. "They make natural boundaries of sorts. Here, between their fast flowing waters, we are peaceable farmers."

"Really?" Edwards squeezed Gabe's fingers and released them with a smile. "That's wonderful to hear. Isn't it, honey?"

"Very comforting." Holy hell, he sounded like a fucking zombie. "What do you grow here between the rivers?"

"Well..." The old man chuckled a little. "We are not like our wealthy American counterparts who plant a single cash crop that make them barrels of money. Because we are small, we must diversify. We have bananas, coffee, cocoa, corn. Many even sell cut flowers."

Like the poppy? Gabe wondered, but didn't verbalize the jaded querry.

"What a wonderful way of life," Edwards said. "Why doesn't Santiago do the same?"

Tevio chuckled. "Perhaps it is the cynic in me, but I believe it may be because he can make a thousand times more money selling coca than cocoa."

"Cocaine," Edwards said.

"Yes." Tevio's expression had turned grim.

"And he grows it just across the river?"

"I fear that is true, so do not venture that way. The roads between the river and his plantation are especially dangerous."

"He has a plantation?"

"If you were to climb to the top of Putumayo you might be able to see his despicable *pozo*."

Edwards shook her head.

Tevio pursed his lips. "Some call it a paste pit. It is where they convert the coca leaves into a gummy substance before completing the cocaine process. You cannot imagine the environmental degradation caused by those dreadful activities."

"I don't understand," Edwards said. "If it's common knowledge that he's making illegal drugs, why hasn't he been incarcerated?"

"Who is going to be rid of him?" Tevio asked. "He is a powerful man with many evil individuals in his employ."

"And I imagine he's extremely wealthy," Gabe said.

"Prostitution, drugs, kidnapping..." Tevio shook his head and sighed.

"Kidnapping?" Edwards asked. Her face was pale.

Tevio stared at her with saddened eyes. "Do not venture to the south, *señora*. I shudder to think what they would do with a sweet lady such as yourself."

The room went silent.

"But my apologies," he said into the quiet. "Where are my manners? Please forgive an old man's worries. I only ask that you be cautious," he said and pushing his chair back, rose to his feet. "Unfortunately, I must be off. I have tasks to tend to in the morning. But Luisa will serve your breakfast after which you are welcome to come and go as you wish. *La Maison* serves a lovely cup of coffee in the village of Inrida. Between here and there you may see all manner of beautiful creatures. I spotted a wooly opossum on one particularly lucky morning, bush dogs and titi monkeys on more than one occasion. But for now I shall bid you *buenas noches,*" he said and bowing with old world charm, shambled from the room.

## Chapter Forty-Three

"So we head south," Edwards said. They were alone in the narrow bedroom. Sheer white curtains rustled in the late night breeze. Outside the sky was as black as molasses.

Gabe nodded. "We'll check Santiago's paste pit first."

She had removed a map from his pack and was spreading it onto the bed. "It's what...about ten miles from here? So maybe four hours to get there."

"Don't forget about the river," he warned and stood to join her by the map.

"I don't habitually fall into them, you know." Her tone was a cross between irritation and apology.

He squelched a grin. "I just meant we're going to have to find a way to cross it."

She nodded slowly and turned back to the map.

"Without you toppling in," he added and kept his gaze front and center.

She gave him a wry look from the corner of her eye. "I like to think I'm earning my wages."

"I couldn't have done it without you." Scowling at the map, he traced the length of the gulch with his index finger. "You think the woman's body was found about there?" he asked but she remained silent.

He turned toward her, brows raised.

The surprise on her face was as clear as daylight and almost made it worth risking compliments. He fought a smile and turned back to the Colombian terrain. "If you're going to cast off, Edwards, you ought to make sure you don't use too much bait."

She stared at him a second. He could feel the heat of her scowl on his face. "I wasn't..." she began then shook her head and shifted her attention away. "Okay, maybe I was fishing a *little* bit." Turning, she sat down on the bed to remove her socks. The mattress shifted beneath her little heart shaped fanny. Mattresses, it turned out, got all the damn luck, Gabe thought but kept his attention front and center.

"If I were a shrink, I would say your parents didn't give you enough praise," he said.

"If I were your patient, I would ask if you're always such a master at the obvious."

"Yeah?" he said and didn't try to keep the surprise from his voice. He could imagine her as a little girl, pigtails askew, freckles scattered like confetti across her pug nose. True, he had been careful with his own accolades, but he had his reasons. For instance, she was scared and out of her element. Praise could make her overly grateful, which could, in turn, cause her do things she would later regret.

And, of course, there was the fact that if they got too close she'd realize what a shithead he could be.

But how on earth would her *parents* fail to adore her?

"Well...just my father really. Mom's pretty great," she admitted.

He scowled, though it was hardly surprising that her old man wasn't all romps and giggles. In his experience, colonels generally weren't. In fact, being human was a bit of a stretch. Shep had said on more than one occasion that Gabe would make pretty good colonel material.

"I always kind of felt that I let her down when I didn't follow through with my medical training," she said.

He deepened his scowl, mildly disturbed by the realization that she would have made a wonderful doctor while he wasn't even a decent *patient*.

"She was always nice about it, though," she said and winced as she pulled off her right sock.

"What's wrong?" he asked.

"What?" She glanced up.

"Do you have blisters?"

"Blisters? No," she said and dropped her toes to the floor.

He swore quietly as he knelt in front of her. "I've never met a woman who was such a piss poor liar."

She opened her mouth as if to argue, but he was already lifting her foot from the scared hardwood. She tried to pull it away, but he held on to her ankle.

The blister on her heel was the size of a dime, red and round and angry. "Why didn't you tell me about this?" he asked.

She tugged again. "Because it's nothing." Her cheeks were pink. He had also never met a woman who blushed as easily as she did. He couldn't help but wonder how low that pink stain went. But he cleared his throat and tried to do the same with his mind.

"Stay there. I'll get some salve," he said and rummaged around in his pack.

"You brought salve and not toilet paper?"

"No room for John Wayne."

She quirked her brows at him.

"Standard military TP," he explained." Rough and ready and takes no shit."

She laughed. The sound shivered through him, easing his myriad aches and pains, but he ignored the magic as best he could.

"Blisters will ruin a mission faster than wet ammo," he said and ferreting out the appropriate tube, returned to kneel by her feet. They were, he thought, about the size of his thumb.

"No room for a podiatrist either?" she asked.

She wasn't the first person to give him flack about the amount of gear he carried. He ignored her jibe and reached for her foot.

"I can do that," she insisted, but he brushed her hands away.

"It's my payment for you learning about Santiago when I was fully focused on the *empagenio*."

She scowled at him, then laughed as she remembered their mealtime conversation. "*Empanada*. I can't believe you haven't learned *any* Spanish."

There was something about her laughter that made his insides do a hard somersault, but he ignored their acrobatics. "Did you think I brought you along for your good looks?"

She was silent. Opening the tube, he glanced up in time to see her look away.

"No," she said finally.

"Good." Squeezing a little ointment onto his index finger, he added, "Because that was just a secondary reason." He immediately regretted his foolish admission, but sometimes the truth was as seductive as a strawberry blonde with a gun.

"You better be careful," she warned, "or I'll get a big head."

Lifting her foot onto his thigh, he smoothed the salve carefully over the blister. But he had squeezed out a little too much and dispersed it onto her ankle. "It would be the only thing on you that was oversized."

She raised her brows at him. He considered knocking himself on the side of the head. "I didn't mean that like it sounded. I meant you're skinny." He tried to hide his wince. "Not skinny," he corrected. "Just…"

"I guess I was wrong," she quipped and tugged her foot from his hands. "It's probably better if I *don't* get too many compliments."

"Sorry," he said and settling back on his heels, drew a long slow inhalation. He'd rather run a gauntlet of pissed off jihadists than participate in this type of verbal combat. "Shep's usually around to make sure I don't act like a complete shit."

"No wonder you want him back so badly," she said but there was laughter in her voice and something in her eyes that made him feel a little drunk. But he sobered immediately.

"Someone ought to kick his ass for this stunt," he said and felt his throat close up at the thought. He'd be lucky if he didn't kiss the fucking son of a bitch if he ever laid eyes on him again.

"We'll find him," she said.

He didn't dare glance at her; her voice alone was as unsettling as hell. Soft, low, and laced with kindness, it made him want nothing more than to pull her into his arms and drink in her essence. And… *Essence? Seriously?*

Keeping his gaze front and center, he cleared his throat and nodded. "How's your other foot?"

"It's fine."

"As fine as the right one?" he asked and reached for her left. She pulled it out of his reach.

"Even finer. Don't you have more important things to do?"

"More important than making sure my troops are battle ready? Not really." He tugged off her sock. "Looks like you've got a blister starting here, too," he said and pushed her pant leg up her calf.

"Don't," she insisted and kicked his hand away.

He tried not to take offense to her aversion even though he had once thought there could be something between them. He leaned back a little. "It should be treated."

"I know. I'll do it. I just…."

He scowled at her. The pink was gone from her face, now. The word scarlet would more aptly describe her cheeks.

"I just…haven't shaved," she said finally.

He stared at her in silence.

"I've been kind of busy." Her tone was prim as she pressed her pant leg firmly against her ankle.

He continued to watch her, trying to get a grip on the situation, on himself, on life. But he couldn't help laughing.

By the time he got his mirth under control, she was glaring at him.

"Are you serious?" he asked finally.

Her lips were pursed, her expression accusatory. If he was any judge of women, which he was *not*, she was beyond serious. But how could she honestly think he would care about her leg-shaving habits? Or notice? Holy shit, in his current state, he'd be lucky to remain conscious if she bared so much as a kneecap.

"Yes, I'm serious," she said. "I didn't pack a razor and my legs are hairy."

"Compared to whose?" he asked finally.

"What?"

"Your legs are hairy compared to whose?" he repeated and tugged up his own pants.

She jerked as if shot. "Holy cow," she said and blinked at his exposed skin. "Were your parents…arboreal or something?"

"Guerrillas," he said. "Of the military nature."

She chuckled at his poor pun then sighed and relaxed a little. "I always wanted a scar like that."

"What?" he asked and glanced down.

"The one on your shin. Where'd you get it?"

He scowled at the blemish in question. "I tripped over a coffee table."

She chuckled. "You're lying."

"It was dark," he said, letting his pant leg drop. "And I might have had one too many beers."

"Not a very sexy story is it?"

Her smile was as warm as sunlight on his skin. "You're probably going to want to embellish it a little if you hope to make any conquests."

"I'll keep that in mind," he said and felt himself falling into her eyes.

She cleared her throat. They pulled their gazes apart. It was like tugging on magnets. "How's your chest?"

Muscular, he thought but didn't say the word out loud. He couldn't deliver a line like that if he had UPS tattooed on his ass. "Healing," he said instead.

"I should take a look at it."

He raised his eyes back to hers, but her expression was no nonsense.

"I lost the GPS," she explained. "I'll never find my way back to Bogotá if you drop dead of septicemia."

"Stop it," he said. "You're making me blush."

She laughed. "Take your shirt off."

God he wanted to, but Shepherd was out there, probably hurting, maybe starving, almost definitely in some kind of big ass trouble. "Listen, Edwards, I'm sorry…about before."

She stared at him, mute for a moment then, "You mean…" She motioned toward the bed where they had so nearly found heaven. "Oh, yeah, don't worry about it. I was just relieved to…" She swallowed. "Learn that we weren't being filmed."

"Yeah," he said but his khakis felt tight at the thought. She'd look damn good on film. And he didn't dare take off his shirt. Not that she'd be uncontrollable if she saw his chest or anything, but… well, hell, maybe she'd be uncontrollable he thought and found that his damned traitorous fingers had already peeled the first button open. "I just didn't want you to get the wrong idea."

She lifted her gaze from his chest and jerked it toward his gargantuan backpack. "No, of course not. I mean, I'm fully aware that this is strictly business."

He managed a nod as he tugged off his shirt.

"We're here to find Shepherd." Lifting out a couple of Telfa pads, she set them aside then straightened and put her palm beside his latest bullet wound. "Nothing else."

He was pretty sure the area should hurt like hell, but her fingers felt as sweet as hope against his skin. "Right." His voice sounded raspy.

"Does that hurt?"

"No."

She made a face. "I'm afraid it's going to sting like the devil when I pull off the bandage."

"It'll be okay."

"All right," she said and gritted her teeth, but in a moment she'd pulled her hand away. "I'm going to get a wet towel."

"What?"

"We'll soak it a little. So it'll come off easier."

"That's not necessary," he assured her but she had already disappeared into the adjoining room.

"Humor me," she said and returned, carrying a dripping washcloth. Supporting it with the towel she'd used earlier, she set it against the bandage. "Pretend I'm your mother."

He raised his brows at her. The idea seemed like a stretch and maybe morally inappropriate.

She smiled. "She must have bandaged your boo boos and kissed your scrapes."

"Sarge?" His tone had gone from guttural to squeaky. There weren't a hell of a lot of people whose memory could put the fear of God into a man like dear old mom.

Her laugh was like falling water, soft and light and soothing. "I forgot her nickname," she admitted. Sitting down on the bed next to him, she lifted her moss-soft gaze to his. Her proximity made him fidgety.

"What nickname?" he asked and scowled into the near distance. It was a hell of a lot safer than looking at *her*. "That's how she was christened."

She laughed again. He didn't know why it made him feel dizzy. "Sarge Durrand?"

"That's Sergeant Durrand to her subordinates," he said. "And everyone's her subordinate."

She was quiet a second. He wanted to glance down, to guess what she was thinking, but seeing her so close to his...everything...did dangerous things to his self-control.

"You miss her," she said.

He jerked his gaze to hers. "What?"

"You miss your mother."

"I'm a Ranger, Edwards," he said and, clasping his hands

behind his back, assumed military rigidity. "Rangers do *not* –" he began, but she straightened with the bandage in her hand.

He raised his brows. Honest to God, he hadn't felt it come off.

"I'm pretty good at kissing boo boos, too," she said.

He stared at her. She was inches away, her expression kind, her eyes warm, but he tried to resist. Honest to God he did.

He just wasn't very strong.

And suddenly he was kissing her.

# Chapter Forty-Four

"So tell me…" Shep said. "Am I handcuffed so I won't escape, or do ya have more depraved reasons in mind?"

Carlotta turned toward him, plump lips pursed, amber eyes as slanted as a wildcat's. He'd known her less than twenty-four hours, but he was pretty damn sure she was going to bear his children.

"I do not know what this depraved it mean," she said and sauntered toward him. She moved with the hypnotic rhythm of a python, every curve undulating.

"Wicked," he said.

She lifted her brows. "You think I have the wicked plans for you?"

He shrugged. The movement made him ache all the way to his ass, which made him think sex was going to hurt like hell. God, he couldn't wait to find out. "Ya know I'm naked under this sheet, right?"

She could smile with nothing but her eyes. It was a sight to behold. "I have been meant to ask you regarding that."

"Really?"

"No," she said and slipping into the chair beside his bed,

settled a bowl onto her lap. She was wearing a candy-apple red dress that clung as if ironed on. He had never been more jealous of a bowl in his entire life. "Now, you must be the good boy and eat your *colada de avena*."

"What if I told ya I don't like..." He glanced into the bowl. The contents looked disturbing reminiscent of vomit. "Whatever the hell that is?"

"I say you will be *muy* hungry by the morning."

"What if I say I'll eat it if ya feed it to me?"

"*Muy muy* hungry by morning."

"Ya wouldn't let me starve, would ya?"

She canted her head a little, making her hair cascade beside her cheeks like a dark waterfall. Her narrowed eyes made her look increasingly feline. "*Señor* worries that you might be a dealer of the drugs."

"The doctor," he said, ignoring the slander. "What is he to you?"

"What is it you mean?" she asked and stirred the awful looking gruel.

"Are ya lovers?"

She glanced up sharply, surprise in her eyes. "This is none of your business."

He raised his brows, gut twisting. "That sounds like a yes."

"It looks to be that you will eat your *colada de avena* alone," she said and rose to her feet, but he managed to grab her arm.

"I'm sorry," he said, "we won't talk about it if ya don't wanna."

She stared at him, debating. "Very good," she said finally and sat back down.

"But ya know he's—" Shep began. She stiffened. He stopped himself from saying more, though gray memories stirred like angry bats in his mind. She was watching him, brow slightly furrowed. "...an old man, right?"

She shifted to stand again, but he chuckled and tightened his grip.

"I'm done now. Really," he said and forced thoughts of Doc from his mind. "Tell me about yourself."

She shrugged and spooned up a bit of porridge. It was as gray as concrete and looked just about as palatable. "What can I tell? I am born here in Solano and this is where I have live the whole of my life."

"Why not Paris?"

She quirked a brow at him.

"Or New York. I hear Victoria Secret is lookin' for models."

She stared at him. "Tell me, do these words of yours work on the women of America?"

"Not on any as beautiful as you."

She rolled her eyes but didn't quite hide her smile. "And what of you, Roy Cherokee? She made the 'r' rumble charmingly when she said his name. Well, his alias anyway. It was the sexiest thing he had ever heard. "You are a cowboy, *sí?*"

"There's no boy in me, *chica,*" he said and took the first spoonful offered by her delicate fingers. "I'm all man."

She snorted and swung her hair behind her back. For reasons he would never be able to name, the motion made his mouth go dry.

"Truly," she said. "You seem to be…" She shrugged. "Not so stupid." The short sleeves of her dress were gathered and clung to the caps of her warm-caramel shoulders. "And not terrible ugly to look upon. Why is it you take to the drugs?"

"Why would *you* take to the doc?"

She pursed her lips but didn't try to rise this time. "He was the friend of my *papi.*"

"Your dad's buddy?" He thought about that while taking another spoonful. "That just makes it creepier," he said. She turned away but he was already apologizing. "I'm sorry. Forgive me. Tell me about your dad."

She drew a deep breath. "My father, he was the farmer. A good one, but it is not easy to make the living on this soil. And when my mother became ill…" She shrugged. Sadness shone in every expressive feature.

Shep thought for a second, drew in a careful breath and spoke. "The old man loaned your father money."

She raised her gaze to his. "You do not understand."

He leaned his head back against the pillows behind him. "Ya could explain it."

"It was much more than the dollars."

He stared at her, dubious, and she went on.

"*Papi* was not the same after *Mami's* death. And Sofia, she needed the father."

"Sofia…" He shook his head once, ambushed by the bubble of uneasiness stirring in his gut. "Your daughter?"

She glanced at him from the corner of her entrancing eyes. "My sister."

The uneasiness slipped away. "So Doc helped ya out."

"He gave me the job in a café. He became the uncle we did not have."

But the old man wanted to be more. That much was as clear as vodka. What would she say if he told her about the man whose eye had been pierced by the sapling? The man the good doctor could so easily ignore as he screamed in agony? And what of Curro, dying in this very room?

"So ya think you owe 'im," Shep said.

"I *do* owe him, but he is too honorable to ask for the payment."

Shepherd kept his opinions to himself, though it was a difficult thing. "Then you're free to leave whenever ya want."

"Of course," she said and shrugged. The scalloped bodice of her dress flirted with her breasts.

"Then why don't you?"

"Who it is to say I wish to?"

"Your eyes," he said and grinned a little. "They're tellin' me all sorts of secrets."

"Oh?" She gave him a sassy glance from beneath forest full lashes. "What is it that they say?"

"That they want me."

She rolled those beautiful eyes.

He sobered unwillingly. "And that ya could do great things."

She stared at him in silence for a second, and then she laughed. "Like bear a conceited American's *bebés*?"

"Maybe." He grinned and kept his tone level, but the idea did unsettling things to his equilibrium. "Or ya could be..." He narrowed his eyes at her, guessing. "A doctor in your own right. Or a teacher. Or a world-famous diplomat."

Her eyes widened in surprise, but in a moment, she snorted.

He smiled. "I'm close aren't I?"

"You are..." She shook her head. "How is it they say..." She was as cute as a puppy when she scowled. "You are the *loco* one."

"Well..." he said and did his best to look pathetic. Which really wasn't that hard since he was wounded, and handcuffed to a bed, and naked. Although, really, he'd rarely found nakedness to be a disadvantage. "I have had a head injury."

Bending at the waist, she brushed the hair from his forehead. Her touch was as light as a summer breeze, bringing back soft memories of lazy sunlit days beside old Mill Creek. He let his shoulders relax against the mounded pillows and spoke softly. "I'd do anything ya suggested."

She tensed a little and raised her brows, but he took the high road.

"If ya were a diplomat," he explained.

She exhaled softly through her nose and offered him more gruel which he took without glancing at it.

"If I am not mistaken, diplomats...they need more than ten years of the school," she said.

"Ya could get your GED online then take classes at Oklahoma State."

For a moment, her dreams were almost visible in her eyes, but finally she laughed. "And what would I do with Sofia while I am become this world famous something?"

"What are ya doin' with her now?"

"Now she is attends the Aspaen Gimnasio Iragua for girls."

"So she's gettin' the education ya didn't."

She shrugged as if it didn't matter. "Someday, perhaps, Sofia will become the attorney and I can be her assist. Until then, I am lucky to have such a job as I do."

He watched her. An attorney. Was that Sofia's dream or hers?

"So you're content to serve coffee for a few pesos a day."

"Sí."

"Martyrs," he said, "usually end badly."

"Not like the runners of the drugs then," she said and rising, left, taking the sunlight with her.

# Chapter Forty-Five

Durrand's lips were hot and firm against Eddy's. His chest felt like sinful heaven beneath her hand, though she had no idea how her fingers had landed there. She kissed him back, because she couldn't help herself, because life was hard and short and...dammit, she wanted to!

He pulled back, chest heaving beneath her palm, eyes staring into hers, giving her a chance to stop, to be sensible, but she didn't want a chance.

Growling, she skimmed her fingers through his hair and dragged his lips back to hers.

After that, there was no stopping. He pushed her up against the wall. Her spine cracked against the plaster, but she didn't care. He was all broad bone and shifting muscle. All hot and vast and... why was he still wearing those damned pants?

They were naked in a second. And then she was straddling him and he was straining and she was gasping... and holy crap!

Eventually, they lay side by side on the bed, though truth to tell she wasn't entirely sure how they had arrived there.

"Don't tell me," she rasped, still trying to catch her breath, "you found a camera after all?"

He shifted his head upon the mattress. The pillows had gone Elvis long ago. "I tried my best," he said.

"No video?"

"Not even a damn peep hole."

"Then what was this for?" She tried to sound accusatory, but perhaps the fact that her naked chest was still pressed up against his made her irritation seem a little less believable.

"This?" he asked and slipped a slow hand down the length of her back.

She stifled a sigh and managed a nod.

He blew out a breath. "This is about losing control."

"Ahh."

The entire length of his body felt as hard as a living oak beneath hers.

"I don't like losing control," he admitted.

She watched him for a second then cleared her throat. "I'm sorry. I shouldn't have—" she began, but he stopped her.

"You *should* have," he whispered and kissed her. "You definitely should have. Even though I'm not near..." His words slipped into silence. His eyes were dark and tortured. As deep as forever.

"Even though what?"

He drew in a long breath. "Maybe *no* one's good enough for you."

She read the nuances, felt his marrow-deep adoration, and cupped his lean face in her palm. "Maybe I'm not good enough for *you.*"

His chuckle was low and mirthless. "I guarantee that's not the case."

"I'll never..." She winced as she slipped her thumb over the scar that nicked his chin. "I'm scared out of my mind half the time."

"You think I'm not?"

"I think it doesn't matter. I think you'll do whatever has to be done to save your friend."

"Whatever has to be done…" He winced. Lifting her hand from his face, he kissed the center of her palm and drew a slow, deep breath. "I want you to go home."

She drew back, inadvertently pressing her hips more firmly to his. "What?"

"Santiago's holding Shep. I feel it in my gut. We know where his property is. You've done your part. It'll be safer if you leave now, let me go in alone."

She stared at him. "Safer for whom?"

"For *me!* It's much less likely that they'll notice a lone—"

"Dad left when Grand was dying."

"*What?*"

She wanted to look away, to hide her emotions, to distance herself from all the sterling qualities that shone from his soul, but she held his gaze. "Colonel Edwards. Everyone thought he was the epitome of honor. But he didn't even have the courage to help Mom through her mother's death. Didn't have the loyalty to stick through the hard times."

"I'm sorry." His words were a quiet rasp of kindness in the darkness. His fingers curled possessively against her neck. His thumb pressed comfortingly into the hollow of her throat.

"I promised myself I'd be different."

"You are," he rasped. "You're everything that's good."

"You don't know me," she whispered.

"I'm a pretty good judge of character, Edwards." He sounded strangely affronted. She couldn't help but smile at him.

"Are you?"

He nodded. "You're the kindest person I've ever met."

Were there tears in his eyes? Her heart felt full to bursting. "You're the bravest."

"I'm not," he said and clearing his throat, carefully lightened his tone. "But I might be the most sex deprived."

She raised her brows. "Well, let's do something about that," she said.

And he did.

## Chapter Forty-Six

"I thought the prettiest girls in the world came from Tulsa," Shep said. "Guess I was wrong." He had no way of knowing exactly how many days had passed since his incarceration. All he knew was that Carlotta had returned.

She turned toward him, as bright as a star.

"Come to Oklahoma with me." The words left his mouth before checking in with his brain, but she just glanced at him askance, dark eyes somewhere between amused and skeptical.

"And what would I do in this…Oklahoma?"

"Besides be bowled over by my country charm?"

Her eyes had gone cynical. "*Sí*, besides that?"

He shrugged. "Ya could be a…hair girl."

"Hair girl?"

"Ya know…one of those women who does stuff with hair. What are they called?"

"Eat your soup."

"Are you sure?" He made a face and shook his head. "That doesn't sound right. Stylist," he said suddenly. "Ya could be a hair stylist. Yours looks especially good today, by the way."

"It does not matter what it is you say," she warned him. "I am not going to make you free."

"Ya don't think I'm just flatterin' ya so you'll take off the cuffs, do ya?"

"No," she said and reached for his pillow. "Sit up." He did so. "I also think you flatter me because you want to have the sex with me."

"What?" He gave her his best shocked expression. "I don't wanna... Well..." He snorted softly. He was a damned good liar. But the devil himself couldn't pull off a whopper like that. "I do *wanna* if *you* wanna, but..." He paused. "Do you wanna—"

"No," she said.

"Oh. All right, well, your hair's still really sexy." It was long and dark with waves that looked as if they could wind around a man's heart and into his soul. "There're about seventy billion American women who'd kill for hair like that."

"I think their deaths would do me little good."

He thought about that for a second. "Well, no, ya probably wouldn't gain a lot if they were TU, but my point is..."

"TU?"

"Ahhh...toes up," he explained, fudging a little. "Anyway, you'd have a pretty good income if ya could make other women's hair look like yours. Even actresses... Hey, I bet ya could be a stylist for the stars."

"Be silent and eat," she ordered.

He stared up at her and felt a little breathless at her nearness. It wasn't that she was beautiful...exactly. Well, okay, it *was* that she was beautiful...exactly... So maybe that was all that was to it. How the hell long had it been since he had been with a woman? *Any* woman? "I *would* eat," he said, but I'm cuffed to the bed." He lifted his left hand, rattling the metal that bound him. "I'm afraid you'll have to help me...again."

"You only need the one hand to eat."

"I've been injured." He tilted his head, hoping he looked harmless and maybe a little helpless. "By your people."

"Herrera is *not* my people." She hissed the words.

"But Doc is."

She pursed her lips. They were as lush as ripe berries. "Señor Tevio, he is a good man."

"No," he said and though he tried to maintain his smile and play it cool, the muzzy memories kept creeping in. "He's not."

She drew herself up. "How is it you dare slanderize his name?"

He watched her, pulled irrevocably into seriousness. A place where he rarely tread. "I dare because ya know it's true."

"I know no such thing as this. He saved my family just as he saved you."

"Why?" he asked.

"Because he does not wish for you to suffer."

"Is that what he told you?"

"*Sí.*"

"He doesn't have any problem with handcuffin' me to the bed."

"He must do so because you are a dealer of the drugs. A man who ruins the lives of innocent children and—"

"Rangers don't deal drugs!"

She scowled. "Rangers? What is this?"

He shifted his gaze toward the door and ground his teeth. He ached to tell her the truth, to raise her opinion of him, but maybe that's why she was here, to learn his secrets, to feed those confessions back to a man who could kill as casually as he could eat dinner.

"Come to America with me," he said.

She shook her head at the abrupt change of subject. "And how would we get there, cowboy?" she asked. "Do you have the fortune in American dollar hid away somewhere?"

Holy shit. Really? After all they'd been through together she was after his money? "No American dollars," he said, "but Durrand will buy the tickets. In fact, he probably has already."

"Durrant?"

"Durrand. He's a friend of mine." He inhaled, careful not to think too hard about the damned know-it-all he loved like an idiot brother. "Makes a habit of saving my bacon."

She looked increasingly confused. "What is this bacon you speak of?"

He grinned at her. "He likes to save my life. Makes 'im feel human."

"Then he had best waste no more time," she said. Her expression was somber, her eyes as bright as Montana silver. "Because *señor*, he will not hold you much longer."

# Chapter Forty-Seven

"You okay?" Durrand was nearly invisible in the darkness. But Eddy could feel the heat of his body, could hear the hard tension in his voice and wished like hell they were still back in Tevio's cozy hacienda. Still entwined on the scattered sheets, sharing secrets and kisses.

She nodded.

"Keep watch," he whispered and glanced toward the front of the corrugated building not thirty yards away. "Call me if you see anyone. I'll do the same when the coast is clear."

She managed another nod. For a moment, she was sure he would reach out, would touch her face, but he only hesitated a moment before he pulled back and slithered beneath the barricade that enclosed Santiago's dynasty. In a moment, he was gone, swallowed by the darkness.

Taking a fortifying breath, she shoved her pack through the hole they'd dug then pressed her back more firmly against the rough bark of a sweet-gum and exhaled carefully. She wished she could be offended by the fact that Durrand had left her behind to stand guard like a frightened child. But gratitude was her overwhelming—

Something touched her thigh. She jumped but managed to keep from yelping just as she realized her cell phone was vibrating in her pocket; Durrand's signal to follow him. She allowed herself one fractured moment of terror before dropping to her belly and wriggling through to the other side. By the time she had reached Durrand, he had already cut the lock to the corrugated building. The door slid open on silent wheels.

"No guard?" she whispered.

He shook his head, but his expression was worried.

She forced a smile. "Not everything has to be difficult," she said, but suddenly, headlights drowned them.

"*Hola*." The greeting was loud and cheery, issued by some unseen force behind the blinding lights.

Eddy ducked. Durrand growled, but they were caught dead to rights, and in a second, a man stepped into the lights. It took several moments for Eddy to recognize him.

"Señor Tevio?"

The elderly man shrugged, expression benign. "You are surprisingly well armed for ones who come only to enjoy the beauty of our country."

Durrand straightened, eyes deadly steady, gun held firmly in his right hand.

"Ponce, if they cause any trouble, shoot the *señorita* first," Tevio said. His voice was conversational though he never shifted his gaze from Durrand. "But do not kill her."

A muscle jumped in Durrand's lean cheek. "Let her go, and I won't cause any trouble."

"Of course, I will let her go," Tevio said and smiled. "Do you think me a monster?"

There was a moment of absolute stillness and then Durrand bent and placed his rifle on the ground."

"Ahhh," Veto said and settled his benevolent smile on Eddy. "So he does care for you, my dear. But is he truly your husband, I wonder."

It was almost impossible to respond, almost beyond her to

push words past her frozen lips. "What's going on?" she breathed. Her voice shook. "I know you told us not to cross the river, but we…we got lost…following a bushbird. It got dark so fast. I was scared and wet. Durrand…" She stopped, mortified by her stuttering mistake. *"Luke,"* she corrected. "Luke didn't want to come here but I was so—"

"Shoot her in the leg," Tevio ordered.

"No!" Durrand yelled, but the word was lost as pain slammed through her.

She staggered backward, stunned, confused as she toppled to the ground.

Another shot whined. She reached vaguely for her own weapon, but someone already stood over her, eyes emotionless, rifle steady. She lay back, strength draining away and rolled her head to the right.

Durrand lay on his side, eyes wide and staring as blood pooled beneath his scalp.

# Chapter Forty-Eight

"Come on, honey, wake up," a voice said, but Eddy just snuggled deeper into her blankets. It was cool outside. Fall was her favorite season. She loved the earthy scents, the vibrant colors, the taste of spiced cider and— "That's an order, Edwards!"

She opened her eyes with a snap, but it hardly mattered. The room where she lay was as dark as a cave. She tried to roll onto her side, but her arms were confined behind her. Craning her neck, she glanced behind her. A chain was attached to her wrists and was strung through a ring set in the solid rock wall. Panic flooded her. She jerked her hands.

"Look at me." The voice from beside her was as quiet as river water, but terror washed the sound away. "Edwards, look at me."

She stilled her movements and turned her head to the left. Durrand was leaning against the wall, knees bent, arms bound behind his back. Blood or some other dark substance caked his face and crackled on his neck.

"Breathe," he ordered.

"You're alive." They were, possibly, the dumbest words she had ever spoken, but it felt good to release them, freeing somehow, allowing her to inhale more readily.

"Take it easy," he said, "Just relax for a minute."

"Are you nuts?" she asked and shifted her gaze along the rock wall. "I'm chained in a cave with no—" Her throat hurt when she gasped.

"Don't look at it," Durrand demanded but she couldn't help it. Manacled to the rock, not fifteen feet away, was a decomposing body. It sat with its back against the stone. A stick protruded from its right eye.

"Edwards..." Durrand's voice was low and steady. "Look away."

It took everything she had to close her eyes, to turn her head, to steady her breathing. For a moment, she thought she would vomit, but she refused the weakness and exhaled shakily. "I think you might have been right about Señor Tevio," she said.

"I wasn't even going to say I told you so."

"Durrand..." She opened her eyes, avoided glancing at the corpse and settled her gaze on his. "I'm sorry."

"For saving my life when I was dumb enough to get shot in the chest?"

She shook her head.

"I sure as hell hope it's not for the sex."

She tried to laugh and failed. "I don't want to die here." Her voice sounded pitifully weak, embarrassingly shaky.

"We're not going to."

"*He* did," she rasped and couldn't resist shifting her gaze sideways.

"He's not us," Durrand said, but horror made it impossible to focus on his words. "Edwards, look at me."

She did so with difficulty.

"You're strong," he said. "Incredible. Nothing stops you once you—"

"No," she said. "I'm not."

"You've beaten carjackers and drug runners and the Amazon already. What's a pair of manacles and a leg wound compared to that?"

"My leg—"

"Is fine," he said. "It'll heal."

"How do you know?"

"If it had hit the femoral artery, you'd already be dead."

She nodded. "Anyone ever tell you that you really know how to make a girl feel better?"

"No," he said. "Never."

Her laugh ended on a sob. Her gaze was being pulled back toward the corpse.

"Focus on me, Edwards."

She did so with an effort.

"Inhale," he ordered.

She tried, then coughed. The air was heavy with decay.

"Exhale."

That was more successful.

"We're going to get out of here," he promised. She nodded though she didn't really know why. "Eventually, someone will come to check on us," he added. "You'll be half naked."

"What?"

"You will have removed your shirt."

"Why?" Her voice sounded childish to her own ears.

"To distract the guard."

She blinked. "Won't it seem..." She shook her head. "Suspicious?"

"You will have used it as a tourniquet for your leg."

She nodded again. The movement felt a little more fluid. "What if he doesn't care?"

"That you're half naked?"

Another nod. This one was almost normal.

"Maybe you haven't looked in the mirror lately." His voice was soft.

She scowled. "I don't know—" she began, but he interrupted her.

"He'll care," he said, voice firm again. "He'll forget all about me and go straight to you. That's when I'll grab him."

"What if there's more than one?"

"I'll shoot them with the gun I take off the first guy."

She nodded, trying to believe, but her mind stuttered with uncertainty. "What if he doesn't get close enough?"

"He will."

"What if—"

"Holy God, Edwards, I've got a head wound. One more question could kill me. Ease up, will—"

A noise from above startled them both. They twisted toward the sound.

Eddy shook her head, frantic, unprepared. But a door was opening. Footsteps were descending. She snapped her attention back to Durrand. His eyes were wide, his mouth open. He twitched.

"Durrand!"

He shifted his gaze to hers and reached frantically toward her, but suddenly his hand fell away. His eyes rolled toward the ceiling and his head smacked hard against the wall behind him.

"Durrand?" She whispered his name. Terror ripped her asunder. "Durrand!"

He didn't move, didn't breathe. His eyes were wide and sightless, his mouth ajar.

"Durrand, no. Don't!" A sob escaped her lips. "I can't—"

"So he is dead."

She jerked her attention to the left. Two men stood against the far wall.

"Help him," she pleaded then switched to Spanish and tried again.

But they laughed. "I do not think so, *señorita*."

"Please," she said but the second man shrugged. Stepping forward, he kicked Durrand's booted foot. It jiggled lifelessly.

"Why would we shoot him if we wished for him to live?" he asked and smiled at her. "You, though, look well worth saving."

Terror swelled up on a fresh wave, threatening to drown her. She scooted back against the wall. "Don't touch me."

"Of course, not," said the tallest of the two and reached for her with a laugh.

But suddenly, he was falling. Durrand's hands snaked out. His chain rattled as it whipped around their tormentor's neck.

The second man snapped off a shot, then stumbled back, gurgling on his own blood. His friend's knife protruded from his throat.

The closest man struggled, feet swinging wildly, but Durrand tightened the chain around his neck. "The American," he rasped. His face looked twisted in the sparse light from above. "Where is he?"

"Go to hell!" the man's voice was garbled Spanish.

Durrand tightened his grip again. The guard squirmed, body jerked atop his captor's outstretched legs. "Edwards, ask him where they're holding Shepherd."

She spoke, voice shaking.

He answered, Spanish rapid-fire fast.

"He says he doesn't know of any other hostages."

"I won't harm him if he promises to do the same and tells the truth. I'll let him get out of here alive."

Eddy caught the guard's frantic gaze. His eyes were beginning to bulge. His knuckles were white where he gripped the chain around his neck. She steadied her voice and repeated Durrand's words.

The man's body went still, but his breathing was raspy. "Señor Santiago has property west of here. A ranch. Few know it is his."

"How far?"

"Two kilometers. Let me go and I will show you the way to—" he began, but Durrand jerked the chain tight. The man gasped, his body juddered and then he fell still.

"No! You promised! You—" Eddy rasped, but Durrand spoke over her.

"Get his keys."

She shook her head, shocked and appalled.

"Get them!"

"I—" she began and shifted her gaze to the corpse. It wasn't until then that she saw the gun their captor had shoved up against Durrand's thigh. She stared at it, unblinking, unmoving as the implication of his lies burst in her brain.

"Eddy," Durrand said. His voice had softened slightly. "We have to get out of here."

She blinked.

"Someone may have heard the commotion." His tone was summer night calm. "Can you reach his pocket?"

The thought of touching the dead body was almost more than she could bear, but she stretched out a shaking hand. Her chain went taut. Pulling her left hand to the wall, she pushed as far as possible with her right but it was no use. "I can't reach it."

"Hold on," he said, and dragging the man by his neck, pulled him over his own body, shifting the corpse's hips toward her.

Eddy closed her eyes and slipped her hand into his pocket.

# Chapter Forty-Nine

"Tell me about this Durren that will come for you," Carlotta said.

Shep had finally been given a pair of drawstring pants. But for reasons entirely unknown, he had been refused a shirt. He liked to think that had been Carlotta's decision.

"Durrand," He corrected.

"That is what I said."

"My mistake."

She gave him a look. He squelched a grin. "Why do ya wanna know about 'im?"

"No reason. I simply try to become not so bored."

"Or you're interested in my life 'cause I'm so damned charming."

"So damned conceit," she said.

"Conceited."

She quirked a questioning brow at him.

"I'm so damned *conceited*," he corrected and snorted, realizing she had played him. "Well, we'll have time to work on your English when we get to Oklahoma."

"Oklahoma?"

"Where all real men are born and raised."

"So this Durren, he is from the Oklahoma, too?" she asked and settled onto the bed beside him. It was wonderfully hard to think when she was so near.

He frowned for a moment, remembering the time Durrand had saved him from a pair of streetwalkers he'd met in Guatemala. Shep would have *sworn* they were born women. "Maybe a couple come from Tennessee, too."

"Does he look like you?"

"Why do ya ask?"

She shrugged. "Hollywood would have us believe that all Americans they are tall and dark and handsome."

"Ya think I'm handsome?"

Another elaborate shrug. "I was ask about your friend. Is he look like you?"

"Well, I don't like to brag."

"I think you lie," she said.

He stared at her.

"I think you like very much to brag. Is he big as you?"

"Durrand?"

She nodded. "I only ask because I am the curious one."

"Well, he *is* tall and—" Shepherd began, but reality throttled him suddenly, stopping him in his tracks. "Shit!" he snarled and caught her hand but she stood, twisting out of his grip, eyes wide, expression troubled.

"What's going on?" His words sounded like a growl to his own ears.

"Nothing goes on," she said.

But he yanked at his cuffs, rattled the bed. "You've seen 'im."

"What? No!"

He searched her eyes. "He's here isn't he?" He stood abruptly, stretching his arm to the side as he skimmed the room. "I need some boots and…" He stopped abruptly, speared her with his gaze. "Come with us."

"What do you talk of?" She waved wildly at his handcuffs. "You are chained to the bed."

He didn't even glance at the manacles. "Where is he?"

"I tell you, I did not see him."

"Carlotta!" he said and grabbed her hand again.

Their gazes met in a clash of emotions.

She squeezed her eyes closed. "I am told there are people in the hole."

"The hole? What hole? What are ya talkin' about?"

She winced. "Some say the *señor* has a pit at his...at his other property. A pit where others are sometimes kept."

"Prisoners?" He swore in silence. "He has other prisoners?"

She winced. He tightened his grip on her hand.

"Carlotta, ya have to leave here. I don't care what he did for your family. You're not safe. The man's psychotic."

"He is not—" she began, but just then there was a shuffling noise outside.

Shep snapped his gaze to the door and back. "Come with us," he said again.

"You are tied to the—" she began but her words stopped in midsentence as the door was flung open.

Gabriel Durrand stepped inside. Blood coated the left side of his face. He was favoring one leg. But the shotgun in his hands looked damned steady. He glanced from side to side. When no one jumped from the shadows, he lowered the muzzle of his semi-automatic a quarter of an inch. "You coming or not?" The question sounded only mildly interested.

Shepherd grinned. "I just need some clothes," he said, but a spatter of distant gunfire tore away their emotional reunion.

"Fuck the clothes," Durrand growled and aiming at the bed frame, pulled the trigger. The metal screeched. Shepherd kicked it apart and pulled his arm free. Durrand tossed him a pistol and swung toward the door.

But Shep turned toward Carlotta. "Please." His throat felt

tight, his heart too large for his chest. "Ya have to come," he breathed.

She shook her head, but there was uncertainty in her eyes, longing in her body language. His arm reached out of its own accord, pulling her close. He couldn't help but kiss her.

"Please." He whispered the word against her lips.

Silence held the world.

"Sooner would be better," Durrand warned, and suddenly Carlotta nodded.

Shepherd kissed her again. Then turning, they charged out the door.

Bullets spattered around them.

"Head toward the river!" Durrand ordered.

They sprang away. Behind them men yelled and swore and discharged their weapons in wild disregard.

But a rifle from up ahead answered back. Bullets whizzed past them. Men grunted and died behind them.

"Is that Sharps?" Shep yelled.

"No," Durrand said and turning, fired again.

A man jumped and fell.

"Halt!" someone ordered. He was close, too close.

But a rifle sang from a few yards ahead. The villains yelped and drew back.

"Indigo?" Shepherd guessed.

"Edwards!" Durrand called, and suddenly a sharpshooter rose from the foliage nearly at their feet.

"Out of ammo," she rasped.

Shepherd jerked in surprise, but there was no more time for questions. Only for running as best they could, stumbling and scrambling through the trees.

Branches slapped them, roots tore at their feet, and three of them were wounded, slowing their pace; their pursuers were already closing the gap.

But they pushed forward until suddenly, they burst onto a

road. They staggered to a halt as a Jeep careened around a curve and skidded to a stop a dozen yards from where they stood.

Timoteo Ortez Santiago stood in the back of the vehicle. Men with rifles flanked him on both sides.

"Americanos! I call a truce." he yelled. "Truly, I wish you no harm."

The sight of Doc Tevio's head of security gasping on the floor following those same words, jerked Shep into motion. "The hell with that!" he snarled and snapped off a shot.

Tevio grasped his chest and slumped sideways. Durrand and his sharpshooter lunged into the trees. Shepherd grabbed Carlotta's hand, pulling her after the others, but she twisted back.

"*Señor!*" she gasped.

Shepherd dragged her with him. "Come on!"

"No!" She jerked out of his grasp.

Shepherd swung toward her.

"Shep!" Durrand yelled and grabbed his arm. "Leave her!"

Shepherd swung around, but Durrand was already raising his weapon. The butt of his rifle collided with the side of Shep's skull. It was the last thing he remembered for a long while.

# Chapter Fifty

"Sure," Durrand said and stared at Shepherd, gaze level, voice dead steady. "Stay here if you want. Maybe this time you can convince your little chica that you're preferable to the drug dealing murderer who financed Miller's whole damn SNAFU."

The too small hostel thrummed with silence. Eddy glanced from one man to the other.

"Maybe Santiago's not the one who hired the hit on Herrera."

"Well, it doesn't really matter, does it?" Durrand asked. "Your girl left you to return to *him*."

Shep ground his teeth. "She doesn't know he's a drug lord."

"Oh, well then..." Durrand said and laughed, a low mirthless chuckle. "Looks like your taste is running toward the usual fare." Rising abruptly, he stared down at the Okie.

"What the hell does that mean?" Shepherd rose, too. He looked as lean and hungry as a wolf.

"Let's just take it easy," Eddy said. They'd just endured two days of hell. Durrand had been sick with worry that he had hit Shepherd too hard. That his friend would never come to. But the cowboy had awakened while they were still traveling. Awakened and nearly tore the Pinto apart trying to return to Carlotta. Threats had been issued. Curses and accusations had followed, but they'd finally arrived in Borgata. Still, it was anybody's guess if they would survive long enough to board their plane in two hours time.

"It means..." Durrand said, head lowered slightly. "She must be dumber than a fucking box of rocks."

"She ain't dumb," Shepherd said. His voice was hollow.

"Then she's a drug lord's wh—"

Durrand never finished the word. Apparently, it's difficult to talk when someone is slamming their knuckles into your jaw. He careened backward, snarled, then hunched forward ready to retaliate, but Eddy stepped in between them.

"Quit it! Just quit!" she yelled and stretched out her arms as if she could hold them back by sheer force of will. They paused for a second, glaring at each other. "Listen..." Her voice was shaky. "My leg hurts like hell, we're running out of time, and there's been enough blood spilled in this country without the two of you acting like morons."

"The fucker cold-cocked me," Shepherd snarled and shuffled to the left, ready to lunge again.

"He couldn't leave you in the jungle, Linus. He only hit you because he cares about you."

"The hell he did!"

"The hell I did!" Durrand echoed. "I hit him because he's a damned idiot who never thinks—"

"And he's sorry," Eddy snapped, wresting her glare from one to the other. "Sorry he hurt you. Sorry he had to leave Carlotta behind. He didn't want to do it. He just couldn't bear the idea of losing you again."

Resentment throbbed in the air like a smashed thumb.

"Is she right?" Shepherd asked finally, eyes hard on Durrand. "Are you sorry?"

"I'm sorry you're such a—"

"See!" Eddy rasped and managed to refrain from rolling her eyes, from smacking Durrand upside the head. "He feels terrible that you were injured, and he blames himself for not convincing you to stay out of Colombia in the first place."

Shepherd faced Durrand, maybe recognizing a whiff of the truth through the stink of testosterone. "It wasn't your fucking decision. You're not my boss," he snarled and took a step forward.

Eddy put a trembling palm against his wall of his chest.

"Not your boss!" she snapped. "Your *friend*." She drew a deep breath, steadying herself. "A friend who'd take a bullet for you. You probably didn't even know he was shot."

Shep's brows lowered but then he snorted. "Ya mean the head wound? Hell, I've had worse mosquito bites."

Durrand crunched his hands into fists. "You've always been an ungrateful son of a—"

"Not the head wound. The *chest* wound. He almost didn't make it," Eddy said. Her throat had grown tight, her voice low. "He nearly died trying to find you. I didn't even know he'd been wounded. He just kept running, leading me through the jungle, despite his injuries. Getting me to safety so he could rescue you, his best friend. He's the most loyal man I've—" Her voice cracked.

Durrand's gaze was steady on her and she knew she should quit. Knew she had no right to think she understood him like no one else. No right to believe they were meant to be together. So what if she felt their souls had melded on that one night in Tevio's hacienda? It had only been sex. So why did she feel like it meant everything?

"He's loyal," she said finally and cleared her throat. "And kind and brave and the best friend an ingrate like you will ever have."

Shep snorted but didn't disagree. Instead, he raised his chin a little, straightened slightly, and studied her with calculating, river-blue eyes.

"So how did *you* get involved with such a paragon, Jennifer Edwards?" he asked.

She didn't answer immediately, but Shepherd continued.

"He came to ya with some sob story about how he was riddled with guilt 'bout my leavin' with Miller, didn't he? How he intended to save me." He nodded. "Yeah. That much is clear. He's hell on wheels when it comes to guilt, but why did ya decide to come along on this little carnival ride through hell? That's the question."

She shrugged. "I'm a trained agent."

Shepherd snapped his gaze to Durrand whose brows lowered another notch.

"Agent?" Shep asked.

She pursed her lips. "CIA."

"Yeah?" He grinned crookedly. "Then why aren't ya CIAin'?"

She shuffled her feet, uncomfortable, though she didn't know why. "I believed at the time that getting your ass out of trouble was a worthy cause."

"And Gabe thought it was a good idea to drag ya into this shit-hole?" Shep stared at her a second then barked a laugh.

Eddy gritted her teeth. She was just about ready to rap the ungrateful son of a bitch in the head herself. "I'm a master marksman," she said.

"Oh, I believe it," Shep admitted and shifted his gaze to Durrand. "If her looks don't kill ya, her sharp shootin' will, huh? And then she's got that whole Spanish thing down, so ya don't have to know shit, right? My question is..." He turned his attention back to her. "Why'd the CIA let a star student like you go?"

She shrugged. "I don't think that's relevant just now."

"Let me guess," Shep said. "They stuck ya behind a desk and ya wanted more. So when this knight in shinin' armor came along with all his do-gooder ideas..." He motioned toward Gabe. "Ya jumped at the chance to get out of Dodge. Is that it?"

"Something like that."

He frowned a little as he assessed her all-American features. "And ya just left the agency high and dry after all that trainin' they gave ya?"

"I *told* them I wanted field experience."

"And they refused?"

"Numerous times."

"Even after ya threatened to quit?"

"They didn't even answer my email."

Shep's brows jumped. "Ya emailed your resignation?"

She resisted fidgeting. "I just…I was upset."

"Are ya sure they got it? I mean…emails go MIA all the time. In fact, McManning can make 'em disappear with the flick of his wrist."

She shook her head.

"He's a dipshit, but he's a magician on the computer. Ain't that right, Gabe?"

"Let it go," Durrand said. His words were little more than a growl, but perhaps Linus Shepherd wasn't the type to heed sensible warnings even if they were snarled like a curse.

"See, we've known McManning since…how long would ya say, Durrand? Ten years? Fifteen?"

"It's not too late to take you back to Tevio," Durrand growled.

Shepherd laughed. "Ya won't do that. 'Cause ya always do the right thing. No matter the cost. And I bet ya agonized about costin' Jenny here a possible promotion, didn't ya?"

"What are you talking about?" Eddy asked.

Shepherd's nostrils flared. "I'm talkin' 'bout Gabe puttin' a call into his old friend. I'm talkin' about him asking McManning to make sure the agency couldn't counteroffer so you'd risk your neck comin' down here to ease old Gabe's guilt."

"He's got nothing to feel guilty about."

"You kiddin' me?" Shep asked and snorted again. "He survived when his buddies died. He let me run off to Colombia before I was ready."

"That's ridiculous," she said. "You're a grown man."

Shepherd laughed but jerked a nod toward Durrand. "Ask him."

"I'm not going to—"

"Go ahead," Shepherd urged. "He's practically incapable of lyin'."

Eddy's stomach felt suddenly queasy, but she turned toward

Durrand. "I don't even know why you bothered to save him," she said. "If I were you I would have—"

"He's right." Durrand's voice was very quiet.

She blinked. "What?"

"My usual detail was dead or wounded. Reynolds was out of the country. But he managed to recommend an agent named Edwards. I needed help. You had the skills. I blackmailed Frank McManning so he'd make sure the agency didn't get your email for forty-eight hours."

She tried to formulate a question, tried to verbalize a response, but instead, she simply grabbed her pack, turned, and headed for the door on wooden legs.

"Edwards!" Durrand said and charged after her, but she pulled out the Glock and pointed it at his chest.

"Follow me," she gritted, "and I swear to God you'll wish you were still in the hole!"

He stepped back a pace.

Eddy left to the sound of Shep's raucous laughter.

# Chapter Fifty-One

*Five months later*

"Eddy's Angels," the receptionist said into the company's landline receiver. Lynn Franklin was a dark-haired beauty with a killer smile, an astronomical IQ, and a black belt in I-can-kick-your-ass-any-day-of-the-week.

Eddy left the door standing open as she headed back inside. It wouldn't hurt business at all if passersby caught a glimpse of the brunette behind the serviceable front desk. Besides, it was a beautiful day outside. In a few months, D.C. would be as hot as a Bogotá nightclub, but right now, it was a pleasant sixty-two degrees.

"How may I save your day?" Franklin asked the caller.

"Ed," Crystal said, just stepping out of an office down the hall. Their little workspace wasn't cheap, but the colonel had offered a sizeable loan. It was impossible to guess how he had even known she was considering starting the agency. "I'm taking off."

Eddy nodded. "Franklin has your itinerary?"

"As close as I could foresee it. I'll be flying into Miami and renting a car, but it's hard to say where things will go from there."

Crystal Hatch was buxom, brash, and a bit of a misandrist. Apparently, being cheated on by two husbands could make a woman a little bitter. If there was anyone who would bring in Bruce Oxer, deadbeat dad, it was Hatch.

"Keep in touch," Eddy said. "Oxer's ex-Army. Don't underestimate him." In fact, several of their clients were connected to the military in one way or another. Apparently, the colonel was sending business her way. And all along she hadn't even been aware her father was *capable* of feeling guilt, much less able to atone for his sins. "If you need backup, let us know immediately."

Behind her, Franklin greeted someone, but Eddy kept her attention pinned on the red-headed Crystal. It wouldn't do for her operatives to fall off the map, and this one was as independent as a mountain lion.

"Will do," she said now.

"I mean it," Eddy warned. "Call me."

Crystal grinned. "Looks like you have a guest," she said and glanced, brows raised, over her boss's right shoulder.

Eddy turned.

Linus Shepherd stood not twelve feet away. He wore a long-sleeved plaid shirt with pearl snaps, and jeans that rode low on his cowboy lean hips. His boots looked to be snakeskin.

"Hey," he drawled.

Eddy caught her breath then chastised herself for the weakness. "Mr. Shepherd." She made sure her voice was low and casual. "I thought you'd be in Oklahoma." She didn't mention the fact that she had wondered a hundred times if Durrand had allowed him to return to Colombia. But it was none of her business. She had done her job, accepted her pay, and moved on. No point letting things get personal. If she had learned anything in Bogotá, it had been that.

"So..." Tall, tightly muscled and fully healed, Shepherd had a grin that could take down most women at fifty yards. Eddy Edwards was not most women. That was the second thing she had learned in Bogotá. "I see ya hung up your own shingle."

She raised her brows at him. "Are you in need of a bodyguard, Mr. Shepherd?"

His grin amped up a notch, screwing up that take-no-prisoners smile. "So far today, my body remains unmolested."

"Need someone to find a missing person or…" She shrugged. "Make a person go missing."

"Holy catfish, girl" he said. "You're a regular Eddy Krueger."

"Not at all," she argued. "But there are a lot of people who wish to be left alone. We can usually convince their antagonists to do just that. Is someone bothering you?"

"Yeah," he said. "Matter a fact, there is. Name's Gabriel Bertram Durrand."

Her breath hitched in her throat for a moment, but she forced a smile. "I'm afraid I can't help you with that," she said.

"Aren't ya even gonna ask me what the problem is?"

"No," she said and turned away.

"Listen…" He grabbed her arm. Franklin raised dark brows, silently questioning.

"I got it," Eddy assured her. The little brunette nodded and turned back to her computer.

Shepherd shook his head. "Is there a factory manufacturin' gorgeous, killer women around here somewhere?"

"I'm afraid I'm very busy, Mr. Shepherd. So if you'll excuse me—"

"He needs you."

Her stomach pitched, but she retained her exterior calm and shook her head. "No," she said. There seemed little reason to pretend she didn't know whom he referred to. Gabriel Durrand was the virtual elephant in the room. "He doesn't."

"Why do ya think that? Because he didn't chase after ya?"

"Chase after me?" Her voice was too loud. She lowered it and laughed. "I'm sure you can find your own way out," she said and turned toward her office. She wasn't hiding, she told herself. She was making a dignified exit. Far better than cursing like a sailor. Light years ahead of bursting into tears. She'd done enough of both of those things in the weeks following her return from Colombia.

But he trailed her into her office. "Hey, I know he's shit at communication. Hell, he's barely human, but..." She turned once she'd reached the far side of her desk. Files lay perfectly aligned on its cross-cut grain. Shepherd glanced out her window to the flowerbeds below. "He ain't cut out to be a mercenary."

"What?"

"A guy named Feinstein is looking for soldiers." Anger jumped in his jaw. "I figure about half of them will come back alive. Maybe a quarter of those will still have all their limbs in the right places."

Panic reared up inside her, but she pushed back the fear, tamped down the nausea. "He doesn't care to see me," she said. "He made that perfectly clear."

"Yeah, he's an ass," Shepherd said and chuckled. "But to be perfectly fair, ya did say you'd shoot 'im if he followed ya."

She fiddled with a manila folder. A Mrs. Eileen Frederickson wanted them to find the daughter she'd given up for adoption fifty-five years earlier.

"Jenny?" Shepherd said, bringing her back to the moment.

"Yes, well...he's been shot before." She breathed in a deep lungful of air and let it out slowly. "He didn't seem all that averse to the experience."

He chuckled. "He's a tough son of a bitch. I'll give him that. Too tough, maybe. Wouldn't know how to apologize if he set your hair on fire."

But he *had* apologized. In a letter. A short but crisp missive sent with her check. *Eddy, I'm sorry to have misled you, but at the time, I felt I was out of options. I have contacted Andrew Richard Mender and strongly suggested that they consider you for any position you desire. You will make a fine operative. Gabriel Durrand.*

The memory almost made her cry again. They'd shared a bed. Shared their lives. Almost died together, Goddammit! And all she got was a *you'll make a fine operative?* Well fuck him!

Shepherd stared at her. "You're right," he said finally and threw up his hands. "You're right. Dumb bastard doesn't know what's good for 'im."

She nodded.

"He cost me the woman of my dreams. Comes ridin' in there like John Wayne. Always has to be the hero. Doesn't think about what anyone else needs. What anyone else wants."

He was right, she thought, but a couple of memories disagreed. She glanced out the window again and gritted her teeth to keep the words at bay, but they escaped. "You *were* handcuffed to a bed," she said.

"Yeah." He chuckled. "And what red-blooded guy don't want that?"

"They would have killed you."

He chuffed a laugh. "I had it all worked out. Carlotta would have set me free. We would have had us the time of our lives. Probably had us a little buckaroo on the way by now."

"Or you would have been hacked into tiny pieces and thrown in the Yari River."

He shrugged as if either option was acceptable. "The point is, Durrand shoulda been mindin' his own business. He's an egomaniac, is what he is. Selfish bastard'd turn on his own mother for a chance to play the damned knight in armor role."

"Selfish?" She stared at him. Her fingers had curled around the engraved letter opener her mother had given her. "Are you kidding me?"

"No, I'm not kiddin'. Shit, you should be madder than anybody. He lied to ya, didn't he? Dragged ya halfway around the world just so he could prove what a hero—"

"He almost got *killed* saving you! If he was any more loyal he'd be canonized on the south lawn of the White House."

He snorted. "Tell that to Oxer."

She felt the blood leave her face, but they couldn't be talking about the deadbeat dad Crystal Hatch was tracking. She didn't believe in coincidence. "What?"

"Oxer," he said. "He was a buddy of ours, but Gabe turned his back on him quick as—"

"*Bruce* Oxer?"

"Yeah. You know him?"

She didn't answer. "Why'd Durrand drop him?"

"I don't know. Something about abandoning his son or something." He shook his head. "Durrand's loopy about kids. Crazy about his niece. Makes him kinda sappy when..." He shook his head. "Anyway, point is, he came outta that whole Colombia deal smellin' like a rose."

"Smelling like a..." She laughed against her will. So what if Durrand had been the one sending business her way over the past few months. She knew *he* was capable of feeling guilt. And he *should* feel guilty, only... "He was shot, twice, chained to a wall, left..." Her voice broke. She cleared her throat and went on. "I would have never made it out of there without him. And neither would you."

He snorted. "Don't let 'im fool y'. Yeah, it maybe seemed like he woulda moved heaven 'n' earth to keep you safe. And no, he ain't looked at another woman since" — he rolled his eyes— "forever! But that's probably just 'cause he's shippin' out in two days. Lockin' up his cabin in Smithville. Fine with me if he comes back in a body bag. It's no more than—" he began, but her hands were already grabbing her bag, her feet already turning toward the door, though her mind had no idea what she was planning. "Hey. Where ya goin'?"

"Franklin, call me on my cell if you need me. If you can't reach me, Candida's in charge."

"Got it."

"See ya later, Jen," Shepherd called. His boots rapped against the floor behind her. In a moment, he was leaning against the front desk. "Hey."

The receptionist raised dark brows at him. He smiled, grin crooked with self-effacing charm.

"And here I thought Tulsa had a rope 'round the prettiest girls on the planet."

# Chapter Fifty-Two

Gabriel Durrand watched the skyline darken as the sun slipped, unseen, toward the horizon. It was going to rain again tonight. But hell, it had rained every day for as long as he could remember. Maybe he should split some logs, start a fire in the woodstove.

He took another sip of beer instead.

"Gabe! You going to answer me or what?"

He lifted his chin and glanced toward his sister. Kelsey was becoming more like their mother every day. It wasn't necessarily a good thing.

"About what?" he asked.

"About the price of pickles." Her sarcastic tone suggested he hadn't been listening. What else was new? Beer, he'd discovered, did not help his concentration. But it had a profound effect on forgetfulness. "Did you get your brains blown out in Bogotá or something? I asked if you're doing your exercises for that leg."

He shrugged.

"'Cause even Feinstein's not going to want you if you can't walk."

"I can walk," he said and took another sip of his beer. He had learned something rather valuable in the months following his return to Tennessee; he didn't really like beer.

She scowled at him and sighed heavily. "Don't go," she said finally.

He gave her a smile, or what passed for one these days. "I'll be fine."

"No, you won't be fine. Your hand's not a hundred percent. Your leg's still healing, and seriously, your mind…"

"I'll be fine," he repeated.

"You signed up already, didn't you?"

He tilted his head back. "Gonna do that tomorrow."

"And what about Shep? He's not going with you?"

"No."

"He know you're going?"

"Maybe."

She gritted her teeth. "If I gave a rat's ass, I'd ask what happened between the two of you."

He gave her a breathy snort.

Her scowl intensified. "What happened between the two of you?"

"Shouldn't you be getting home to Zoey?" he asked.

She glared at him. "You don't have to be such a…" she began but stopped and shaded her eyes with the flat of her hand. "Who's that?"

He glanced to the left. A white Prius was just pulling into his driveway. "Don't know." He didn't add that he cared even less.

The car slowed. A woman got out. She was slim. Her hair was strawberry blond. And her eyes…

Something sizzled in the core of his being. Something that cared a whole hell of a lot.

"Gabe?" Kelsey said.

He was standing, though he didn't remember rising. His throat felt tight. Beside his thighs, his hands had curled to fists, as though in self-defense.

"You know her?" his sister asked.

She was coming up the steps. Her hair was pulled into a sassy ponytail that bounced when she walked, as if she didn't have a care in the world.

It was damned difficult to breathe.

"Durrand." Her voice was low and breathy.

"Edwards." He could barely force out the word.

Silence followed, heavy and long.

"You look good," he said finally. It was the understatement of the century. She looked like sunshine, like home. Like an angel sent from heaven.

"So do you," she said.

"He looks like shit," Kelsey countered. "Who are you?"

Eddy widened her eyes, and for a moment, Gabe thought she would step back. The Durrand women were not to be trifled with, but Edwards straightened her back and caught his sister's eye with a steely gaze. "I'm the person who saved his ass in Colombia," she said and jerked up her chin a notch. "Who the hell are you?"

"You were in Bogotá?" Kelsey asked and yanked her gaze from one to the other.

"I asked who you were," Edwards said.

Kelsey may have answered, but Gabe never heard her words. Hope had sparked in the marrow of his bones and burst through his system like a roman candle. And although he knew there were a thousand things he should do, a million things he should say, he didn't do any of them. Instead, he stepped forward, wrapped Eddy in his arms and kissed her.

There was a moment of hesitation, a lifetime of uncertainty, and then she kissed him back, holding onto him like a life raft in a thunderstorm.

"You should have come after me," she whispered.

"I'm a fucking idiot," he agreed and kissed her again. "How'd you find me?"

"Shepherd," she rasped.

"Dammit! Now I owe him again."

"Can't be helped," she said. "Who's the woman?"

"If I say she's my sister will you let her live?"

"That depends. You going to ask me in or what?"

He felt his throat close up but managed to squeeze back the tears. "If you're deluded enough to want me to."

"There's mental illness in my family."

"Thank God," he said and lifting her against his chest, carried her into his life.

# Discover More By Lois Greiman

**Chrissy McMullen Mysteries**
Unzipped
Unplugged
Unscrewed
Unmanned
One Hot Mess
Not One Clue
Uncorked
Unleashed
Unhinged

**Home in the Hills Series**
Hearth Stone
Hearth Song

**Hope Springs Novels**
Finding Home
Home Fires
Finally Home

**European Historical Romances**
The Princess and Her Pirate
The Princess Masquerade
Seducing a Princess
Highland Hawk
The Fraser Bride
The MacGowan Betrothal
The Warrior Bride
Highland Jewel
Highland Flame
Highland Wolf

# About the Author

Born on a North Dakota cattle ranch, Lois Greiman graduated from a high school class of sixty students before moving to Minnesota where she professionally trained and showed Arabian Horses for several years. Since that time she's been a high fashion model, a fitness instructor, and a veterinary assistant. But an incurable case of writing fever put a stop to all those occupations. Her Highland novels have received Affaire de Couer's Critic's Choice Award, Romantic Times K.I.S.S. Award, and been nominated for Romance Writer's of America's prestigious Rita. Her titles have appeared on Barnes and Nobles Best Selling Romance list and won her the Midwest Fiction Writer's Rising Star Award.

http:/www.loisgreiman.com,
http://www.facebook.com/lois.greiman,
**http://www.facebook.com/ChrissyMcMullenMysteries,**
**Follow Lois on Twitter @loisgreiman2**

Printed in Great Britain
by Amazon

20131772R00173